HARLEQUIN® *Super*ROMANCE®

939
SEP

FOREWORD BY JENNIFER BLAKE

Snow Baby

Brenda Novak

9 MONTHS LATER

$4.50 U.S./$5.25 CAN.

D0030089

HARLEQUIN®
Makes any time special ™

AVAILABLE NOW:

ISBN 0-373-70939-0

HARLEQUIN SUPERROMANCE
Celebrates its 20th Anniversary

*Two decades of bringing you the very best
in romance reading.*

*To recognize this important milestone,
we've invited six very
special authors—whose names you're sure to recognize—
to tell us how they feel about Superromance.
Each title this month has a foreword
by one of these authors.*

New York Times bestselling author Jennifer Blake
says that Superromance novels "present a broad
spectrum of romance stories from the heart-pounding
to the heartwarming." She talks about the books'
"innovative plot lines and fresh new voices"—
qualities that definitely appear in the work
of Brenda Novak.

Snow Baby is Brenda's second book
for Superromance. She's achieving a reputation
for realistic and moving stories with a strong focus
on family relationships.

Publishers Weekly has described her writing as
"energetic" and her characters as "appealing."

Her peers also acknowledge her talent. The well-
known writer Merline Lovelace calls Brenda's books
"must-reads." Vicki Hinze (author of Acts of Honor)
says this about Brenda's stories: "Real people. Real
problems. Complex and genuine. Brenda Novak
shoots straight for the heart—and captures it!"

Dear Reader,

As an author, the question I get asked most often is "Where do you get the ideas for your stories?" Sometimes it's a specific location that inspires me, or an unusual event. Sometimes it's something as remote as a friend's retelling of an experience that happened to another friend's sister's aunt's neighbor! Well, this story strikes a little closer to home for me. It was inspired by my own sister. She and Chantel, the heroine, have many things in common. They are both tall—almost six feet—consider themselves "ugly ducklings" (although the rest of the world sees a swan) and battle the unique insecurities that come with towering over most other women and turning heads everywhere they go.

Take that kind of character and put her in a story where she and her sister are in love with the same man, and you have the backdrop for *Snow Baby*. To keep from destroying relationships that mean a great deal to them, Chantel and Stacy Miller and Dillon Broderick all wrestle with their individual needs and desires. But only when each is ready to sacrifice his or her happiness for the other two do they establish the kind of bond that transcends the selfish and the ordinary and becomes something truly special.

And it's all because of an unexpected *snow baby*…

I hope you enjoy my latest Superromance. I'd certainly love to hear from you. You can write to me at P.O. Box 3781, Citrus Heights, CA 95611. Or simply log on to my Web site at www.brendanovak.com to leave me an e-mail, check out my book signings or learn about my upcoming releases.

Best wishes!

Brenda Novak

FOREWORD BY JENNIFER BLAKE

Snow Baby
Brenda Novak

HARLEQUIN®

TORONTO • NEW YORK • LONDON
AMSTERDAM • PARIS • SYDNEY • HAMBURG
STOCKHOLM • ATHENS • TOKYO • MILAN • MADRID
PRAGUE • WARSAW • BUDAPEST • AUCKLAND

For my sister, Debra Cundick, a beautiful child, a beautiful
adult, the inspiration behind this book.

Sometimes in life we meet people who encourage us, who
teach us that we are worthy of our dreams, who set an
example for us of courage and determination in the face of
formidable challenges. I married one of those people—
and that is something for which I will always be grateful.

ISBN 0-373-70939-0

SNOW BABY

Copyright © 2000 by Brenda Novak.

Visit us at www.eHarlequin.com

Printed in U.S.A.

FOREWORD BY JENNIFER BLAKE

Romance novels serve different purposes for different people. Depending on the category or type, they provide fantasy adventure for those in need of escape from everyday tensions, trust in a future filled with love and joy for readers who have not yet found these things, a sense of home and family for women who have either lost theirs or never had any, remembrance of intimacy for those whose memories may have dimmed, and more—so much more. These so-called simple stories reaffirm the magic of living and loving. They illustrate that women can survive and prosper and find their hearts' desires. They provide a promise that women and men can share a close relationship and the implicit pledge of a wonderful future. They give people a life goal that, even when it seems least attainable, still causes the senses to quicken and the world to seem good and bright.

Some would say that romance novels create unrealistic expectations, that a real personal relationship can never live up to the fantasies presented. What a shortsighted view! Those who hold it fail to see that in striving for the Holy Grail of a perfect love, men and women may overcome incredible odds to discover tolerance and acceptance of each other's foibles and find rich moments of laughter, passion and devotion. They can become better lovers solely from the attempt. All great endeavors begin with a fantasy. If you never dream of climbing the highest mountain, then you'll never reach the heights. If you never dream of a fine romance, then you will surely never feel the magic.

In my own experience, however, romance authors seldom write their stories with the idea of creating romantic expectations. They write for the pleasure of the words flowing through their brains, for the joy of creating their own special worlds and inviting readers into them. They write to show others with a romantic frame of mind the charming, funny or exciting stories that they create to entertain themselves and to share the romantic joy they feel inside. If they can entertain readers while doing these things, then that's more than enough.

Superromance novels like the one you hold in your hands explore the promise of love in all its many varieties. They present a broad spectrum of romance stories from the heartwarming to the heart-pounding. They are as close to mainstream as it's possible to come in category romance, and have been the proving ground for many authors who have gone on to have bestsellers in the broader fiction market. With innovative plot lines and fresh new voices, they provide more fully developed reading experiences. I hope you enjoy this story—*Snow Baby* by Brenda Novak—and that you find it in whatever joy and romance your heart may be seeking.

Jennifer Blake

Jennifer Blake is a four-time *New York Times* bestselling author, whose first book was published in 1970. She has published well-known historical romances like *Love's Wild Desire*, as well as contemporary mainstream novels, the most recent of which is *Roan* (MIRA Books, July 2000). Jennifer has received many awards and accolades; among these are the fact that she was appointed Writer-in-Residence at Northeast Louisiana University in 1982, and in 1997, was chosen as the recipient of Colorado's Frank Waters Award for Achievement in Fiction. Jennifer Blake understands, respects and values romance fiction—and romance readers—as her success has repeatedly proven.

CHAPTER ONE

I'M NEVER GOING to make it.

Chantel Miller hunched forward, trying to see beyond the snow and mud being kicked up onto her windshield by the semi next to her. She could barely make out the taillights of the Toyota Landcruiser she'd been following for miles, and she longed to pull over and give her jangled nerves a rest. But the narrow two-lane highway climbing Donner's Summit was cut into the side of a cliff, and she didn't dare stop. Not in a storm like this.

In the back of her mind she heard her father, who'd been dead for nearly five years now, telling her to slow down, keep calm. He'd taught her to drive and had offered all the usual parental advice—never let your gas tank get below half, keep your doors and windows locked, never pull over in the middle of a storm.

God, she missed him. How could so much have happened in the past ten years? At twenty-nine, she already felt battle-weary, ancient.

She shrugged off the memories to avoid the regret they inspired, and focused on her driving. Her sister, Stacy, was waiting for her in Tahoe, only an hour away. She'd be able to make it that far as long as she could get past the big rig that was churning up the mountain beside her, nearly burying her car with sludge.

She gave her red Jaguar—her only concession to the life she'd left behind—some gas and shot around the semi, then eased down on the brake. The road was covered with black ice. Her stomach clenched as the Jaguar fishtailed, but then its tires grabbed the asphalt and the taillights that had been her beacon appeared in front of her again.

"Hello, Mr. Landcruiser," she breathed in relief, and crept closer, determined to stay in the vehicle's wake. The plows were long overdue. Snow was beginning to blanket the shiny road.

Stretching her neck, Chantel tried to release some of the tension in her shoulders, then cranked up the defrost. A pop station played on the radio, but she barely heard the familiar lyrics as she listened to the wind howl outside. Ice crystals shimmered in the beam of her headlights, then flew at her face, clicking against the windshield.

She shouldn't have left Walnut Creek so late. If it hadn't been her first week at her new job, she would have insisted on heading home when everyone else had, at five o'clock. But she not only had a new job, she had a new profession, back in her home state of California, clear across the country from where she'd lived before.

Changing careers was probably the most difficult thing she'd ever done, but Chantel was determined to overcome her insecurities and be successful at a job that required a brain—if for no other reason than to prove she had one.

Overhead a yellow sign blinked *Chains required over summit.* To the right, several cars waited, engines running, as their owners struggled in the cold and wet to get chains on their tires. A couple of men wearing orange safety vests worked as installers for those willing to pay for help.

Chantel was studying the shoulder, looking for a place to pull over, when brake lights flashed in front of her. She screamed and slammed on her brakes, but the car didn't stop. It slid out of control. With a bone-jarring crunch, her Jag collided with the Landcruiser ahead of her.

Pain exploded in Chantel's head as her face hit the steering wheel. She sat, breathing hard, staring at the black snowy night and the back end of the white Landcruiser, which was now smashed. Then someone knocked on her window.

Dazed, she rolled her head to the side and saw a tall dark-haired man looming above her. "Are you all right? Unlock the doors!" he shouted.

Immediately her father's warnings echoed back: *Always keep your doors and windows locked....*

When she didn't respond, he scowled at her through the glass and tapped again. "Did you hear me? Open the door!"

She let her eye-lids close and put her hand to her aching head as her senses began to return. She'd just been in a car accident. This was probably the other driver. She had to give him her driver's license and insurance information, right? Of course.

With trembling fingers, she sought the automatic door lock and heard it *thunk* just before the man flung her door open and leaned inside.

A freezing wind whipped around him and flooded her car, carrying the smell of his aftershave with it—a clean masculine scent, far different from the trendy fragrances used by the male models she'd worked with not so long ago. Then a firm hand gripped her chin and tilted her face up. "Your lip's bleeding, but not badly. Any other injuries?"

She struggled to rearrange her jumbled thoughts. Stacy, accident, aftershave, blood... "Just a lump on my head, I think."

"Good." He stood and jammed his hands into the pockets of his red ski parka, frowning at the crushed metal in front of them, and it suddenly dawned on Chantel that he was angry. Really angry. The signs were all there—the terse voice, the taut muscles, the furrowed brow. "Is something wrong?" she asked.

He looked at her as if she had two heads. "You mean other than what you just did to my SUV?"

She winced. "I'm sorry. I'm worried about my car, too. I haven't owned it more than a year. But you stopped right in front of me. There was nothing I could—"

"*What?*" He whirled on her, the furrow in his brow deepening. Ice crystals lodged in the dark stubble of his jaw gave his face a rugged appearance, but the long thick lashes fringing his eyes looked almost feminine. "You're kidding, right?"

"No, I'm not." Chantel's tongue sought the cut in her lip. She reached across the console to the glove box and retrieved a napkin to wipe the blood from her mouth. "How could you expect anyone to stop so fast in this kind of storm?"

He stiffened. "I managed to miss the car ahead of me. And you want to know why? Because I wasn't tailgating him for the past thirty miles!"

"I wasn't tailgating you," she said, but a memory of her struggle to keep up with his taillights raced through her mind and made her wonder if she'd been following too closely, after all. She'd hardly been able to see anything— except his lights.

"Regardless," he said abruptly, "we have to move off to the side. We're stopping traffic. Are you okay to drive?"

She nodded, shivering despite her navy wool coat. "I think so."

"Just pull over there." He indicated a couple of spots other cars had just vacated. It seemed to Chantel that his initial anger had softened to mere irritation.

Feeling jittery, she slowly eased the Jaguar over so the traffic behind them could get through. A couple of motorists paused to see what had happened and a chain installer jogged over and hollered something at the guy she'd hit, but the weather was too bad for anyone to linger. No ambulance, no fire trucks. The accident wasn't nearly as interesting as it could have been.

Thank God!

Chantel watched the man from the Landcruiser stride toward her and wished she was safe in her new condominium in Walnut Creek, curled up in front of the television. She was exhausted and cold and rattled. But she had to make it to Tahoe. After all the years she and her sister hadn't spoken, Stacy was finally ready to give her another chance.

I won't blow it, Stace. I've changed, grown up. You'll see.

She lowered her window as the Landcruiser's owner gave her car a skeptical frown. "You look like you belong on the streets of Beverly Hills," he said. "I bet you've never driven in snow."

"Listen, I come from New York. You've never seen snow until you've spent a winter back East." She didn't add that she hadn't owned a car for most of the ten years she'd lived in the Big Apple. Taxis, public transit or, more often, limousines had always carried her where she'd wanted to go, but she wasn't about to volunteer that information. He didn't need to know how precisely his accusation had hit its target.

"Excuse me," she said to get him to step back. "I want to see the damage." She buttoned up her coat and scrambled out of the car, wincing as her white tennis shoes sank deep in the cold slush. Her vision swam for a moment, but she kept one hand on the door for support and soon the world righted itself.

Like most people, the Landcruiser's owner did a double take when he saw her at her full height. His gaze started at where the snow buried her feet, then climbed her thin frame until it met the withering glare she reserved for gawkers.

She raised a hand before he could make any comment. "I know, I hear it all the time. I'm almost six feet, so you don't have to ask." She gave him a glacial smile to cover the way her body shook with reaction to the blizzard and the accident. "That doesn't make me a freak, but it does intimidate some men."

He grunted. "Short men, maybe."

Chantel had to admit he didn't look like a man who could be easily intimidated. Similar to her in age, he had shoulders twice the width of her own and was taller by at least four inches. But she'd always hated her height, even when she stood next to bigger people. She'd grown up to taunts of "Daddy Long Legs" and "Miller High Life" and couldn't see herself as anything but gangly and awkward, despite a successful modeling career.

She shut her door and leaned into the wind, fighting the weakness of her legs as she trudged over to check out the damage. "Ouch," she said, sheltering her face from the snow so she could view the Jag's crumpled front bumper and broken headlight. The Landcruiser sported a smashed right rear panel. "Well, my car certainly got the worst of it, don't you think?"

He cocked an eyebrow at her, but didn't say anything. He didn't have to; she could guess what he was thinking.

"It was your fault, too," she said, irritated by his smug attitude, which reminded her too much of Wade, even though this stranger looked nothing like her ex-boyfriend. "You slammed on your brakes for no apparent reason."

He gave an incredulous laugh. "The car in front of me stopped. What did you want me to do? Drive off the cliff?"

Is it too late to consider that option? Chantel bit her

tongue, knowing her hostility was spurred by the memory of Wade and not this stranger. Not really.

Glancing at her car's smashed front end a final time, she hurried back into the driver's seat. The accident had caused some expensive damage, but it was still pretty much a fender bender. She wanted to swap information and be on her way, or Stacy would think she wasn't coming.

She hoped this guy wouldn't insist on waiting for the Highway Patrol.

"Why don't you grab your driver's license and insurance card and come get in my truck?" he called after her. "It'll be drier and warmer than trying to do it out here."

Never get in a car with a stranger, her father's voice admonished.

Especially such a powerful-looking stranger, Chantel added on her own.

"I'll just write it all down and bring it to you. You're not planning to wait for the police to arrive, are you? There's really no need. In a collision like this, the rear ender's always on the hook."

He smiled, transforming his expression from a Terminator-style intensity to the guilelessness of an All-American boy. "There's a good reason for that, you know."

"Okay, so I might have been following a little closely, but in a storm like this, calling the cops could hold us up for hours. Can't you just file a report in the morning or something?"

"No problem. I want to get out of here, too."

"Great." She gave him a relieved smile—a semblance of the smile that had made her a living for the past ten years—and hurried back to her car. After scribbling down her policy number, insurance agent's name and phone number, license-plate number and driver's license number, she walked toward his truck.

He rolled down his window and glanced at the slip of paper she handed to him. "What about *your* name and telephone number?"

"My agent will handle everything."

"No way. You're not leaving here until I have your name, your number and your address. Just in case."

Chantel fought the wind that kept blowing her long blond hair across her face. "In case of what?"

"In case I need to contact you."

"I don't think my husband would like me giving out that information," she hedged, blinking the snow out of her eyelashes.

He scowled. "I'm sorry, but you just rear-ended my truck. I want to know I can get hold of you. And I don't care whether your husband likes it or not."

This could be a dangerous world, and she was completely alone in it. But what were the chances she'd just rear-ended another Ted Bundy? With a sigh, Chantel gave him the information he'd requested, hoping he'd fallen for the imaginary-husband routine.

He passed her a card. "I wrote my cell phone number on the back. You can reach me on it anytime."

"Fine." She glanced down and read, "Dillon Broderick, Architect," before shoving the card into the back pocket of her jeans to keep it from getting wet.

"Are you *sure* you're okay to drive?"

She was still a little rattled but determined to fulfill her promise to Stacy, despite the storm, despite the accident, despite everything.

"Yeah. You?"

"I'll have a stiff neck tomorrow, but I'll live. Take it easy," he said, and pulled away before Chantel made it back to her car.

Dillon Broderick put his Landcruiser into four-wheel drive and merged into the traffic heading up the hill, cursing under his breath.

As if his week hadn't gone badly enough. Now he had the bother of getting his truck fixed—the estimates from body shops, the insurance claims, the rental car—and beyond all that, the maddening knowledge that his new Landcruiser would never be the same.

"'I wasn't tailgating you,'" he mimicked. She'd dogged him since Auburn, when it had started to snow. He'd flashed his brake lights several times, trying to get her to back off. But she'd come right up again and again, nearly riding on his bumper. If a man had done that, he'd probably have broken his nose for risking both their lives, but what could he do with a tall, beautiful woman?

Grin and bear it, just the way he did with his ex-wife.

He glanced at the paper where Chantel Miller had written her name and address. She lived in Walnut Creek, not far from his own house in Lafayette. At least they were both local. That should make things easier.

He shook his head at the thought of the damage the accident had done to her Jaguar XJ-6. What a sweet car! Her husband wouldn't be pleased when she got home.

If she got home.

The thought of Chantel Miller heading up the mountain with only one headlight caused Dillon a moment of guilt. It was difficult enough to see the road with two working lights. He probably should have waited to make sure she had chains and could get them on. But he was already late. His friends had been expecting him for hours.

He flipped open his time-planner and turned to the page where he'd jotted down the information about their rental cabin. He punched in the number, and a cheerful voice greeted him on the other end. "Hello?"

"This is Dillon. Is—"

"Hey, guy! It's Veronica. We were afraid you'd gotten into an accident or something."

"Actually I did, but no one was hurt."

"Omigosh! What happened?"

"I'll tell you when I get there. I just wanted to let everyone know I'm still a half hour away. Traffic's been moving pretty slow in this mess."

"Don't worry, the drive'll be worth it. The ski resorts are getting something like sixteen inches of snow."

He smiled. He needed a rigorous physical vacation to steal his thoughts away from his ex-wife and all the dirty custody tricks Amanda was playing on him with their two little girls. "That sounds great."

"We'll see you when you get here."

He was just about to hit the "end" button when his call waiting beeped. He looked at the digital readout on his caller ID, wondering who'd be phoning him this late, but didn't recognize the number. He switched over. "Hello?"

"Mr. Broderick?"

"Yes?"

"This is Chantel Miller. You know, the woman who just…well, we were in an accident a little while ago."

How could he forget? He pictured her almond-shaped eyes gazing up at him, the high cheekbones, the small cut on one pouty lip, and refused to acknowledge how incredibly beautiful she was. Only, she sounded different now, almost…frightened. "Is everything okay?"

"Well, um, I really hate to bother you. I mean, you don't even know me and I can't have made the best impression—" she gave a weak laugh "—but, well, it looks like I'm lost and—"

"Lost! How could you be lost? I left you not more than fifteen minutes ago. Aren't you on Highway 80?"

What was this woman? Some kind of trouble magnet?

"No. Actually I turned off about ten minutes ago. I've got directions to a cabin where my sister is staying, but it's so difficult to see through the snow. I must have taken a wrong turn somewhere."

"Can't you call your sister and find out?"

"The cabin's just a rental. I don't have the number. I was in such a hurry to get going tonight and the directions seemed so clear. I never dreamed the weather would be this bad. It's been nothing but sunny at home."

It was March. Who would have expected a storm like this when it was nearly spring? He hadn't checked the weather himself, but then, he had a four-wheel drive and probably wouldn't have checked it even in the dead of winter. "Do you have your chains on?"

'Yeah, I paid one of the installers to put them on just after you left, but they're not doing any good."

"What do you mean?"

"My car's stuck."

"It's *what?*"

"Stuck. There hasn't been a plow through here for a long time, and the drifts are pretty deep—"

"And you drove into that?"

Silence. "I'm sorry. I shouldn't have bothered you," she said softly, and with a click she was gone.

"Dammit!" Dillon tossed his phone across the seat. How stupid could this woman be? Anyone who drove a wrecked sports car onto an unfamiliar side street in the middle of a storm like this had to be a few cards short of a deck.

"Let her call the Highway Patrol," he grumbled, and tried to forget her, but another mile down the road, he saw the dim shadow of an exit sign. He'd left Chantel Miller not more than fifteen miles back. She couldn't be far. It might cost him another hour, but he could probably find her more easily than anyone else. More quickly, too.

Veering to the right, he headed down the off-ramp. All roads, except the freeway, were virtually deserted and lay buried beneath several inches of snow.

He stopped and flipped on his dome light to study the sheet of paper with Chantel's personal information.

She hadn't included a cell-phone number. He tried her home, hoping he could at least get hold of her husband. Someone should know she was in trouble, just in case she didn't have sense enough to call the Highway Patrol or tried to walk back to the freeway or something. A person could easily freeze to death in this weather.

After five rings, a recorder picked up, and Dillon recognized Chantel's voice telling him to leave his name and number. He hung on, waiting to leave a message for her husband, and was surprised to hear her continue, "Or, if you'd rather try me on my car phone, just call—"

Bingo! He scrounged for a piece of paper and a pencil and jotted down the number, then dialed it.

Chantel answered, a measure of relief in her voice. "Hello?"

"It's me, Dillon Broderick. I'm coming back for you. Tell me where you are."

She paused. "It's all right, Mr. Broderick—"

"Dillon."

"Dillon. Maybe I need a tow truck. I'm thinking about calling the police."

He thought of her sitting in her wrecked Jag, the cold seeping into the car, the storm howling around her, and for some reason, remembered her smile. This woman had just smashed the back end of his truck, but for a moment that didn't matter. She was alone and probably frightened.

"Well, maybe you should do that, but I'm coming back, anyway, just to see that you're okay."

"Are you sure? I feel really bad. I mean, for all I know, your wife and kids are waiting for you, worried…"

"No wife and kids, at least not worried ones." Just the rest and relaxation he'd been craving. He thought of his friends sitting around the fireplace, drinking wine, laughing and talking, listening to Janis Joplin or Patsy Cline, and turned around, anyway.

"Now," he said, "how did you get where you are?"

CHAPTER TWO

"FORTY-FIVE BOTTLES of beer on the wall, forty-five bottles of beer, take one down, pass it around, forty-four bottles of beer on the wall."

Chantel gave up trying to distract herself with the repetitive chant and glanced impatiently at her watch—again.

She'd talked to Dillon Broderick more than a half hour ago. Where was he? Her hands and feet were frozen, but she dared not run the car's engine any longer for fear she'd use all her gas. Fueling up was one of those things she hadn't had time for when she'd dashed out of the house four hours earlier. Now she could only stare, disheartened, at the gas gauge, which read less than a quarter of a tank.

Closing her eyes, Chantel rubbed her temples and willed back the tears that threatened. She'd been so stressed with the move and her new job, and so focused on reaching Stacy at a decent hour, that she hadn't done *anything* right. Now her new car was wrecked, and she was stranded on some nameless street in the middle of a snowstorm.

She let her head fall forward to rest on the steering wheel, hearing Wade's voice, despite her best efforts to banish it from her mind. *That's what you get when you don't use your head. You never think, Chantel. Never. What would you do without me?*

Well, she was finding that out, wasn't she? She'd left him six months ago, and despite all his calls and letters, she wouldn't take him back. She was fighting for the person she used to be, before Wade and modeling had nearly destroyed her—the girl her father had raised.

But it all seemed so hopeless sometimes. Or at least it did right now.

She glared miserably at her car phone. She didn't even have anyone to call. The only friends she'd had when she and Wade were living together in New York were *his* friends. The only hobbies, his hobbies. He'd made sure her whole world revolved around him, and she'd been as stupid as he always told her she was, because, to save their relationship, she'd let him. *You're just another pretty face, Chantel. Good thing God gave you that.*

The phone chirped and Chantel grabbed it.

"Hello?"

"I can't find you. Are you sure you turned right and not left at the second stop sign?'

It was Dillon Broderick. He was still coming.

She said a silent prayer of thanks and tried to retrace in her mind the route she'd taken. When she hadn't been able to find the street her sister had written down, she'd taken several turns, always expecting the cabin to appear around the next corner. Now it was hard to remember exactly what she'd done.

"I turned right," she insisted with a sigh of defeat. She was tired, so tired she could barely force herself to stay awake. After six months she still wasn't completely recovered, she realized. "I don't know why you can't find me."

He didn't say anything for a moment, and Chantel pictured his face, with its strong jaw, chiseled cheekbones and light eyes, which had been filled with anger about the accident. Would he get frustrated and decide not to continue searching? Her stomach clenched at the thought.

"Did you call the police?" he asked.

"Yes, they said they'd send a car."

"And you gave them the same directions you gave me?"

Chantel felt another pang of despair. "You're saying the police won't be able to find me either, right?"

He cleared his throat. "Let's not jump to any conclusions. They certainly know the area better than I do and might have some idea where to look. I'll go back the way I came and try another route from the freeway."

Chantel knew that courtesy demanded she tell him to return to his original route and not to trouble himself further. The police were coming—eventually. But the snow piling ever higher on the hood of her car would soon block out everything else. And she already felt so alone.

"Dillon?"

"Yeah?"

She wanted to ask him to keep talking to her, not to hang up, but her more practical side admonished her against running up his car-phone bill, to say nothing of her own. She wasn't in any real trouble, not with the police on their way. She didn't need anyone to hold her hand. "Nothing. Thanks for trying."

"That sounds like you think I'm giving up. I can't let anything happen to you. How do I know your insurance will take care of my truck?"

He was teasing her. Chantel heard it in his voice and smiled. Fleetingly, she wondered about his wife and kids—the ones he'd said weren't worried about him.

"Where were you headed before you came back for me?" she asked.

"Tahoe. I'm going skiing for a week. What about you?"

"Same here. Just for the weekend, though."

"So you know how to ski?"

She got the impression he was just being nice to her, trying to calm her down, but she didn't care, not as long as his voice hummed in her ear. "Yeah. My dad used to take us when we were kids."

"You ever been to Squaw Valley?"

"Not yet. I grew up in Utah and used to go to Snowbird or Alta."

"That's some great snow there. My buddies and I took a trip to Utah when we were in college."

"I'll bet college was fun." Chantel fought the chattering of her teeth, not wanting to let him know how terribly cold she was.

"You didn't go to university?"

"No."

"Hey, you got your headlights on?"

"You mean headlight, don't you?"

He laughed. "Yeah. Otherwise, with this snow piling up, I won't be able to tell you from any other car sitting by the side of the road."

"It's on."

"Good. What about the heater? It's pretty cold outside."

"No heater. Not enough gas." This time, the chill that ran through her echoed in her voice. "And it *is* cold."

"How much gas have you got?"

"Just enough to make it to Tahoe once you pull me out of here."

"Listen, this is what I want you to do. Dig through your luggage and put on all the layers of clothing you can. I don't want to find an ice cube when I get there, understand?"

"I've already done that."

"What about gloves and boots?"

Chantel curled her toes and frowned when she could no longer feel them move in her wet tennis shoes. "No such luck. I was going to buy all that once I reached Tahoe."

"Damn. This just keeps getting better, doesn't it?"

Pinching the bridge of her nose, Chantel swallowed back a sigh. "I guess I wasn't very prepared."

"I can't believe you had chains."

"I did only because I bought them shortly after I got the car and stuffed them in the trunk."

He chuckled. "Too bad. Otherwise you'd have been forced to turn back."

"I couldn't turn back," she said, thinking of her promise to Stacy.

"Why not?"

"There's something I have to do in Tahoe."

"What's that?"

Penance.

DILLON SQUINTED as he tried to see beyond the pale arc of his headlights. White. Everything was white—and stationary. He called Chantel again and told her to honk her horn, then rolled down his window, hoping he'd hear something, but the wind carried no sound other than its own vehemence.

What now? Dropping his head into his hands, he rubbed his eyes. He'd been searching for two hours. He would have given up long ago, except that the police hadn't found Chantel, either, and he could tell from the sound of her voice that her initial uneasiness was turning to panic.

He called her cell phone again. "I'm going to return to the freeway and start over."

"No!" She sounded resolute. "You're crazy to keep looking for me, Dillon. I never should have called you. I thought it would take you a few minutes to come and pull me out, nothing more. I never expected anything like this."

"I know, but you can't be far away. If I could just spot you, we could both be on our way to our respective vacations—"

"Or you could get stuck, too. The police called to say

they can't look for me anymore, not until morning. The storm's too bad.''

"What? Why not?'' She could freeze to death before morning!

"They don't want to risk anyone's life, and I don't want you to risk yours.''

What about *her* life? Dillon wondered.

She took an audible breath. "You're going to have to head back, before the roads get any worse.''

Dillon maneuvered around a parked car that looked like a small snow hill. His tires spun, then finally propelled him a little farther down a road that was quickly becoming impassable. The slick ice and heavy snow were making him nervous, but he'd canvassed the area so completely, he could only believe he'd find her in the next few minutes.

"You can't be far,'' he muttered.

"It doesn't matter. The police know what they're doing. Anyway, they told me not to use my car phone. I'll need the battery when they resume the search.''

Conserving her battery made sense, but cutting off a frightened woman did little to help her. "I'd better let you go, then.''

Two hours ago Dillon had cared only about making it to the cabin in time to enjoy the party. Now he could think of nothing but Chantel Miller, a beautiful young woman stranded alone in the middle of a snowstorm. He sighed. "It's hard for me to give up after all this.''

"Just think about what I did to your truck. That should make it easier.'' She attempted to laugh, and Dillon had to admire her for the effort.

"You'll probably be on the news in the morning, talking about how some brave fireman saved you,'' he said.

"Yeah. I'll be the tall one.''

"The tall one with the knockout smile and the sexy

voice," he added, "but I probably shouldn't say that to a married woman."

"Dillon?"

"Uh-huh?"

"There's no husband. I just…you know, a woman can't be too careful."

"Are you telling me I look like an ax murderer?"

"Actually I think you look like Tom Selleck."

He laughed. "It's the dimples. I hated them when I was a kid, thought they made me look like a sissy. When I was five or so, my mom dressed me up as a girl for Halloween, and I never lived it down—or at least I didn't until I passed six feet and could grow a full beard."

"I'll bet no one teases you anymore."

He could hear the smile in her voice, and it made him feel slightly better. "No, they don't." He paused, wondering what to do next. "Damn, Chantel. I'm sorry about this mess. You must be—"

"Anxious for morning. That's all."

"Sure." He continued to steer his truck through the fresh powder and felt his tires give more than they grabbed. He knew that if he stayed out any longer, he'd get stuck, too. "Well, I won't use up any more of your battery."

"Okay."

The edge that crept into her voice reminded him of the way his little girl sounded whenever she didn't want him to leave her, and that made it hard as hell to hang up. He and Chantel Miller might have been complete strangers three hours ago, but now they seemed like the only two people in the world."

"I'll call you tomorrow."

"Right."

"Goodbye, Chantel."

"Hurry back to the freeway, Dillon…and thank you. I'm

sorry about your truck. I've got your card. I'll send you a thank-you note.''

Yeah, you can say, "Thanks for nothing."

THIS IS WHAT HAPPENS, Chantel, when you try to do something without me, Wade sneered.

Chantel covered her ears with her hands, even though she knew the sound came from inside her own head. "Shut up," she whispered. "You're gone and I'm glad."

His laugh echoed through her mind, and she almost turned on the radio to block it out. She hadn't seen Wade in six months, but they'd spent ten years together before that—ten years that weren't easy to erase.

She blew on her hands, then hugged herself again. She'd taken off her wet shoes and pulled up her knees so she could warm her toes with her piled-on sweaters, not that it made any difference. She was freezing. If it got any colder....

She pictured Stacy at the cabin and wished she could reach her sister. Her car phone lay in her lap, cradled against the cold and darkness, but the number for the cabin was at home, on the easy-wipe board next to the refrigerator. Why hadn't she transferred it to the sheet of directions Stacy had given her? Why hadn't she gone back when she realized she'd left it?

She'd been in too much of a hurry, that was why—but it was useless to berate herself now. Except that it kept her from succumbing to the exhaustion that tugged at her body. The police had warned her not to go to sleep. If she did, she might never wake up.

She thought about Wade and the choices he'd encouraged her to make and all she had suffered because of them—the low self-esteem, the anorexia, the past six months of constant effort to become healthy again. If she was going to

die, why couldn't she have done it in the hospital, before
the long haul back?

Because that would have been too easy. She needed those
experiences. The past six months had made her a stronger
person than she'd ever been before.

That truth blew into her mind with all the force of the
raging storm, then settled like a softly falling snowflake.
Yes, she was stronger. When the nurses told her she'd probably die from her disease, she'd decided it wouldn't beat
her. She'd given up modeling. She'd left Wade. She smiled,
knowing, in the end, that she'd surprised them all.

But the past had left its scars. Her illness had cost her the
one thing she wanted more than anything....

She winced and shied away from the longing. She wasn't
ready to deal with it yet. A new career, a new life. That was
enough for now. Then, perhaps someday—

Suddenly Chantel sat bolt upright and tried to see through
the snow on her windshield. Her headlight had gone out,
hadn't it? The police had told her to turn it off, to conserve
the car battery, as well as the telephone battery, but she
couldn't bring herself to relinquish the one thing that might
actually get someone's attention. Without it, the Jaguar
would look just like every other car, every *empty* car.

Gripping the steering wheel with numb hands, she shifted
to her knees to see above the mounded snow, then squinted
down at her instrument panel. The lights were dimming. She
could barely make out the fuel gauge. The white needle
pointing to ''E'' wasn't the most comforting sight, but without it, she'd be sitting in complete darkness, alone, as the
storm continued to bury her alive.

She should start the car and recharge the battery. She
needed the heat, anyway. What good was saving gas now?
Either she made it until morning when the police would
come for her. Or she didn't.

Turning the key in the ignition, she heard the Jag's starter give a weak whine, then fall silent. She was too late. The battery was already dead.

Should she get out? Look for help on foot? She fingered the phone, wishing Dillon would call—he was the only one who might—but she knew he'd never risk using up the rest of her battery. By now he was probably sleeping beneath heavy quilts in a cabin that smelled of pine and wood smoke.

She imagined him bare-chested, the blankets coming to just above his hips, a well-muscled arm flung out. Would there be a woman beside him? A woman who'd been waiting for "Dillon Broderick, Architect" in Tahoe?

Chantel shook her head. It didn't matter. Only sleep mattered. Her body begged her to close her eyes and simply drift away.

Soon her lids grew so heavy she could barely lift them. She couldn't feel her nose anymore, could no longer see her breath fogging the air. She tried to sing the *Titanic* theme song, but even that was too much effort. Instead, she heard the melody in her head and told herself her heart would go on. And her father would be there to greet her. Her father…

Why hadn't she left Wade sooner?

I'm free, Daddy. And I'm finally coming home…to you.

With a strange sense of eagerness, she closed her eyes, but a persistent thump on the outside of the car pulled her out of sleep's greedy clutches.

"CHANTEL! IT'S ME, Dillon!"

Dillon wiped all the snow off the window and flashed his light inside. It *had* to be her car. How many smashed Jags could there be with one dim headlight still reflecting off the white flakes falling from the sky?

"Dillon?" He heard her voice through the glass and

breathed a sigh of relief. He'd found her! He couldn't believe it. He'd turned around and tried to drive back to the freeway, but he hadn't been able to leave her behind. And now he was elated to think he'd beaten the odds.

She fumbled with the lock and opened the door, and he pulled her out and into his arms.

Pressing her cold face against the warmth of his neck, she held him tightly.

"You all right?" he asked.

She didn't answer, just clung to him, and he realized she was crying.

"Hey, what kind of a welcome is this?"

"I'm sorry," she mumbled, drawing back to swipe at her eyes. "I just, I just…" She began to shake from the cold, and he knew he had to get her warm and dry—as quickly as possible.

"Let's go. You got anything else in there we can use to keep you warm?"

She shook her head. "I'm wearing everything I've g-got."

He chuckled at her mismatched and odd-fitting layers. "Good girl. We're out of here, then."

He took off his ski hat and settled it on her blond head, carefully covering her ears. Then he shoved her hands in the leather gloves he'd been using.

"My hands b-b-burn," she complained.

"That's good. At least you can feel them." Then he saw her feet. "Where the hell are your shoes?"

She blinked down at her toes. "They were w-wet. I had to t-take them off."

"You have to put them back on, at least until we make it to my Landcruiser." He reached inside the car for her tennis shoes.

When he finished tying her shoelaces, she glanced around and frowned. "Where's your truck?"

He raised his brows, wondering how to tell her the truth of the situation. "You're not still worried that I'm an ax murderer, are you?"

"Why?"

"Because I've got some good news and some bad news. The bad news is that my Landcruiser's stuck. We're not going to get out of here tonight." He grabbed her cell phone from the car, took her hand, and started to pull her over to where he'd left his vehicle. "But the good news is, you're no longer alone."

"That's not such g-good news for you," she said.

He grinned and looked back at her, admiring the unique shape of her amber-colored eyes. "It's not as bad as you might think."

CHANTEL LET DILLON lead her up the side of a sharp incline through waist-deep snow. Pine trees stood all around them, tops bending and limbs swaying as they fought the same wind that flung ice crystals into her face. Her clothes and shoes were soaked through, and even with gloves on her hands, she didn't have enough body heat to warm her fingers. Never had she been so cold, not in ten years of New York winters.

She slipped and fell, and Dillon hauled her back to her feet. "Come on, we've got to hurry. I don't want you to get frostbite," he said, pulling her more forcefully behind him.

Chantel angled her face up to see through the trees in front of them. Other than the small circle from Dillon's flashlight, everything was completely dark. The falling snow obliterated even the moon's light, but the night wasn't silent. The wind alternately whined and howled, and tree limbs scratched and clawed at each other.

"Are you sure you know wh-where we're going?" she called. It felt as though they were scaling a mountain, heading deeper into the forest, instead of toward civilization.

"I'm taking a more direct route, but we'll get there."

"I d-don't think I can walk any farther." The air smelled like cold steel, not the pine she'd been anticipating, and suddenly Chantel wondered why she'd ever wanted to go to Tahoe in the first place. She had enough to take care of in the valley. She wasn't ready to deal with the issues between her and Stacy yet.

"We gotta keep moving. It's not much farther." Dillon sheltered her with his large body and tugged persistently at her arm.

"I'm freezing!"

"So am I. Come on, Chantel, we need to keep walking. Talk to me. That'll keep our minds off the cold."

She looked at the man who'd risked his life to save her. Hadn't she wrecked his car earlier? Yet here he was, trudging through the snow, pulling her along, telling her to talk to him. Without him...

Chantel didn't want to think about what might have happened without him. "You're c-crazy, Dillon. Why didn't you leave me?"

"Freud would probably say I'm trying to prove my masculinity."

She thought he was smiling but couldn't see his face in the darkness. "There are easier ways to do that."

He laughed. "I've always had to do things the hard way. My poor mother used to shake her head in exasperation and tell me how wonderful my sisters were to raise."

"F-F-Freud would probably have something to say about that, t-t-too."

"No doubt. Only I don't think being a troublemaker has anything to do with my sexuality."

"I think it's the t-testosterone. My c-cousin once kicked a hole in the wall when I put him down for a nap."

Dillon paused. "How old was he?"

"Three. It was my f-fault, really. I forgot to take off his cowboy boots."

Dillon put his arms around her waist and half carried her over a fallen log. "Your cousin's my kind of kid. But girls can be hellions, too. My littlest is a spitfire."

"How many—" Chantel could barely form the words "—children do you have?"

"Two girls, nine and seven."

She pictured him with a couple of dark-haired, blue-eyed daughters. If they looked anything like their father, they would be beautiful. "So you're m-married?"

"Divorced."

"I'm s-sorry."

"So am I."

Chantel fell silent again. She had no strength left.

"Tell me about you," Dillon suggested. "Is there a man in your life?"

"No." Wade was too long a story, and she was far too weary to expand on her answer. "I can't g-go any f-farther," she said, sinking to her knees in the snow. Somehow she wasn't cold anymore. She just didn't care. There wasn't anything left inside her with which to fight. "You g-go on…"

"I'm not leaving you." A strong arm swept her to her feet, but she pulled away again, shaking her head. *I can't,* rang through her thoughts, but she could no longer speak. Her mind seemed clouded, her senses dulled. Her body simply slowed and stopped moving, like a cheap windup toy.

"Chantel!" The command cut through her hazy thoughts, but she refused it. *Let this be over.*

The second time Chantel heard her name, she knew Dil-

lon would not be denied. Weakly she tried to move toward
to his voice, then felt the world tip and sway as he lifted
her in his arms.

"So you're going to make me carry you, huh?" he
breathed, his chest heaving as he bore her weight through
the wind and snow.

Silence fell for what seemed a long time. Then, from
somewhere far above her, Chantel heard Dillon again. "Stay
with me, baby," he whispered urgently. "Don't go to sleep!
Fight the darkness, Chantel."

Chantel wasn't sure she wanted to stay, let alone fight,
but something about his voice enticed her toward his
strength. *Don't let me go...I won't let go.*

"I see it now."

His words made no sense, caused no reaction in Chantel.
She only knew that he'd left her. But he was close. She
could hear him talking to himself, moving a few feet away.
A car door slammed, twice, then she felt herself being jos-
tled about as he pulled and tugged at her arms, her legs,
her...

What was it? What did he want from her?

Then it all came clear. He was stripping off her clothes.

CHAPTER THREE

CHANTEL'S BODY burned as it warmed by degrees, slowly turning from what felt like dead wood to living flesh again. She didn't know how much time had passed, only that she was in some sort of sleeping bag, crushed against something strong and hard—an expansive chest? Two sinewy arms circled her as large hands chafed her back. A rough stubbled chin grazed her cheek as thickly muscled legs became entwined with her own, moving constantly, trying to warm her lower extremities.

She was being held by a naked man. And he was warming a great deal more than her extremities.

She stiffened.

"Chantel? Are you back with me?"

The voice identified Dillon immediately, but still she raised her head to make out his face in the darkness. "Wh-What happened?"

Closing his eyes, he shamelessly hugged her to him, belly to belly. It was then that Chantel realized how fast his heart was beating.

"What's wrong?" she asked, still disoriented.

"Are you kidding? I thought I was going to lose you. It was nip and tuck there for a while."

Slowly the memory of being stranded in her car came back to her. She remembered how Dillon had rescued her, remembered trudging behind him through the snow. Then there was nothing but blackness until the burning and tingling started and grew painful in its severity.

"How do you feel?" he asked.

"Like I'm on fire."

"That's good."

"Where are my clothes?"

"I don't know. Outside somewhere. I wasn't concerned with what happened to them. I just knew I had to get them off you—fast."

"Because..."

"Because you were soaking wet and freezing to death. And that's what you're supposed to do with someone in that situation." His voice sounded slightly defensive, as though she'd accused him of being some kind of pervert.

Realizing he'd just saved her life, Chantel tried to act nonchalant. She wasn't sure he'd needed to remove *every* stitch of their clothing, but he'd obviously acted in what he thought was her best interests. "I've seen it before on television," she admitted.

"How's the burning in your arms and legs? Getting any better?"

"A little."

Chantel shifted to remove her lower body from contact with Dillon's, which was nearly impossible in the snug bag. While modeling, she'd seen a score of naked men, changing from one outfit to another, and lots of men had seen her doing the same thing. But somehow she couldn't treat being with Dillon as indifferently as she'd handled working around those fellow models, photographers, costumers and artistic directors. Especially since his body felt good enough to melt her bones.

"Relax."

Though nervous and vulnerable, she tried to do as he suggested, but ended up simply keeping as still as she could.

It had been almost a year since she'd been with a man. She'd gotten so skinny in her final months with Wade that he hadn't wanted her, at least sexually. And the memory of it made her even more self-conscious than she would normally have felt in this particular dilemma.

"I'm sorry I got you into this mess," she said to break the awkward silence.

His chuckle rumbled in her ear. "Don't be. From my perspective, there are worse things than having a beautiful woman in my arms."

Chantel smiled. So he was generous, as well as kind. "What do we do when we're warm?"

"Wait for morning."

The thought of spending the entire night in Dillon's arms sent a shiver up Chantel's spine. He hugged her closer and began to rub her back again, as though he assumed her reaction had something to do with the cold. But Chantel knew it had much more to do with the man holding her, stroking her.

"That feels good," she whispered.

Dillon's shallow breathing—and more obvious proof lower down—told her he agreed. "I guess this might get a little awkward," he said, knowing, of course, that she couldn't possibly miss his arousal. "But don't worry. I won't, you know, try anything."

She smiled at his attempt to reassure her. "We just have to relax, like you said."

"Unfortunately, even that won't change some things."

"I know," she whispered. "It's okay."

Chantel had felt exhausted only moments earlier, but now her blood zipped through her veins and wouldn't let her lie still. "We're not going to be able to rest," she said, "if we feel we can't move."

"We can move."

"I know, but I'm hesitant to put my arm here or my leg there..."

"Do whatever makes you comfortable."

Sighing, she snuggled closer, laying her head on his chest and slipping one cold foot between his. The burning in her arms and legs had eased, but her fingers and toes still felt like ice. "Thanks," she said. "I guess we should probably get some sleep. I'm a lot warmer now, aren't you?"

"I'm plenty warm," he told her, but to Chantel his body didn't feel as though he was ready for sleep. His muscles were taut, his chest rising and falling too fast.

Dillon's breath stirred her hair, but he said no more. Chantel listened to the storm outside until sleep began to woo her. Then, when she was finally warm, she drifted slowly toward it. As her brain lost its override on her body, she relaxed even more and pressed closer to the muscled chest beneath her hands, the powerful limbs entwined with her own. The steady beat of Dillon's heart lulled her that final step, and she fell into peaceful oblivion.

DILLON STARED into the darkness, willing his body to forget the soft flesh pressed against his, to block out the smell of woman that filled his nostrils. He and Chantel Miller were merely two strangers surviving the storm together. Morning would come and everything would be the way it was before.

Still, he had to admit that the person he held in his arms was no everyday woman. She was slender and elegant, but it was her smile and her eyes that appealed to him most. Unique, exquisite, haunting.

Beautiful. She was simply beautiful. And, of course, her body did nothing to change that overall impression. Long legs, smooth and shapely, slid against his own; her small perfect breasts were crushed against his chest. He'd longed to touch them from the moment he'd taken off her shirt, to feel them in his palms...

She smashed my truck. She smashed my truck. She smashed my truck. And she made me miss the party at the cabin.

He repeated Chantel's shortcomings over and over to himself, but nothing quelled the hot desire that smoked through his veins. To make matters worse, he'd begun to feel a little proprietary toward her. He had found her. He had saved her. It was that old *finders keepers, losers weepers* thing, and he knew it. But no matter how many times he told himself no, his groin tightened, insisting on a different answer.

If it hadn't been so long, he wouldn't be like this, he told himself. He and Amanda had divorced two years ago, and he hadn't slept with a woman since. He'd come close a few times, but the commitment that went with sex had always pulled him up short—because he didn't want to give his daughters any competition. He owed Brittney and Sydney his wholehearted loyalty. Divorce was hard enough. He knew firsthand how difficult it could be to get along with a stepparent. Why would he do the same thing to his kids that his parents had done to him?

Chantel stirred. One of her hands climbed across his ribs, and he had to stop himself from cupping the roundness of her derriere and pressing her more firmly against him. It was simply the most natural of responses. But she was sleeping peacefully and had no idea she was driving him mad.

And he'd promised he'd be good.

A sweet mewling sound came from Chantel, but her eyes remained closed. She was probably dreaming. He gazed through the darkness, finding the curve of her cheek, the silky spray of hair that fanned out over his arm, and caught sight of her lips. They were slightly parted...and wet.

He clenched his jaw. It was going to be a long night.

THE CELL PHONE broke the silence, waking Chantel with a start. Next to her, Dillon stirred and they both fumbled around until Chantel came up with the phone, which turned out to be her own, and answered it.

"Hello?"

"Miss Miller?" a man's voice said.

"Yes?"

"This is the police dispatcher just checking to make sure you're okay. The storm hasn't lifted yet, but I want you to know we'll get there as soon as we can."

"Okay."

"You sound tired, Miss Miller, but I can't stress how important it is that you not fall asleep. With the windchill factor, it's well below zero outside."

"I understand, but I'm not alone anymore."

"What?"

"I, um... A friend of mine came to find me. Only he's stuck now, too."

"The two of you are together?"

Dillon shoved himself up onto one elbow. "Give me the phone so I can tell them where we are."

"We're sheltering in a Toyota Landcruiser," she said into the receiver. "Here, he wants to talk to you."

Chantel listened as Dillon identified himself and gave the dispatcher directions. When he ended the call, she looked at him expectantly. "What did he say?"

"To sit tight. Someone'll be here as soon as the storm lifts." He flicked on a flashlight and looked at his watch.

"What time is it?"

"Three o'clock."

Chantel groaned. "No wonder I'm still tired. Did you get any sleep?"

"I dropped off about five minutes before the phone rang."

Now that she and Dillon were both awake, Chantel felt her earlier self-consciousness return but fought it back. They might as well get used to each other. According to the dispatcher, the police were going to be a while yet. "What kept you up?"

She thought he arched a brow at her, but couldn't see clearly enough in the darkness.

"You don't want to know," he said.

"What—was I snoring?"

He laughed. "You didn't have to."

Catching his meaning, Chantel felt her face flush and tried to sidle away, but he wrapped an arm around her and pulled her down beside him. "Come on. It's too cold for that."

She put a hand on his chest, keeping a slight distance between them. "Tell me about yourself, Dillon."

"What do you want to know?"

"Well…tell me about your daughters."

He opened up easily to that question. His voice warmed as he talked about his girls and their accomplishments. His fourth-grader had just competed against a sixth-grader for student-body treasurer and won. She played the clarinet in band and sang in the school choir. His second-grader was in gymnastics and could already do a back flip.

Chantel felt something tug at her heart and knew she should have steered the conversation away from kids. It was always this way when…

Dillon fell silent right in the middle of describing a family trip they'd taken to Disneyland just before the divorce.

"And then what?" she prompted.

He didn't answer, and Chantel berated herself for not listening more closely. What was it he'd said? Something about promising his girls they'd go back every year. Wasn't that it? "Dillon?"

"What?"

"You didn't finish."

"I know. I don't want to talk about it anymore."

"What's wrong?" She propped herself up to look in his face, but in the darkness, she couldn't decide whether his expression was as stony as his voice suggested.

He shook his head. "I'm just angry. It has nothing to do with you."

"It's that damn Mickey Mouse, right? You hate him."

He gave her a grudging smile. "No."

"Then what?" Chantel studied him again and guessed that what she saw was pain. "Forget it. You don't have to talk about it," she said. "Divorce is a hard thing—for everyone."

"I never thought I'd be divorced," he admitted. "I never wanted to be."

"I don't think anyone ever plans on it."

"It's funny how someone you love can turn into someone you don't even know, isn't it?"

"Oh, I see. You're not over your ex-wife yet." For some reason she wanted to pull away, but there was no room to do so.

He laughed harshly. "Wrong. I'm completely over her. I got over her shortly after her second affair, which, ironically enough, was with the mailman."

"You're kidding."

"No. Well, technically speaking, he wasn't our mailman, but he worked for the post office."

"How did she meet him?"

"At the gym."

"Ouch."

He laughed, but his voice was edged with bitterness. "I used to think that sort of thing could never happen to me."

"Does it hurt to talk about it?"

"Not anymore. At first I thought I'd never recover. I blamed myself. We got married too young. I was gone too much, working, trying to put myself through school. I think she was lonely and bored and found the wrong kind of friend. She and the woman next door, who was already divorced, started going out together in the afternoons, visiting bars. I could see what was happening, but I thought I could stop it. I thought if I was meeting her emotional needs, she wouldn't turn to other men. She admitted she didn't love them."

"Did you ever find out why she did it?"

"She said she liked the thrill of it. I think she was on boyfriend number three then, and she was leaving the girls with baby-sitters to spend the day at the gym or tanning. I cut back on my hours at work, but she resented the hit our budget suffered because of it, and her behavior only got worse. I finally realized she had affairs because it fed her ego that other men found her attractive. And she liked my jealous reaction."

"I take it the two of you aren't friends now."

"Actually I'm just trying not to dislike her too much. Not for the old stuff, her betrayal of me—that's history. It's the problems we're having now that make me mad. It kills me that I'm missing so much of my girls' lives. Their mother changes boyfriends like she changes underwear and insists Brittney and Sydney welcome each new guy with open arms. Sometimes she even makes them call whoever it is 'daddy.'"

Instinctively Chantel reached up to caress his cheek. "You sound like a wonderful father. Can't you gain custody somehow?"

"I've spent thousands of dollars trying to do just that. California is touted as being liberal, but the judge still won't award me custody. I'd have to completely discredit Amanda to get them, and I just can't bring myself to destroy my daughters' mother."

"What about visitation rights?"

"I pick up the girls whenever I legally can, but a lot of the time Amanda takes off so that they're not home when I arrive. Or she leaves them at her mother's, who thinks I've let her daughter down and won't even open the door to me."

"Fighting all of that must get old."

He paused. "I'd rather fight it than not see them. Now Amanda is trying to get permission from the court to move to Iowa."

"Iowa!"

"Yeah." He scrubbed his face with his free hand. "I'm sorry. I don't know why I'm telling you this."

"Because it's the middle of the night, and we're naked and huddled together in your sleeping bag."

"I'm fully aware of the naked part, but how come I'm the only one baring my soul?"

So I don't have to tell you about the skeletons in *my* closet.

"Do you like being an architect?" she countered.

"I love my work, but we're going to talk about you now. What do you do?"

"I work in the district office of my state senator."

"Were you involved in politics in New York?"

"No."

"'No'? That's it? What, were you a stripper or something?"

"I was a model."

"Really? Who'd you model for?"

Chantel bit her lip, reluctant to discuss her modeling experience because she was afraid of where the conversation would lead. "Let's talk about something else."

"Why? You didn't like modeling?"

"I loved it."

"Then tell me about it."

Cocooned against the weather, Chantel breathed in the smell of the aftershave she'd first noticed when Dillon had leaned into her car, and smiled. She could trust him. He'd come for her despite the storm, even after the police had given up.

"I did runway modeling, and some work for high-end catalogs. I was in the *Sports Illustrated* swimsuit issue a couple of years, used to model for Calvin Klein a lot. Oh, and I was on the cover of *Vogue* once."

"Wow, sounds like you were pretty successful. What happened?"

Chantel thought of Wade and his demands, demands that increased with her success. "I had a boyfriend...well, more like a husband, really. We lived together for the ten years I was in New York. He modeled, too, and when he didn't get the breaks I did, he became fanatically jealous. He insisted I cancel contracts I never should have canceled, had me refuse jobs I should have taken. I did it to preserve the relationship, to prove he came first. We'd talked about having a family, and I wanted to get married, but he kept putting me off. He said he didn't see the point of making it official since all that mattered was what we felt, not some piece of paper. The harder I tried to please him, the more difficult he became. And then I got sick and had to quit altogether."

"What kind of sick?"

Chantel sighed. She hated telling people what had happened to her and usually didn't. They didn't understand anorexia, were generally frightened of the self-hate that spurs it on. "It wasn't anything communicable."

"I wasn't thinking that." He smoothed the hair off her forehead, and Chantel closed her eyes, wishing he'd go on caressing her until the devils from her past were forgotten. "Tell me what happened," he whispered.

"I had anorexia."

"How bad?"

"I had to be hospitalized. The doctors didn't think I'd make it. Neither did Wade."

"Wade's the man you were living with?"

She nodded. "Wade Bennett. I believe, deep down, he was hoping against me. Maybe that's what made me decide to prove them all wrong."

Dillon was silent for a long while. "Where's Wade now?"

"In New York, still trying to make it, I guess. I won't open his letters."

Dillon's arms tightened around her. "And you're well now, aren't you? You look... I mean, I've never seen a more beautiful woman."

She'd heard those words before, over the years, from numerous men who'd tried to pick her up. But Dillon sounded sincere. "Anorexia is like alcoholism. You're never really cured. It's a constant battle."

"It's a battle you'll win."

Unable to stop herself from giving him a simple gesture of affection, Chantel played with the hair on his arm, then slid her hand up to his shoulder. "I think your wife must've been crazy."

He laughed and rolled her onto her back. In the process

his hand brushed her nipple, which immediately drew up hard and tight.

"Chantel?'

"Mmm?''

"Are you seeing anyone now?''

The huskiness of his voice told her he wanted her, and Chantel felt an answering warmth in the pit of her stomach. "I'm not dating anyone. I only recently moved back to California.''

"Good.''

"Why?''

"Because I'm going to kiss you.''

His head descended and his lips found and molded to hers, tasting her, teasing her, gently prodding. The practical side of Chantel screamed that she'd known this man for mere hours. But her heart felt as though she'd known him for years.

She opened her mouth to welcome his tongue, surprised that the small cut she'd received in the accident didn't bother her, and he deepened the kiss until the warmth blooming in her belly began to spread out to her limbs. He tasted the way his breath smelled, like spearmint gum, she thought lazily, and began exploring his mouth. Circling his neck with her arms, she let her hands delve into the thickness of his dark hair, threading the short silky locks through her fingers, tugging him closer.

When she groaned, he made an identical sound in his throat, and quickened the pace of their kiss until Chantel was so hungry for more she was shaking. She shifted, pressing her body more fully against him, then gasped when his large rough palm clutched her breast.

Two fingers flicked across her nipple as he trailed kisses down her throat, whispering how wonderful she felt and tasted and looked. Chantel arched toward him, wanting him to kiss her breasts.

He read her need quickly and easily, and responded with an eagerness that made her desire spiral even higher. His mouth clamped on to her nipple, and as his tongue darted and teased and suckled, hot jolts of pleasure went through her. "That's good," she murmured.

He moved to the other breast, and she kneaded his powerful shoulders, reveling in the way his body fit perfectly against hers. Dillon's size made her feel small for the first time in her adult life. And what he was doing to her—it was so fulfilling. Dillon had already touched something deep inside her, something Wade had never reached.

"Chantel?" Dillon's raspy breath tickled her ear as he nuzzled her neck. "Do you want me to stop, Chantel? I know I said I wouldn't touch you, but I never dreamed it would be so…"

She wrapped her legs around his so he couldn't put any space between them. "No, don't stop," she whispered.

"What about birth control?"

"We don't have to worry about it." Chantel swallowed hard, willing back sudden tears. "I can't have children."

He paused above her, as though trying to see her face in the darkness. "The anorexia?"

"They told me in the hospital that my reproductive system has shut down and will never work properly again. I haven't had a real period for over a year." She drew a shaky breath, and then realized she was crying.

"I'm sorry," he murmured, kissing her forehead and her cheeks. "That's a tough break, especially if you want kids."

"There's nothing like a baby, right?" She tried to sound flippant, but couldn't stifle the sob that gave her true feelings away.

The sympathetic tone of Dillon's voice caressed her as effectively as the fingers that found and wiped away her tears. "There are other good things in life," he whispered.

Her arms tightened around his neck. "Show me one, Dillon. Show me this one," she said, and pulled him down for another mind-numbing kiss.

CHAPTER FOUR

IT WAS THE SILENCE that woke him.

Dillon blinked and raised his head to listen. The wind had died. What time was it? Difficult to tell. The snow piled on top of the truck kept the inside dark, but he'd bet it was morning.

He shifted slightly, trying not to wake Chantel as he let some of the blood flow back into the arm she was sleeping on. It had been quite a night! He grinned, remembering Chantel's first warm willing response and the times he'd made love to her since. Sometimes she was a little shy and reserved, sometimes she played the temptress. But the crazy thing was that he couldn't get enough of her. Even now, just looking at her face, sweet and passive in sleep, he wanted to wake her and lose himself in her arms again.

"Is the storm over yet?" she asked, her eyelids fluttering open, despite Dillon's decision to let her sleep.

"I think so."

"Darn."

He kissed the tip of her nose. "What does that mean?"

"They'll be coming for us."

"Isn't that what we want?"

Her large eyes gazed up at him, and he caught his breath. Was it possible to fall in love in only one night?

"I don't want reality to intrude," she complained. Then she sighed. "I have to go see my sister. You have your friends waiting for you." Her silky limbs wrapped around him again, and she kissed his neck. "Mmm, I guess we got a little sweaty last night. You taste salty."

He laughed. "We got a lot sweaty, among other things."

"It was incredible, wasn't it?"

"Good enough that you won't forget me before we get home?"

"How could I forget the man who saved my life?"

"Hey, that's right! Doesn't that make you my slave or something?"

"No!" She tried to wriggle away, but he restrained her.

"Come on, slave, I'm getting hungry for more of you..."

She groaned. "You're insatiable! Not again! I'm tired." Running her fingers up and down his spine, she massaged the stiff muscles in his back, then pulled him down for a long searching kiss.

Dillon savored the taste of her, wishing they were at his place so they could get up and take a hot shower together and eat something. "If we were home, I'd make you breakfast in bed," he told her.

"Where's home?"

"Lafayette."

"We live that close to each other?"

He ran a hand through his sleep-tousled hair. "Yep. And then, after breakfast, I'd get you in the tub and lather your hair and massage your scalp and lick water off the tips of your breasts..."

"Hmm...maybe I'm not as tired as I thought," she said, but before Dillon could take her up on the invitation, they heard some kind of heavy machinery moving toward them.

Chantel groaned. "A snowplow. They're here, aren't they?"

Dillon listened to the noise get louder and louder as the plow made its way through the heavy snow. "That's my guess."

She sighed and studied him, looking somber for the first time that morning. "I haven't thanked you for coming back for me, Dillon. Who knows how long I would've had to wait before the police found me? I couldn't even give them good directions. What you did was so brave."

He wiggled his brows to make her laugh again. "And I've been handsomely rewarded."

"Roll over and let me hold you," she said. "Just until they get here."

He obeyed, and she curved her body, spoon-fashion, along the back of his.

"What are we going to do about clothes?" she asked, the noise of the plow nearly drowning out her voice. "I don't like the idea of being caught in such a vulnerable position."

"Don't worry. I'll get out and take care of everything. You can stay modestly covered back here."

"Thanks, Dillon."

"Chantel?"

"Uh-huh?"

"Can I call you when we get home?" he asked, half-afraid she'd refuse him for some reason only she knew.

But a *yes* sounded in his ear, and he smiled and pulled her arms more tightly around him.

CHANTEL DREW a deep breath and stared up at the A-frame log cabin that corresponded to the address on the directions Stacy had given her—and wished she was still with Dillon. After all the highs and lows of the past night, she felt physically and emotionally spent. The last thing she wanted to do right now was face her sister.

If only she hadn't given her word and could simply head back home—

"Omigosh, Chantel, what happened to you?" Stacy appeared in the doorway and frowned at the damaged Jaguar. "Now your car doesn't look any better than my Honda."

Chantel gave her a tired grin, feeling awkward and unsure of how to greet her sister. Should she rush over and hug Stacy as though they hadn't been estranged for ten years? Just smile and wave "hello"?

Remembering her sister's cold response the first time Chantel had contacted her—when she'd just returned from New York and had blubbered her way through a painful apology—she opted for the smile and jammed her hands in her pockets. "Would you believe I got stuck in the storm last night and had to wait for the police to bring a tow and get me out?"

"Are you kidding? Why didn't you call me?"

I've been worried. For a split second, Chantel hoped to hear those words, but Stacy didn't add them. "I drove off without the phone number." She chuckled, feeling her palms start to sweat and wishing, more than ever, that she could climb back in her car and drive away.

"Are you okay?"

I've been worried.

Again the words didn't come. Chantel clenched her fists in the pockets of her baggy jeans. Her sister would never say anything that indicated that she still cared. Why hope? "I think I'll be better after I shower and have something to eat. Tell me this place has hot water."

"It does. Everyone else left to go skiing, so the bathrooms are free."

"Oh! I'm sorry if waiting for me made you miss the fun."

Stacy paused halfway between the door and the Jaguar. "No, actually I'm expecting someone else. He'll be here anytime."

Chantel felt a blush heat her cheeks. What had she been thinking? She forced a smile. "So you've met a guy, huh?"

"Yeah."

"You never mentioned him on the phone."

"There wasn't any reason to go into it. I told you I was inviting a few friends, and I did."

"Well, tell me about him," Chantel said, trying to act like any normal sister would. Besides Stacy's father, who lived a hermit's life somewhere in New Mexico, they had no family left. Whether either of them wanted to admit it or not, they needed each other.

Stacy shrugged. "What do you want to know?"

"Where did you meet?"

"At the hospital. We've known each other for a couple of years."

"He's a doctor?"

"No, he was there for a meeting with one of the doctors. He was handling the majority of the tenant improvements for the medical building next door."

"And you really like him?"

For a moment Stacy's hard shell cracked and she gave Chantel a genuine smile. "Like him! You should see him! I've never been so head over heels in love. I'm going to marry this one or die trying."

Chantel laughed. "Wow. He must be something. I can't wait to meet him."

The shadow of old pain fell across Stacy's face, making Chantel regret the simple offhand remark. "Stacy—"

"I know. You'd better have that shower," she said briskly. "Let's take your stuff inside."

Trying to remember the warmth and approval she'd felt with Dillon, Chantel focused on his parting kiss and his promise to call her as soon as she arrived home.

She could do this. She was only staying in Tahoe till

Sunday, and thinking of Dillon would get her through the weekend.

Thinking of Dillon could get her through anything.

HAD STACY'S BOYFRIEND arrived? Chantel stepped out of the shower and listened for voices in the living room as she pulled on the jeans and long-sleeved T-shirt she'd had her sister toss in the dryer, but heard nothing beyond the distant drone of the television.

"Stace?" she called out.

A light step sounded in the hall, and her sister poked her head into the bedroom just as Chantel began to work the snarls out of her long hair. "You done?"

"Yeah. It felt great. Is your friend here?"

"Not yet. He called to say he stopped off for a late breakfast. He'll be here any minute."

Chantel smiled at her sister's barely concealed excitement. "You still want to get married, Stace?"

"If I want kids, I don't have a lot of time to waste. I'm already thirty-two." She fingered Chantel's expensive leather luggage.

"That's only three years older than me." *Only, I don't have to worry about getting married...or having kids.* Instinctively Chantel pressed a hand to her stomach. The ultimate price. She wondered if Stacy would more easily forgive her if she knew, then rejected the idea. She wouldn't play on her sister's sympathy. That was cowardly. She'd gotten what she deserved. Wasn't that what Wade had said the last time she'd seen him?

For once in his life he'd been right.

"After age thirty, three years counts for a lot," Stacy said, plopping down on the bed while Chantel applied lotion to her face.

"While the rest of us were dreaming of having careers,

you always wanted to marry and settle down,'' Chantel murmured.

"Ever since I graduated from high school, but all too often I made the mistake of bringing them home. Then they'd see you.''

And what had stopped her from finding a husband during the past ten years, while Chantel was in New York?

Chantel stifled the defensive retort. She didn't want to start a fight. She was here to rebuild her relationship with Stacy, not destroy it. "I'm sorry, Stace. I can't understand why anyone would rather be with me than you.''

Her sister sighed. "Look in the mirror, Chantel. That explains everything.''

Chantel gazed into the mirror that contrasted her tall lean form with her sister's short slightly stocky build, her light eyes with her sister's chocolate-colored irises.

"We're as opposite as night and day, aren't we?'' Stacy said.

"My father was tall and blond, yours short and dark. Mother loved them both. We didn't get to place an order. I certainly never asked to be six feet tall.''

"And I never asked for saddlebags. Them's the breaks, I guess.''

Chantel glanced at her sister's curvy figure. "You don't have saddlebags. I've always wanted to be petite, like you.''

A knock from the front of the cabin interrupted them, and Stacy jumped to her feet. "He's here!''

Waving her out of the room, Chantel said, "You go enjoy him. I'm pretty tired after last night. I think I'll lie down for a while. Which bunk is mine?''

There were two unmade beds and two that hadn't been touched. "Take your pick of those,'' Stacy said, already on her way out. At the door she turned back. "On second thought, why don't you meet him before your nap? We may as well get it over with.''

Chantel cringed at the tone of Stacy's voice. She sounded as if she'd rather have root-canal work than introduce her sister to her boyfriend, but Chantel threw her shoulders back and took a deep breath.

Stacy was in love. It was time to meet her sister's Mr. Right—and to let him know he'd better not so much as throw a friendly smile in her direction.

Following her sister, she headed into the small cluttered living room, filled with a half-dozen pieces of mismatched furniture surrounding a black fireplace insert. Through the front window overlooking the drive, she caught a glimpse of a white sports utility vehicle. But the sight struck no chord in her until Stacy opened the door, and she saw Dillon Broderick standing on the front porch.

CHAPTER FIVE

"CHANTEL! WHAT ARE YOU doing here?" Dillon looked from Stacy to Chantel and back again. There were hundreds of cabins in the Tahoe area, and thousands of people came up on any given weekend to ski. What were the chances of running into her again? Not that he was unhappy about it. He'd been thinking about the new woman in his life ever since they'd parted, missing her, already looking forward to calling her. It just wasn't a pleasant surprise to find Chantel in company with the woman he'd been dating for the past few weeks.

Stacy's brows knitted together. "You two know each other?"

Dillon smiled uncomfortably. "Actually we—"

"Got in a car accident coming up here," Chantel cut in, her voice brisk. "We don't really know each other, just met briefly out in the storm to exchange insurance information." She shrugged. "I'm sorry about our little fender bender, by the way."

Just met briefly out in the storm? After what happened last night? Dillon wasn't sure how to react. The time he'd spent with Chantel meant something to him. *She* meant something to him. At the same time, he'd been dating Stacy for the past few weeks, and while they hadn't become serious or exclusive or anything, he wasn't sure exactly what she expected of him.

"I'm sure the insurance will take care of the Landcruiser,'' he said shortly. "How do you two know each other?''

"Chantel's my sister,'' Stacy replied.

Dillon wished he could step back into his truck until his head stopped reeling and he could catch his breath. Stacy's sister? He'd just slept with Stacy's *sister?* His gaze flew from Chantel's elegant fine-boned face, now devoid of color, to Stacy's pixie cuteness, and he wondered where the family resemblance was. He and Stacy had been friends for two years, but he couldn't remember her ever having mentioned a sister.

"It's cold outside. Come on in and tell me about last night," Stacy said with a quick welcoming hug.

Dillon glanced helplessly over Stacy's head to Chantel, but she wouldn't meet his eyes. Jamming her hands in the pockets of her jeans, she stared at the carpet.

Stacy hooked an arm through his and pulled him inside. "When Veronica said you'd called and weren't going to make it, I thought you'd turned back. What's this accident all about?''

Normally Dillon didn't mind Stacy's demonstrative nature, but today it grated on his nerves. Her touch seemed more familiar, more *possessive* than he'd noticed before. "It wasn't a bad one," he said simply, setting down his large duffel bag. "Is everyone else already on the slopes?''

"It took them a while to dig out from under the snow, but they're at Squaw Valley now. I told them we'd meet them after lunch.''

"Great.'' His eyes darted to Chantel again. Her hands were still in her pockets, and she was sidling toward the hallway.

"I'm going to go blow-dry my hair,'' she said before ducking out of the room.

Dillon tried to keep his gaze from following her, but it

was virtually impossible. He was too taken with her after last night. He was too concerned about the revelations of the morning.

"I gather the accident was my sister's fault," Stacy said, studying him.

Dillon rubbed his neck. "Not really. It was the storm more than anything. Where should I put my stuff?"

"You can room with Bill and Tony, if that's okay. There're four bunks in the back."

"Fine." Dillon let Stacy lead him down the hall. The high-pitched whir of a blow-dryer came from behind one of the doors they passed, tempting him to barge in and try to explain his relationship with Stacy to Chantel. But he told himself there'd be a better time and kept moving until they came to a small square room with two sets of bunk beds pushed against the walls. Cheap comic-strip curtains hung over one window, and a few well-worn rugs covered the wooden floor—standard furnishings for a rental cabin.

"How come you never mentioned having a sister?" he asked Stacy as he dropped his duffel on a wrinkle-free bed.

"Because, for a long time, I didn't," she replied.

WAS SHE IMAGINING IT or had Dillon's eyes really lit up the moment he saw Chantel? Stacy stood in the hall outside Dillon's room, chewing her upper lip. He was just surprised, she told herself. Not every man she met was going to throw her over for her sister. Still, she couldn't shake the feeling of foreboding that had shot through her veins when she'd introduced the two of them a few minutes ago.

Maybe she shouldn't have invited Chantel to join her this weekend. She simply wasn't up to living in her sister's shadow again.

Closing her eyes, Stacy took a deep breath, remembering Chantel's apology when she'd returned to California. The way she'd offered it, humbly and without hope, had melted Stacy's heart, reminding her how much Chantel had meant to her while they were growing up. Life was okay back then, better than okay, until one incredible year—when the tall gangly Chantel had suddenly become a stunningly beautiful woman.

Then things began to change. Stacy and her sister couldn't go to the mall anymore without boys falling all over themselves in their eagerness to get close to Chantel. They couldn't go dancing together without Stacy playing the wallflower while Chantel was swept onto the floor by one boy after another.

And now Chantel was back, and Stacy feared she'd find herself right where she used to be, playing second fiddle to the golden girl of the family. Life was almost easier when she and Chantel weren't speaking. If not for seeing Chantel's face plastered on the front of countless magazines, Stacy could almost convince herself that she didn't have a sister. And after what Chantel had done, she felt perfectly justified in doing so.

And yet…sometimes Stacy longed for the old days. The Christmas Eves they'd whispered together in one big bed, too excited to sleep. The Halloweens they'd poured all their candy into one common pot. The summers they'd spent together—the trees they'd climbed, the lemonade stands they'd run, the games they'd played.

They'd lost so much since then. Where had it gone?

Pushing away from the wall, Stacy crossed to her sister's door. The blow-dryer was quiet now, but she could hear Chantel moving around the room. She knocked softly. "It's me."

At her sister's invitation, Stacy slipped inside and sank onto the bed. "So what do you think?" she asked.

Chantel stood in front of the dresser, brushing her hair. "About Dillon?"

"No, about the price of eggs in China. Of course about Dillon."

Her sister smiled at her in the mirror. "He seems pretty special. I think you've chosen a great guy this time."

Stacy waited, sensing something more in her sister's voice, but Chantel didn't elaborate. "Are you going to tell me what happened last night? About the accident?"

"Oh, that." Chantel set the brush down and turned to face her. "Unfortunately I rear-ended him. It was so snowy and slick, I just couldn't stop in time."

"And then?"

Chantel cleared her throat. "And then I gave him my insurance information."

"But you said you got stuck."

"That was after the accident."

"What happened to Dillon?"

"I don't know."

Chantel had spoken so quietly, Stacy could barely hear her. "What?"

"I said I don't know. Maybe the Highway Patrol closed the freeway. I've heard they do that sometimes.

"Yeah, they do." Stacy toyed with the fringe on one of the throw pillows that decorated the bed. "So, do you want to go skiing with us today?"

"Actually I think I'll stay here and read, or just take it easy. Last night was pretty traumatic."

"Okay." Stacy tossed the pillow aside and stood to go, feeling instantly relieved—and hating herself for it.

CHANTEL COULDN'T STOP shaking. Long after Dillon and Stacy had left, she sat in the living room, staring out the window at the crumpled fender of her car and wondering how much more could go wrong before something finally went right. She'd almost died last night. If not for Dillon, she would have fallen asleep and never awoken. But he'd come for her, risked his own life to save hers, and his sacrifice and all they'd shared afterward had forged a bond so quick and sure Chantel wasn't sure how to sever it. She only knew that she had to. For Stacy.

How ironic that it would come to this, she thought. Or maybe it was simply justice.

The telephone rang, and Chantel glanced at the Formica counter where it sat on top of a narrow phone book. She had no desire to talk to anyone. She had even less energy. But the ringing wouldn't stop.

After several minutes she climbed to her feet and walked slowly across the room to answer it. "Hello?"

"Chantel?"

It was Dillon. Chantel's breath caught at the sound of his voice, and the memories of last night crowded closer. Memories of a rough jaw against her temple, words of passion in her ear. "I thought you were skiing."

"I'm in the lodge. I wanted to talk to you."

"Where's Stacy?"

"She took the lift up with the others."

There was an awkward pause.

"Listen, Chantel, I just want to say that I was sincere last night, that it was real. I didn't mention Stacy because she and I have only dated a few times. And nothing's ever happened. I mean, we haven't had sex or anything, in case you're worried about that."

Part of Chantel was relieved to think he hadn't slept with Stacy. A bigger part of her cringed to imagine what her sister would do if she found out about the two of them. "She cares about you, Dillon."

"I care about her, too. We've been friends for almost two years."

"So you wouldn't want to hurt her."

"Of course not."

Chantel took a deep breath. "Then you understand why this—whatever it is that sprang up between us—can't go on."

Silence. Then, "I'm not sure I understand at all."

"Stacy's my sister, Dillon."

"A fact I'm not likely to forget and one I wasn't very happy to discover. But I'm not sure I'm willing to give up a relationship that could work for one that wasn't going anywhere to begin with."

Chantel blinked against the tears welling in her eyes. She thought they'd shared something special; it was gratifying that Dillon felt the same way. But it made no difference in the end. Because nothing mattered except regaining Stacy's trust and proving herself a true friend and sister at last. She needed to do that for herself as much as her sister. "I just…can't."

"Why? I'm not saying we have to do anything right now. We can give it some time, let things cool off—"

"No. I don't want to be responsible for you backing away from Stacy. Last night was a mistake. I'm sorry, Dillon."

Chantel hung up while she still had the mental fortitude to do so. She didn't want him aware of the turmoil inside her. If he sensed her doubt, he'd push, and she couldn't afford that. Couldn't afford to be tempted into forgetting all her new goals and desires. Especially her desire to be the type of sister she should have been in the first place.

The phone rang again, but Chantel refused to answer it. She wouldn't open the door between her and Dillon, not even a crack. She was going to be bigger than she'd been before. Stronger and better. Safer.

"It's too complicated, Dillon," she whispered, even though she knew he couldn't hear her.

The phone kept ringing, on and on. Finally she covered her ears and wept.

HOW SHE MADE IT through the weekend, Chantel didn't know. They were some of the hardest days she'd ever spent, and she'd had her share of hard days in the past year. But she'd managed to keep Dillon at arm's length. He'd tried to talk to her several times and had watched her closely, his confusion and desire showing clearly in his eyes.

She'd turned a cold shoulder to him, refusing to entertain memories of their time together or to consider any contact in the future. He was Stacy's. Off-limits. Period. There was no margin for error in that.

Kicking off her shoes in the middle of her own living room on Monday evening, Chantel turned on the television before going into the kitchen to root through the refrigerator. At least work was getting easier. Today she'd forwarded several letters to Congressman Brown from constituents who needed help on federal issues. There wasn't much a state senator could do to assist someone with the IRS, except to pass on the request. She'd responded to myriad letters on child-support reform, somehow managing to figure out how to do a mail merge on her computer. And she'd learned how to handle the scheduling for the congressman so she could fill in if Nan, in the capitol office, was ever away.

She was beginning to think there was life after modeling. But she still regretted that she had no education. Stacy was a nurse, with a good job in the maternity ward at the hospital. Chantel envied her the pay but knew she could never work so closely with newborns. Always seeing someone else go home with what she wanted most would cause her constant pain.

A knock at the door interrupted her consideration of a frozen burrito. "Who is it?"

No answer.

Frowning, Chantel shut the freezer door and went to peek through the peephole. Whoever it was was standing too far to the right. She could make out nothing more than part of one denim-clad leg. Another solicitor for some worthy cause? They always seemed to come at dinnertime.

Chantel opened the door as far as the chain would allow. "Who is it?"

Wade shifted so she could see him. "It's me. Can I come in?"

Chantel's stomach dropped. *Oh, no. Not now.* It had only been six months since she'd left him in New York, but already he looked different. His hair was bleached blond, an earring dangled from his left ear, and he'd obviously been hitting the weights again. "No. How'd you find me?"

He gave her the grin that had won her heart when she was only nineteen. "We're both from this town. Where else would you be?"

"So what do you want?" she asked warily.

"Just to see you. We didn't part on the best of terms, and..." He ran a hand through his short thickly gelled hair. "I owe you an apology for not being there for you when you were in the hospital."

"I didn't want you with me in the hospital. I told you that."

"I know. You said it was something you had to do for yourself, but that's crazy. For all intents and purposes, you're still my wife, Chantel."

"I was never your wife, Wade."

He jammed one hand into the pocket of his Tommy Hilfiger jeans. "My folks would like to see you."

"I'll try and stop by," she replied, but she said it only

to placate him. Visiting the people she'd once considered her in-laws would prove too awkward. She liked them, but they'd never spent much time together, and she needed her break with Wade to be as clean as possible.

"Steve wants to know if you're coming back. He says he could put you to work right away."

Steve Morgan had been her agent, was still Wade's, evidently, and one of the few people Chantel actually missed. "Tell him I appreciate the thought, but I don't want to model anymore. You both know that."

"Well, I've gotten a few covers. Have you seen them?"

Chantel shook her head. She purposely stayed well away from the magazine racks at the grocery store. The allure of New York was strong enough without reminding herself of the life she'd led there. The easy money. The glamour and the parties. The attention. In those respects, the Big Apple had more than its share of appeal, but that kind of life was lethal to her. She couldn't keep herself well when everything depended on her looks. And when she was there, she couldn't stay away from Wade. He was an addiction as dangerous as any drug, because he thrived on her destruction.

"Are you going to keep me standing outside all day?" he asked. "Can't we at least be civil about this?"

A voice in Chantel's head urged her to refuse him. She supposed that was the voice of wisdom. Instead, she listened to her heart, which told her they'd been together for ten years and should be able to speak kindly to each other now. Closing the door just long enough to slide back the chain, she opened it again, and Wade stepped in.

"I thought you liked contemporary decor," he said, studying her living room, which could have been featured in the magazine *Country Living*.

"*You* like contemporary," she said simply, which pretty

much summed up their problems. Wade had to have everything his way. No one else mattered.

"Well, what you've done here is nice. You look great, by the way."

Chantel had no intention of returning the compliment, even though he did look good. He'd always looked good. And he smelled even better. The Givenchy that was his favorite cologne invaded her senses, bringing back memories she would rather forget.

"Where are you working now?" he asked.

She perched on the edge of a plaid wing-back chair, wishing he'd say whatever he'd come to say and then just go. "I work for a state senator."

"Wow. How'd you get that?"

He thought she wasn't smart enough to do a real job. That hurt her, as always, but she kept her shoulders straight and her head high. "I applied."

"Good for you."

"Are you going to tell me why you're here?"

"You don't know?"

"If it's to talk me into coming back, you can save your breath." Chantel knew she sounded much tougher than she felt and hoped he couldn't see through her.

"How come you never answered any of my letters?"

"Because I never even opened them." She didn't add that she'd saved them, though. They were all lurking in a drawer in her bedroom.

"Why?"

"You know why."

"You think this whole thing is my fault, don't you?" He propped his hands on his narrow hips. "What did I ever do but love you and take care of you?"

And criticize and punish me. "I don't want to go into it anymore."

A fleeting look of fear crossed his face, but he quickly masked it. He'd probably thought she'd come crawling back to him eventually, unable to function without him. Well, she *was* functioning, perhaps not well but adequately, and she was going to continue to stand on her own two feet if it killed her. Even though, after what had happened with Dillon, she felt weaker now than ever. More alone...

"It's Stacy, isn't it?"

"It's you. It's me. It's us. We just don't work. I wish I'd seen it years ago."

A knock at the door interrupted them. Grateful for the reprieve, Chantel ducked around Wade to answer it.

"Hi." Dillon stood on her front stoop, wearing a pair of faded jeans and a chambray shirt, the wind ruffling his hair. The sight of him made Chantel's heart skip a beat and then go into triple time, even though her head warned her he was as dangerous to her peace of mind as Wade.

"Dillon."

He slanted her a crooked smile. "Can we talk?"

Chantel threw a glance over her shoulder, wondering what to do. Wade, always the jealous type, might say something to embarrass her, even though private punishment was more his style. When they were a couple, he'd withhold his affection and pout if he thought she'd paid too much attention to another man. Or, more times than not, he'd just get back at her by being obvious about the petite dark-haired groupies he sometimes slept with.

But none of that mattered anymore, she reminded herself. Opening the door, she let Dillon in.

"Dillon, this is...an old friend, Wade Bennett. He just got here from New York and stopped by to say hello."

Dillon's face grew shuttered, speculative, telling her he recognized Wade's name, but he nodded.

"Wade, this is Dillon Broderick."

Wade didn't bother to smile. Instead, he eyed Dillon from the top of his dark head down to his leather Top-Siders. Just over six feet, Wade wasn't exactly a small man, but Dillon had a few inches on him, broader shoulders and a more powerful build. He also looked far less groomed. While Wade had no doubt checked the mirror only moments before to make sure every hair was in place, Dillon had probably come after a long day at work without bothering to fuss about his appearance. His hair was unruly, as though he'd been running his fingers through it, and a five-o'clock shadow covered his jaw. His ''take me as I am'' air made him all the more appealing, in Chantel's opinion.

''What's he doing here?'' Wade demanded.

''Wade, don't,'' Chantel said, placing a hand on the door-knob. ''You were on your way out. Don't let Dillon stop you.''

''I just want to know what's going on. Is this guy trying to move in on my turf?''

''You have no turf, at least not here,'' she responded.

''So what? You think he just wants to be friends?'' Wade chuckled. ''Then you don't know guys. He's just trying to get in your pants.'' Wade spoke to Chantel, but his stare was a challenge, directed at Dillon. And Dillon seemed more than ready to answer it. His jaw tightened and his right hand curled into a fist.

Chantel stepped between them. The crudeness of Wade's words brought a heated blush to her cheeks, but she wasn't about to let the two of them start fighting. ''That kind of talk's not going to help anything,'' she said. ''And you have no right. Now, please go.''

Wade looked from her to Dillon and back again.

Dillon put one hand on the door, opening it wider. ''You heard her, buddy. Out.''

''Who the hell do you think you—''

Without even waiting for him to finish, Dillon grabbed Wade by the shoulders and tossed him outside. Chantel gasped, expecting her ex-boyfriend to come up swinging, but Wade merely scrambled to his feet, called them both a few choice names once he was out of range, and took off.

CHAPTER SIX

DILLON TOOK a deep breath, waiting for the adrenaline pumping through his body to subside. "Are you okay?" he asked, watching Chantel make her way over to the sofa and sink into it.

"I'm fine. I just thought… I didn't think he'd go without a fight."

"Guys like him never fight. They talk tough, but when someone calls their bluff, they run."

"Not Wade, at least not if he thinks he can win."

Dillon tried a smile, hoping to calm Chantel down. She'd lived with Wade for something like ten years, if he remembered correctly. "A man who's that concerned about what he sees in the mirror is going to be pretty careful," he said. "Gives whole new meaning to saving face."

Chantel blinked up at him, then laughed. "Can you always tell so much about someone you've just met?"

"Not everyone's that transparent. Take you, for instance. I've only known you four days, but I'm already confused." He took the seat next to her. "I was hoping you could explain a few things."

A certain wariness entered Chantel's eyes, but she nodded.

"I want to know how you could cut things off between us so quickly and easily. I thought you felt something that night. If I wasn't dreaming, you *told* me you did."

"That was before I knew about you and Stacy."

"There is no me and Stacy."

"Dillon, you were dating my sister. I hope, for her sake, that you still are."

"You want me to pretend to feel something I don't?"

"No…yes." Her fingertips flew to her temples as though she had a headache. "I don't know. I just want you to do whatever you would've done if you'd never met me. Stacy's a wonderful person. She'd make someone—you—a great wife."

The alarm that had gone off in his head when he'd first realized who Chantel was rang louder. All weekend he'd been telling himself that they just needed some time to talk, time alone. He'd been sure he could convince her that they should tell Stacy what had happened, explain that it was beyond their control and gain her blessing to keep seeing each other. Now he doubted he could reach Chantel, after all, and wondered if she'd ever open up to him again. "You can say that, after Friday night?" he asked.

She stared at the carpet, and her voice was soft when she answered. "I can't say anything else."

Dillon stood and began to pace. "Chantel, I've already made love to you." He whirled to face her. "I want to do it again, here, now, tomorrow, the day after that and the day after that. I can't forget how it felt to hold you, our bodies joined, and hear you cry out my name. I lost myself in that moment—"

"Stop!" She covered her ears, and when she looked up at him, he saw the tortured expression in her eyes. "It was a mistake, Dillon. We didn't even know each other. I nearly died that night. You saved me. It was an unusual situation. Things happened that otherwise wouldn't have."

"That's bullshit and you know it! It wasn't a passing attraction kindled by the heat of the moment. The spark is still there."

"What? What do you want from me?" Tears started down Chantel's face, and Dillon wanted to kiss them away as he had the night they'd been stranded in the storm. He remembered the silky feel of her cheek beneath his lips, the salty taste of her tears. She'd closed her eyes and given herself up to his comfort. He wished she'd do the same now.

"I want what we had."

"It was an illusion! *I'm* an illusion! Don't you know that? If not, ask the guy you just threw out of here."

"I don't give a damn what he thinks." Dillon knelt before her and tried to pull her into his arms, but she resisted. "Look at me, Chantel."

"You don't know me," she insisted. "If you did, you wouldn't want me. Men like you are a dime a dozen. They like the idea of having a fashion model to hang on their arm. Big man bags model. That's all."

The insult stung, bringing Dillon's anger back full force. He shoved away and got to his feet. "I didn't know you were a model when I went back for you. How can you say that?"

"Because if you cared about me, you wouldn't ask me to hurt my sister!"

Dillon let the words hang in the air. Was he being selfish to fight for what they had, what he thought they could have? "Stacy can't care that much for me. We've only dated a few times."

"She thinks she's in love with you."

"But that's crazy!" He turned away to stare at the Thomas Kincaid painting above the fireplace. "How?"

Chantel gazed up at him. "Easily," she murmured.

"What about you? Don't your feelings count for anything? Or are you trying to tell me you don't have any feelings for me?"

Dillon held his breath, waiting, hoping she'd give him a crumb of encouragement. But she spoke only of Stacy.

"I almost lost her once, Dillon, my only sister, my only living family. Our mother died of breast cancer when we were in junior high. Stacy's father took off when she was only three. Then my father—the father who raised her—died of a heart attack five years ago. I'm all she has left. And family is family. I'm going to be the type of family she can count on, through thick and thin. I'm going to be there for her, even though she doesn't think I have it in me. Because I love her. And because it's my duty. And because I owe it to her for the past."

He ran an impatient hand through his hair. "What do you mean? What happened in the past?"

"I told you. I nearly lost her."

"How can you *lose* a sister?"

"By stealing her fiancé and running away with him to New York!"

Dillon stared at Chantel's bent head. She was openly crying now. "Wade?" he asked numbly.

She nodded.

DILLON STARED at the ceiling of his bedroom, trying to figure out what he should do. He cared about Stacy, but he didn't love her. He thought he could love Chantel, but she wouldn't let him. And regardless of all the other confusing emotions swirling around in his head and his heart, he wanted Chantel physically, and more powerfully, than he'd ever wanted any woman.

With a groan he rolled over and faced the wall, seeing the crest of an early-morning sun through the branches of the crepe myrtle outside his window. He'd told himself over and over that he wouldn't get emotionally involved, not with anyone. Considering the way Amanda was acting, his two daughters needed him, not more competition for his time and attention. In the two years since his divorce, he'd dated and had fun, but no woman had come close to unlocking his heart. Until now.

Ironically enough, Chantel held the key and didn't want it.

Damn, life could be difficult.

He pictured Stacy's bright smile, the dimple that dented her cheek. He didn't want to hurt her any more than Chantel did, didn't want to ruin their friendship. He liked her, maybe even loved her in a brotherly sort of way, but after meeting Chantel, he knew he had to distance himself. Just in case there was ever a chance—

The telephone on his nightstand rang, and he picked up the receiver, hoping it was Chantel. He'd scribbled his home number on a slip of paper and placed it on her counter when he'd left. But deep down he knew she wouldn't use it. She'd already made up her mind, and her past experience with Wade, along with her drive for self-respect, wouldn't let her change it.

"Hello?"

"I can't believe I finally caught you home."

Dave, his uncle. Dillon smiled. "I went out for dinner last night. Have you been trying to reach me?"

"I've called half a dozen times, just never bothered to leave a message."

"Why not?"

"I hate answering machines."

Dillon released an exaggerated groan. Some of the older generation resisted change more than others. Dave, with his hulking build and gray crew cut, looked like some kind of tough guy. And he was. He was a childless retired marine with a history of promotions and a heap of awards. But Dillon knew him to be a gentle and compassionate man.

The type who talked little but meant every word he said. Dave had made a world of difference in Dillon's life. Though he'd never told Dillon he loved him—he wasn't vocal enough for that—Dillon had never doubted it. Despite all the stepfathers who'd sworn Dillon was worthless, Dave had believed differently. And Dillon had finally decided to prove him right. "I guess e-mail's out of the question, too, huh?"

Dave chuckled. "Damn computers. It's not enough people got 'em in every room in the house. Now they're packing 'em along everywhere they go."

"How's Reva?"

"Still badgering the hell out of me. Won't let me eat my steak and eggs without fussin' about the cholesterol. Weighs all the damn food. I swear, the farm looks as good as it does because work is my only refuge."

Dillon didn't believe that for a minute. Dave loved his Vermont farm, his retirement haven. And he loved Reva as much as any man could love a woman. Dillon knew that if anything happened to her…well, he didn't want to think about what would become of Dave.

"She still make you that chicken-and-broccoli casserole I like?"

"Yeah. I guess she has her moments."

Dillon could hear Reva saying something in the background and knew Dave was catching hell for what he'd said. He smiled to himself. "Tell her I appreciate that she's trying to take good care of you, even if you don't."

"If you call naggin' takin' care of a man…"

"She's the only one who could put up with you."

"That may be true."

Dillon could hear the smile in Dave's voice. They went on to talk about sports and the weather. His uncle never approached subjects any deeper than that, but beneath the surface of everything they said, Dillon felt the strong bond between them.

"When you comin' back this way?" Dave asked.

Dillon had visited the farm twice since the divorce, had taken the girls both times, and knew he'd go back again this summer. Brittney and Sydney loved running around with the dogs, climbing on the tractors and pulling carrots out of the garden. And he loved being with Dave and Reva. "I'll come for a week sometime in July or August."

"Good. Reva will make that casserole you like."

Of course she would. And she'd also make pies and bread, salads with the vegetables in the garden and, despite the cholesterol, they'd grill steaks. They'd drink lemonade on the porch after dinner. Dillon would try to pretend that Dave wasn't getting on in years. And he'd know they were some of the best days of his life.

"Gotta go. Reva says it's time for breakfast."

Dillon smiled again as he hung up and decided he might as well get out of bed. But the telephone rang again before he could so much as move.

"Hello?"

"Dillon, this is Helen."

Helen? His mother-in-law Helen? She hadn't called him once since the divorce. He sat up and propped himself against the headboard. "It's six o'clock in the morning. What's wrong, Helen?"

"It's Amanda." She coughed, then continued in her throaty smoker's voice. "She went to Las Vegas for the weekend with a...friend."

The way she said "friend" let Dillon know it was a man. With Amanda, of course, it would be. "And?"

"And she was supposed to be back last night, but I haven't heard from her."

"Where are the girls?"

"Here. With me."

"Did she leave you a number, tell you where she was staying?"

"No. She called on Saturday morning, but that was it. I'm worried. Brittney and Sydney missed school yesterday, and I missed work. I thought she'd be home anytime, but now…I don't know what to think. I can't miss another day of work or I'll lose my job."

"I'm coming to get the girls," Dillon said, dressing as he spoke. "Do you know the name of the man she went with? Maybe we can call the hotels to see if—"

"She said his name's John Heath, but I've already called all the hotels I can think of. None have a John Heath registered."

"Are the girls upset? Do they know what's going on?"

"They're still asleep. They know we've been waiting for their mother to come back, but they don't seem too worried. They're used to being here with me…a lot."

Dillon clamped down on the anger he felt at that statement. They didn't have to be at Helen's—ever. He wanted all the time he could get with his daughters, but Amanda kept them from him out of sheer spite. That her mother went along with it only added to his frustration and fury. He often wondered what Amanda had told Helen to poison her so completely. "Have you called the police?"

"They said I could file a report tomorrow, but they didn't sound like they were going to do anything about it. I filed one last year when Amanda disappeared for a few days, but it turned out to be nothing, so they think this is just the same kind of…situation."

"I never heard about that. Where was she?"

"Palm Springs."

"With a man?"

"What do you think?"

His poor girls. Their mother had degenerated into a complete mess. What had happened to the woman who used to read to them and play with them and rock them to sleep? "Are you going to let me in this morning, Helen? In the past I haven't caused a scene, for the girls' sake. But this time I won't go away. I'm taking my girls home and—"

"I called you, didn't I?"

"Yes." He sighed. "And that's exactly what frightens me."

Because you wouldn't have done it unless you felt you had no other choice.

"STACY? IS THAT YOU?" Chantel called from the bedroom when she heard the front door open and close. She hadn't expected her sister to drop by the condo this morning, but Stacy lived only fifteen minutes away and she had her own key. Chantel had asked her to keep it in case she ever needed a spare. Stacy had never used it before, but who else could this be?

"Yeah, it's me. Aren't you going to be late for work?"

Chantel glanced at the digital clock on her nightstand as she slipped on her shoes. It was almost eight o'clock already. She'd been up most of the night, unable to sleep because of Wade's sudden appearance and Dillon's disappointment when she'd sent him away. She'd finally drifted off in the wee hours of the morning and then had difficulty waking up when her alarm clock went off at six.

"Darn."

"What?"

Chantel heard Stacy walking down the hall toward the bedroom. "I *am* going to be late. And it's only my second week."

"What happened?"

"I took a sleeping pill."

"Why?"

"Why do most people take sleeping pills?" Chantel said as she brushed past her sister on the way to the kitchen. "Don't you have to work today?"

"No. I only work Thursday through Sunday this week."

"Must be nice."

"Do you want me to come by at lunch? We could go out."

Chantel's breath caught at the casual, offhand invitation, simply because it sounded so natural. Finally Stacy was beginning to trust her again, or at least to like her a little. She turned and threw both arms around her sister in a quick, impulsive hug, the first in more than ten years.

Stacy stiffened, but after a moment, she patted Chantel's back. It wasn't the warmth Chantel was hoping for. But it was a start.

"What's up with you?" she asked as Chantel broke away and grabbed her car keys.

Everything. Nothing. "I'm just glad to see you."

"You're not going to embarrass me today at lunch, are you?" Stacy teased.

Chantel laughed. In her current frame of mind, there was no telling what she might do. "I can't give you any guarantees."

"I brought you a bagel."

Food? Chantel grimaced to herself. She hated food. She waged a constant war with herself—trying to eat when normal people ate, forcing herself to consume amounts that resembled normal portions. She wasn't going to bother this morning. "Thanks, but I'm not hungry. Is that why you came over? To make sure I ate?"

"No, I came over because someone called me last night, and I wanted to talk to you about it."

Chantel paused at the door. "Who was it?" she asked without turning around.

"It's too late now. We'll talk about it at lunch."

DILLON SAT in his newly remodeled kitchen and watched his daughter Brittney frown at her oatmeal. She'd scoop up a bite, stare at it for a moment, then let it drop off the end of her spoon.

"That will do you more good if you eat it," he said, setting the morning paper aside.

"I hate oatmeal."

"It's healthy. Doesn't your mother ever make you hot cereal?"

"No."

"What do you normally eat for breakfast? Eggs?"

"Fruity Pebbles."

"Your mother gives you sugared cereal every morning?"

"No. She tells me to get it myself so she can sleep."

Dillon rubbed his forehead. "Who feeds Sydney?"

"She gets her own, like me."

"I see. Do you get yourselves to school, too?"

"Mom drives us."

Dillon wondered how Amanda managed to get out of bed for that. "Well, I'm going to take you this morning, okay?"

Brittney nodded as the toilet flushed and Sydney came out of the bathroom.

"Did you wash your hands, kiddo?" Dillon asked his youngest daughter.

"Oops." Sydney went back in and emerged with her hands dripping wet. Dillon dried them with a paper towel, then pulled out a chair for her at the table.

She sat down and studied her cereal with the same morbid interest one might view a dead bug on the windshield. "What is it?" she asked at last.

"Oatmeal," her sister replied, the disdain in her voice revealing that it was nothing she was going to like.

"Oh." Sydney glumly considered the prospect of her breakfast. "When's Mom going to be home?"

Dillon wondered which they missed more—their mother or their Fruity Pebbles. "Your grandma and I aren't exactly sure. She's been delayed, but it shouldn't be too much longer." He stood to clear away the dishes, wondering what he was going to do about getting his daughters picked up from school. He had a full day planned at the office, complete with an afternoon of meetings that would be difficult to cancel on such short notice.

"Do you still go home with Mary Beth Hanson after school sometimes?"

Brittney nodded, but Sydney wrinkled her nose. "Mary Beth's mean."

"Only because she doesn't like you always tagging along with us. You should play with Jeremy. He's your age," her sister told her in a condescending voice.

"But he's a boy!"

Dillon gave Sydney a mock wounded look. "Hey, what's wrong with boys?"

"Well, there's nothing wrong with you," she clarified.

"Do you want me to call Mary Beth and see if we can go over there today, Daddy?" Brittney asked.

"Actually, why don't I call so I can talk to her mother."

He dialed the number Brittney recited, but no one answered. "Don't they have an answering machine?" he asked.

"Yeah. Their mom's always on the phone, though. She's probably talking to someone else and just not switching over."

"Great." Dillon took one last look at the list of appointments he had scheduled for the day and sighed. He transferred the Hansons' number to his day-planner, then herded the girls toward the bathroom to get their teeth brushed. They'd come to him with only one change of clothes, which had been dirty, and no toothbrushes. A stop at the drugstore had remedied the toothbrush situation, and a load of laundry at seven this morning had provided clean clothes, but Dillon couldn't help wondering what Amanda was spending all his child support on. Twenty-five hundred a month should stretch far enough to include toothbrushes.

The girls said little on the ride to school. Were they afraid for their mother? Dillon was starting to worry himself. Amanda wasn't the best parent in the world, but he believed she loved the girls. She should have called by now.

He remembered Helen's mentioning that Amanda had disappeared on one previous occasion, and wondered how many things had changed since they'd lived together. Amanda hadn't taken her marriage vows very seriously, but she'd been a responsible mother. Was she still? Or had she become so immersed in a life that wasn't conducive to raising children that she was neglecting the girls? He'd tried to ask Helen this morning, but Amanda's mother was too protective to say any more than she'd already said on the telephone.

"Here we go," he said, pulling over to the curb behind a station wagon and a string of minivans.

The girls piled out, toting their backpacks.

"Do you have your lunches?" he asked.

Brittney waved two brown paper bags at Dillon, then handed one to Sydney. "Dad made them."

"Is there a treat inside?"

Dillon chuckled. "There's a turkey sandwich, carrot sticks, pretzels and apple slices. Plus a juice box." Another item from the drugstore.

Sydney groaned. "No cookies or potato chips?"

"Not today." Dillon looked at his daughters' freshly scrubbed faces. In their own ways they both resembled Amanda, but Brittney, with her dark hair, piercing blue eyes and long limbs, looked a great deal like him, too. Sydney, on the other hand, was petite and blond, with dark brown eyes and a small turned-up nose.

For a minute the doubt that had festered like a sliver beneath his skin prickled Dillon again. Was she his? Short of doing a blood test, there was no way of knowing, and he refused to go that far. Amanda would certainly never admit that there was any question, not while she had him on the hook for so much child support. But every once in a while he wondered—and was tempted to find out for sure.

Until he thought through all the ramifications. What if Sydney *wasn't* his? Would he love her any less? Would he see to Brittney's needs and not Sydney's?

No. Regardless of the genetic reality, he'd committed himself to be her guardian, her protector, her *father*. He wouldn't back out on her now. Which meant he would never seek the truth. And if they were both lucky, she'd never notice the physical dissimilarities between them.

"We'll go out for ice cream tonight, okay?" he told them. This proposition met with squeals of approval, just as Dillon had expected. At the sound of the bell, they gave him a hug and a kiss and hurried off.

As Dillon sat and watched them cross the schoolyard, concern for their well-being flooded his heart. He'd never wanted to be a part-time father. He'd always imagined himself as the kind of parent his own dad hadn't been—kind, loving, a source of unlimited strength, and an equal partner with his children's mother.

But Amanda hadn't made the kind of commitment marriage entailed. She'd turned to other men, and his marriage had fallen apart. During and after the divorce, he'd refused to let the children be used as pawns, which meant he'd given in to most of Amanda's demands. Only now he wasn't so sure he'd done what was best for the girls. Amanda was getting too wrapped up in her own life and wasn't taking proper care of them.

Maybe it was time he took the gloves off.

Except, if Sydney wasn't his and Amanda knew it, he could never win. He'd lose one daughter trying to save the other. And he wasn't sure he was willing to take that chance.

CHAPTER SEVEN

"SO WHAT DOES AN AIDE to a state senator do, anyway?"
Stacy asked, standing just inside the lobby of the office
where Chantel worked.

Chantel slung her purse over her shoulder and slid her
chair under her desk. "A little bit of everything, really. I'm
not a true aide, in that I don't represent the senator at district
functions. The field representatives do that. I just open all
the mail and schedule their appearances and—"

"Do you do the scheduling for the senator, too?"

"No. Nan at the capitol office in Sacramento does that."

"Is the senator ever here?"

Chantel nodded. "He works in the district office on Fri-
days and whenever the legislature isn't in session."

"This is a nice place." Stacy surveyed the burgundy-and-
gold wallpaper, the molding along the ceiling and the expensive drapes that made the office look more like someone's personal library.

Maureen smiled up at them from her desk across the
room. "California senators are treated like princes, although
an office this nice is a bit unusual. We got this on a sublease
from some attorneys. Our capitol office certainly looks more
standard."

Chantel introduced Maureen Ross, the office manager, to
Stacy.

"Chantel's doing a great job," Maureen volunteered. "She's particularly good at helping constituents."

Stacy raised her brows. "I should probably know what that is, but I don't."

"A constituent is anyone who lives in the senator's district," Chantel answered. "The people he represents can call or write us when they're having a problem with one of the state agencies, and we sort of act as a liaison to see that the problem gets worked out fairly."

"Like what kind of problem?"

"Oh, for instance, this morning Chantel helped a guy who needed to get his real-estate license right away," Maureen said. "He didn't have time to wait until the Department of Real Estate got around to scheduling the test, so he called us."

"If he didn't get his license quickly, he was going to lose his job," Chantel added. "He works for a mortgage company."

"And did you fix everything up?" Stacy asked.

Maureen motioned to the flowers sitting on Chantel's desk. "She sure did. He takes his test next week. Sent those to thank her."

Chantel smiled, feeling a genuine pride in her job. She certainly wasn't making the kind of money she'd made in New York, but she was doing good things for people and learning a lot about the political process. She even planned to participate in the senator's election campaign next year. "Are you ready for lunch?" she asked Stacy.

"Where do you want to go? Riley's?"

"Sounds good."

They both said goodbye to Maureen, then headed out the front door to Stacy's Honda.

"Do you think I should call and ask Dillon to join us?" Stacy asked, settling herself behind the wheel.

Chantel focused on getting in and snapping her seat belt. While she hoped Stacy would be happy—to the point of allowing her sister the relationship with Dillon she desired herself—Chantel didn't particularly want to spend much time in their company. She didn't know if she could watch the two of them get closer and wonder if she and Dillon might have had a chance if he hadn't met Stacy first.

"If you want to," she said, trying to sound neutral.

Stacy started the car and shifted into Reverse. "Well, I was just thinking it might not seem like I'm asking him out that way, since there's two of us. I don't want to come on too strong, you know. He's met you already, and it could be like three friends getting together for lunch. No big deal."

"Sure. That's great." Chantel couldn't help the lack of enthusiasm in her voice. Fortunately Stacy seemed too busy concentrating on merging into traffic to notice.

"Will you dial the number for me?" She pulled into the street, then handed Chantel her cell phone and recited the number from memory.

Her heart sinking, Chantel dialed. "Ready?"

Stacy sent her a nervous smile and took the phone. "Here goes."

Propping her elbow on the door, Chantel leaned her head on her hand as she listened to Stacy give her name to what must have been a receptionist. After a minute Dillon came on the line.

"Hi, this is Stacy. Chantel and I were just heading out to lunch and thought it might be nice if you joined us. Any interest?"

Please, no, please, no, please no… Chantel chanted to herself. *Come on, Dillon, don't do this to me.*

"…right now…we're going to Riley's Pub… Yeah, it's by the mall… Okay, great! We'll see you there in fifteen minutes or so."

Chantel choked back a groan. Dammit! He'd accepted, just as she'd known he would.

"He's coming," Stacy announced, beaming with excitement. "Do I look okay?"

Stacy's cream sweater and slacks set off her dark hair and eyes and shaped her figure nicely. "You look beautiful. He'll be dazzled." *And I'll be sick.*

"He's *so* handsome, don't you think?"

Damn, was Chantel going to have to sing Dillon's praises every time she saw her sister? Weren't things hard enough? "He's very handsome," she repeated. *And fantastic in bed and courageous in an emergency, and strong in all the right ways, and soft when it really counts…*

"I mean, he's not like Wade," her sister went on, telling her with a fleeting glance that after ten years she was finally able to talk about him. "Wade was probably the most *perfect* looking man I've ever met. Until Dillon, I thought he'd always be the standard by which I measured other men. But for me, he was almost too fussy, you know? I mean, you were with him for ten years. Don't you think he could be too picky, too compulsive about looking good?"

"Definitely." Wade's weaknesses extended far beyond his vanity, but Chantel still carried too much pain and doubt inside her to really open up and discuss him. Reaching across the console, she squeezed Stacy's arm. "I'm sorry, you know. For what I did. Truly."

Stacy kept her eyes on the road. "You've already apologized. And that's not why I brought him up."

"He called you, didn't he? He's the person you were talking about this morning."

She nodded.

"What did he say?"

"That he's still in love with you." She shot Chantel a sideways glance and took a deep breath. "That he wants you back. That you belong together. He thinks your guilt over me drove the two of you apart. He wants me to convince you that it's okay for you to be with him. That I'm over it and I've forgiven you."

"And?" Chantel fidgeted with the pleat on her slacks.

"And he's right. If you still love him, I want you to go back to him. I don't want you to break up because of me."

A whirlwind of conflicting emotions assaulted Chantel. She felt guilty for not having made the sacrifice Wade and Stacy credited her with. She felt inadequate because she'd tried to make her relationship with Wade work—after all, she'd certainly paid a high enough price for it—and had failed in spite of her tremendous effort. And she felt angry that Wade would involve Stacy after what they'd both done to her.

"Was it difficult to talk to him?" she asked.

Stacy pulled into the pub's lot and angled the car into a parking place. "It felt weird at first."

Chantel could imagine. Probably the last time he and Stacy had talked, Stacy had been wearing his engagement ring.

"So? What do you say?" Stacy dropped the keys into her purse and leaned back without making any move to get out of the car.

Chantel glanced longingly at the restaurant. She didn't want to talk about Wade. She didn't want to analyze the many reasons she couldn't go back to him. She wasn't even sure she could explain all of them if she tried. "I can't," she said simply.

"He said your agent has more work for you. You could be on the cover of *Vogue* again. Doesn't that appeal to you anymore? It was all you talked about once you turned sixteen or so."

Chantel stared out her window, picturing their agent, Steve, and the photo shoots and the limousines and Wade waiting for her at their artsy apartment.

"Why would you want to give that up to work in a state senator's office?" Stacy asked. "Think of the money."

Finally Chantel met her sister's eyes. "I can't go back, Stace. For a while there...I was sick."

"What does that mean? You don't have AIDS, do you?" She sounded panicky.

"No. Wade's the only man I've ever slept with, not that I couldn't have gotten it from him." She laughed weakly, but Stacy didn't even crack a smile.

"What kind of sick, Chantel?"

Chantel grabbed her purse and opened the door. "It doesn't matter. I'm better now," she lied.

DILLON PAUSED at the entrance to Riley's to allow his eyes to adjust to the dark interior. He liked this place, with its Tiffany lamps, hardwood floors, brass railings and noisy crowds. The food was good here, the company was usually better. Today he didn't really have time for lunch, especially if he had to pick up his girls at three, but the prospect of seeing Chantel again had motivated him to massage his schedule enough to squeeze another hour out of it. She'd asked him not to call her or come to her house again, and he planned to respect her wishes. Which meant he wasn't about to miss an opportunity like this one, even though see-

ing her in Stacy's presence promised to be awkward, the
way it had been at the cabin.

"Dillon!"

Stacy waved at him just as the hostess approached.

"It looks like I've found my party," he said, and weaved
through the room to the table where Stacy and Chantel sat.
Stacy smiled broadly at him as he sat down, then handed
him a menu. Chantel barely acknowledged him before beginning an avid study of the restaurant's offerings.

"How's work going?" Stacy asked.

"Busy," Dillon admitted.

"Well, we're flattered you took the time to have lunch
with us, aren't we, Chantel?"

Chantel mumbled something unintelligible, then excused
herself to go to the rest room. As she left, Dillon couldn't
help but admire how good she looked in her classy suit.
And he wasn't alone. She turned a number of heads, both
male and female.

Knowing Chantel hated the stares her height inspired, Dillon forced his attention back to Stacy. "What's the occasion?" he asked.

"No occasion. I thought it would be nice to have lunch
with my sister."

"Thanks for letting me join you."

She smiled, a little too brightly, and Dillon remembered
Chantel's saying that Stacy thought she was in love with
him. He hoped she'd wake up one day soon and realize it
was just a crush. It had to be. They'd kissed once, but
there'd been no real sparks, at least not on his side. Which
made it hard to imagine that she'd felt something different.

He studied the colorful ten-page menu, wondering what
the chances were of Stacy's meeting someone else. Regardless of the fact that Chantel insisted he not back away from

Stacy because of her, things had changed. Rescuing Chantel, making love to her, had made a huge difference in his life. There was no going back now.

"Are you guys ready?" A young waitress, wearing a red-striped golf shirt covered with pins and buttons, a short black skirt and running shoes, stood at his elbow, pad in hand.

"I'm ready," Chantel said, answering his questioning look as she returned to her seat.

Stacy pulled absently on one of her curls. "I'll have the chicken enchiladas."

Chantel ordered the oriental chicken salad. Dillon asked for the Cajun pasta, then passed the waitress their menus.

"You don't have to work today?" he asked Stacy.

"Not until Thursday."

"Must be nice to work only four days a week, huh?"

"Chantel wouldn't have to work even that many if she went back to New York," Stacy said. "Her boyfriend's a model, too, and he's in town right now, trying to talk her into going back with him. He insists she'll be on the cover of next September's *Vogue* if she does."

Dillon felt a prickle of alarm. There might not be any hope for them right now, but he didn't want to see Chantel go anywhere, especially to New York with that jerk he threw out of her house. Especially when she was still fighting the anorexia that had nearly killed her. Even for the cover of *Vogue*. "Is that a possibility?" he asked.

Chantel shook her head. "Not right now."

Stacy drank some of her water. "Personally I think she's crazy if she doesn't go."

"Maybe there's something here she cares more about than fame," Dillon suggested mildly.

"I doubt it. Wade's the love of her life. And fame and

fortune are pretty alluring to Chantel. Or at least they used to be."

"Fame and fortune are pretty alluring to everyone," Dillon said.

"Wade's not my boyfriend anymore," Chantel pointed out, although she said nothing in her own defense. She tried to act indifferent, but Dillon knew Stacy's barb had hit its target, and he hurt for her. If only Stacy knew how hard he and Chantel were working to avoid a repeat performance of what had happened with Wade. He wanted to give Chantel's knee a squeeze to reassure her, but he kept his hands to himself.

"Wade still thinks you belong to him," Stacy said.

"Wade has a hard time understanding the word *no*," Chantel replied.

"Well, Wade's not the only man in New York, you know. Giving up your boyfriend doesn't mean you have to walk away from your career."

Chantel anchored a lock of hair behind her ear. "We talked about this outside, Stacy. I don't want to go back, okay?"

Stacy shrugged. "Suit yourself."

The waitress brought their food, and they fell silent as they started their meals. Stacy moved quickly through her enchiladas, but Chantel mostly picked at her salad, doing more stirring and rearranging than she did chewing and swallowing. Eating was probably hard enough for her when she *wasn't* upset, Dillon thought.

"How are your girls?" Stacy asked.

He swallowed and wiped his mouth with his linen napkin. "They could be better. I had to pick them up from their grandmother's early this morning. On Friday, their mother went to Las Vegas with one of her boyfriends, and she hasn't come back. We're trying to locate her, but until we do, I'm pinch-hitting."

"But you're not used to having them during the school week, are you?"

Dillon barely heard Stacy's question. Chantel had looked up at him with those incredible eyes, turning her full attention on him for the first time since he'd sat down. He managed a crooked smile. "Not really. But I'm improvising."

"Who picks them up after school?" Stacy asked.

"Actually I'm going to have to do it today." He checked his watch. "In just a couple of hours, as a matter of fact. Sometimes they go home with a friend, but I've called and called and haven't been able to reach anyone at Mary Beth's house."

"That means you'll have to leave work early."

He nodded.

"There's no need to do that. I can pick them up for you."

Dillon took a drink of his Coke, just to stall for time. What should he say? He could certainly use the help, but he didn't want to accept anything from Stacy that she might later resent. "That's okay. I'm going to take some work home with me."

Finished, Stacy shoved her plate away. "But there's no need. They know me, so they should feel comfortable about it, and I have the entire afternoon yawning before me with absolutely nothing to do. You know I'm not working today. Let me pick up the girls and help them get their schoolwork done. Then you can come by on your way home." She grinned. "If I'm super-industrious, I might even be able to manage a hot supper for the three of you."

Which sounded entirely too domestic to Dillon. He cleared his throat to refuse, when Chantel lent her support to Stacy.

"Stacy's great with kids," she said. "And she makes a mean lasagna."

"Really, it's no problem for me to—"

"Dillon, stop," Stacy said firmly. "I think your girls are great. I *want* to do this. Now if you'll excuse me, I need to use the ladies' room."

As soon as Stacy was out of sight, Dillon shot an accusing glare at Chantel. "I don't want her to pick up Brittney and Sydney," he said. "That could mislead her into thinking that…I don't know, that there's something more between us than friendship."

"She's already too far down that road."

"But what about this dinner thing?"

"You're making a big deal out of nothing. She's an attractive woman with plenty of prospects—"

"Which is exactly what I keep trying to tell you. She certainly doesn't need me."

"—so it's not like she's going to attack you."

"I'm not afraid she's going to attack me! Attacks I can handle. I'm afraid she's going to accuse me of using her when she realizes I don't reciprocate her feelings."

"Then maybe tonight would be a good time to talk about how you both feel."

"You say that like you have no personal stake in it."

Chantel played with the condensation on her glass. "I don't."

STACY STUDIED HERSELF in the bathroom mirror and groaned. How could she be so stupid? She'd wanted to counteract Chantel's incredible beauty by making her appear shallow.

Instead, she'd made herself look bad and caused Dillon to become defensive of Chantel. She had to get a grip on herself. One minute she felt sorry that she and Chantel weren't closer and wanted to forgive her for everything. The next she did her best to drive a bigger wedge between them.

Love…hate. Love…hate. How did she really feel about her sister? And how badly was she willing to treat her to keep her away from Dillon?

If she kept going on like this, she'd probably chase the two of them right into each other's arms. Somehow she had to calm down and try to develop some confidence. How could Dillon fall in love with her when *she* couldn't think of one reason why he should?

Leaning closer to her reflection, she stared at the small wrinkles that were forming around her eyes and mouth. Laugh lines, she told herself. But they spoke more of age than laughter. She wasn't getting any younger. If she wanted marriage and a family, she needed to coax a proposal out of Dillon—sooner rather than later.

He loved children. Over the past two years, she'd seen him with his daughters lots of times, heard the loving way he spoke of them and to them. They were the center of his life.

Right where she wanted to be.

Stacy pulled her lipstick out of her purse and applied it. She needed some sort of advantage. Something to reassure her that he wasn't going anywhere. Something to make him realize what she already knew: that they'd be perfect together.

She put her lipstick back in her purse and quickly brushed her hair.

Maybe that something should be a baby.

Stacy started to walk out of the rest room, then slumped back against the door, unable to believe her own thoughts.

Was she really that desperate? She'd never tried to trap a man before, and she wouldn't stoop to that level now. But if it happened naturally...

She forced a smile to her lips and headed back to the table. If it happened naturally, well, she wouldn't do anything to stop it.

CHAPTER EIGHT

''I HOPE THAT'S a frown of concentration.''

Chantel glanced up to see Maureen standing over her desk. She'd been thinking about how Stacy had treated her at lunch. She knew she deserved anything her sister decided to dish out, but that didn't lessen the melancholy that had settled over her in the two hours since then. On top of everything, it had been more difficult than Chantel had ever imagined to see Stacy touch Dillon's arm when he said something funny, or brush against him as they left the restaurant, or smile as though they shared an inside joke. At the cabin they'd had a bunch of friends around and had behaved just like part of the group, but Stacy had treated Dillon differently at lunch.

What if he did as she'd told him to and pursued a relationship with Stacy? What if they got married?

Chantel would have to stay well away. She doubted her attraction to Dillon was something that would ebb with time, but she hoped it would. Especially because she couldn't get close to Stacy if she was always trying to avoid contact with her sister's boyfriend—or husband.

''Are you stuck?'' Maureen asked.

Gazing down at the stack of invitations she'd been trying to sort through, Chantel held up one she'd set aside. ''I know I'm supposed to schedule the field reps to attend only the functions in their individual areas, but Layne has a chamber mixer at the same time as this ribbon-cutting ceremony. Should I ask one of the other reps to fill in?''

''That'll work. If no one can go, send our regrets. Or pin on a badge and go yourself if you want.'' She checked the invitation. ''It doesn't look like it's going to be that big an event. They're not asking for anyone to speak or anything.''

Chantel had secretly hoped to attend some functions in the district. She needed to get out more, meet people. But she hadn't been working for the senator long enough to feel confident representing him. She wasn't even sure of his stand on some issues, only those she'd heard the others talking about over the past two weeks. ''Maybe when I've been around a little longer,'' she said.

''That's fine.'' Maureen went back to her desk as Lee, another of the senator's three field reps, came in the door.

''Hi, Chantel. Any messages?''

Chantel handed him a couple of slips of paper. ''There's more on your voice mail.''

''Got those. Thanks.''

She was about to ask him if he wanted to attend the ribbon-cutting ceremony, but the telephone rang just then.

''Senator Johnson's office.''

''Chantel? It's Stacy.''

''Hi, Stace. Did you find Dillon's kids okay?''

''Yeah. I've got them with me now. They're beautiful girls, really sweet, and we're having fun. But you're never going to believe what's happened.''

''What?''

''The hospital called. They need me to come in to work. And I'm not expecting Dillon until six-thirty or so.''

''Can't you call him?''

''I've tried a couple of times, but the receptionist says he's in a meeting.''

''Tell her it's about his kids. I'm sure she'll interrupt.''

"I hate to do that. He was so relieved that I was going to do this for him. He must have thanked me three times."

"So you're calling me because—"

"I was hoping you could take them for a little while."

"Stacy, I don't get off until five, and sometimes I stay much later than that."

"You don't have to stay late. No one at the office expects you to."

But they expect me to know something about current events and how to work a computer, and they've given me a huge stack of letters to read and answer. I have so much to learn to make up for the ten years I spent being oblivious to everything but fashion. "I'm just trying to ensure that I'll be successful here."

"You'll be successful. Don't worry. It's not like I'm asking you to get off early or anything. I just want to drop the girls off as soon as you get home so I can run a quick errand at the mall and make it to the hospital by six."

Chantel sighed. She didn't want to take Dillon's kids, because she didn't want to know them. She didn't want to know them, because she didn't want to care about them, or him. She wanted no more links between them.

But this was the first favor Stacy had asked since they'd started speaking again, and she couldn't refuse. "Okay. Will he pick them up at my place at six-thirty, then?"

"Yeah. I'll leave him a message."

"Another call is coming in. I've got to run. See you after work."

Chantel put the call through to Lee, then tried to concentrate on the scheduling again, but it was nearly impossible. Later today she'd meet Brittney and Sydney, the girls she'd heard Dillon talk about with such tenderness that night in his truck. She already felt an emotional connection with them.

How? She and Dillon had had a one-night stand, nothing more, she told herself sternly. And even if what they'd shared was much more than that, she had to get over it.

STACY SMILED to herself as she hurried through the crowded mall, searching for the lingerie store she knew was somewhere near Macy's at the far end. She'd never planned to seduce a man before, but just the prospect of sleeping with Dillon made her feel reckless and excited and aroused. She'd been wanting him to take their relationship into the physical realm for a long time now, but just as he seemed about to get there, he'd suddenly backed off—ever since the cabin in Tahoe. There, they'd gotten into the jacuzzi together, skied together, stayed up late talking and laughing, but there'd been no privacy and he hadn't made a move to touch her since that one chaste kiss after their last date.

That was all going to change, she promised herself. She just needed to buy something he'd find irresistible, make him a great dinner, serve an excellent wine and hope he'd figure things out from there.

Stepping into Monique's Lingerie and Hosiery, Stacy began to admire the filmy nighties and teddies that surrounded her.

"Can I help you?"

A tall thin blonde, who looked a little like Chantel, came forward. For a moment Stacy felt guilty for using Chantel to get the kids out of the way without telling her sister her real plan. But she knew Chantel would only try to talk her out of it. *He'll make the move when he's ready.* That was her favorite line, but Stacy was sick of hearing it.

And she was tired of waiting.

"I'm looking for something that will show my figure to its best advantage," she said.

"A negligee?"

"Or a teddy or something."

The girl's gaze ran up and down her body, assessing her attributes. "Why don't we try something that slims the hips and enhances the bust line? Like a black corset?"

"Fine." Stacy watched the girl select three possibilities, then held them up in front of her while she gazed into a floor-length mirror. A red see-through baby doll with panties was tempting. The feather trim at the top concealed her small breasts. But she wanted something even more wanton, more wicked. Something in black.

"How about this?" the salesgirl asked, presenting Stacy with a black lace push-up bra and matching garter belt to be worn over a pair of thonglike panties. "There's not much fabric here, but it will accentuate your figure in all the right places. Add a pair of silk stockings and high heels, and you'll look absolutely fabulous."

Stacy smiled. Fabulous. That was how she wanted to look. Just like Chantel.

She pushed the thought away. She was short and stubby, with dark hair and ordinary eyes. She could never look like Chantel.

But no man in his right mind could refuse her in an outfit like this.

DILLON SIGHED as he put his briefcase in the backseat and climbed into his rented Taurus. It had been a busy day. He was glad he hadn't had to reschedule all his appointments to go and pick up Sydney and Brittney, especially since he and Jason had just landed another big job this afternoon— drawing the plans for a set of twin towers in downtown Walnut Creek. But he had no doubt Stacy would have dinner waiting for him, and he wasn't looking forward to accepting more of her hospitality while trying to avoid further romantic entanglement. It made him feel like a jerk—even though he would have helped her, had the shoe been on the other foot. They were friends, after all. He just hoped friendship would be enough for Stacy.

Fortunately the girls were going to be there, he reminded himself, missing them. They would make good chaperons and what with homework, baths and school in the morning, they'd provide the perfect excuse for leaving right after dinner. He also wanted to take them shopping for some new clothes tonight. If they left Stacy's early enough, maybe they could swing by the mall before it closed.

Picking up his cell phone, he dialed Helen's number then started his car and eased into the busy street.

"Hello?"

"It's me, Dillon. Have you heard anything?"

"No. I filed a police report today, but like I said, they don't seem to be too worried. They act like she'll turn up when she's ready."

"What do you think's going on?"

There was a long silence. "I don't know. I'd like to think Amanda's not capable of abandoning her children, but I'm not so sure anymore. She really liked this guy."

"She's liked them all. Why is he any different from the rest?"

"He wasn't interested in the girls. Treated them like excess baggage. Amanda always had me take them when he was going to be around."

Dillon was more than eager to have his kids back, especially without further legal complications, but he couldn't imagine the hurt they'd suffer if they ever learned their mother had walked out on them. "Maybe something's happened to her," he suggested.

"Maybe."

It sounded like Helen was crying, but she was a proud, hard-bitten woman, and he knew she wouldn't like him knowing it. "Do you think I should hire a private investigator?" he asked.

"You'd do that?"

"I'm thinking about it." He hadn't made a decision yet. Maybe he and the girls were better off not knowing. For now. But what about later? Amanda would come back eventually. She didn't stay with one man long enough to give Dillon any confidence that things with this new boyfriend would work out.

Either way, the girls would lose, which gave him one more thing to hold against his ex-wife.

"I'll let you know what I decide. Call me if you hear anything," he said.

"I will. Do you want me to take the girls for you next weekend?" she asked.

"No. I'm glad to have them home. I want to keep them."

"Dillon, don't get any ideas about going to court again...."

For a moment, her old hostility was back, but the emotion seemed to falter, along with Helen's words. "Never mind. We'll deal with the custody issues when Amanda gets back. Just be good to them," she said. "And let me see them once in a while, okay?"

How does it feel to have so little control? he was tempted to ask. Dillon had felt almost powerless for two years, but telling Helen how wrong she and Amanda had been wouldn't help the situation now.

"We'll come by on Sunday."

"Thanks," she said softly, and hung up.

Dillon ran a hand through his hair. He needed to work out a car-pool arrangement and a safe nurturing environment for Sydney and Brittney during the afternoons until he could get home from work. Mentally he went down his list of prospects: Children's World, Kindercare, Aunt's Bee's Day-care. He'd have to take time off tomorrow to visit each place, because even if Amanda came back, he wasn't going to let the situation return to the status quo. He wanted his girls, and for their sake, he was finally ready to do whatever it would take to make it official.

"CAN WE RENT a movie?" Brittney asked, setting down the crayons Chantel had bought to entertain them until Dillon arrived.

"Probably not tonight. Your father should be here any minute."

"Where's Mommy?" the younger girl, Sydney, asked her.

It was the first time either of them had mentioned their mother, but after hearing what Dillon had said about her at lunch, Chantel felt a twinge of pity. "I'm not sure, sweetie. She'll probably be back soon, though. Look, I'm making spaghetti and meatballs. Are you hungry?"

They'd already had a snack. Chantel had stopped on her way home from work and bought some chocolate milk and oatmeal cookies, but it was past six-thirty and time for dinner. She'd made an extra large batch of spaghetti, thinking Dillon would be tired and hungry after a long day at the office, but she didn't want to admit to herself that she was doing exactly what Stacy had wanted to do for him.

"Something smells good," Sydney said. "Is it the spaghetti?"

"I think it's the garlic bread. And I've made a little salad. Why don't you girls help me set the table?"

Pleased by the prospect of helping, the two of them put their crayons and coloring books away and started setting out the silverware. "Are you my daddy's girlfriend?" Brittney asked.

Chantel hid a smile. "No. We're just, ah, friends."

"He sure has lots of friends," Sydney said.

"I'll bet he does," Chantel muttered, figuring he classi-fied all his romantic interests as friends. It made sense that he'd downplay his relationships, considering how angry it made him that his wife was doing the exact opposite and having the girls call each new boyfriend "Daddy."

"Should we set a place for Dad?" Brittney asked.

Chantel considered the table, wishing she had some flow-ers for the center. "Yes. I'm sure he'll be hungry."

"Do we have to wait for him? I'm starving," Sydney announced.

Chantel glanced at the clock. Dillon was already twenty minutes late. "There's no need to wait. He can eat when he gets here." As the children washed their hands, she filled their plates. Then she sat down with them and ate some salad while they dug into their spaghetti.

"This is good!" Brittney declared. "I love the meat-balls.'"

"I make them out of sausage. Gives them more spice."

It was a quarter after seven when they finished dinner. Leaving a plate for Dillon, Chantel cleaned up the kitchen while the girls watched television. When she was through with the dishes, she decided to read to them. "Anyone got a good book?" she asked.

"We're reading *Charlotte's Web* in school," Brittney said.

"Do you have a copy?"

"It's in my backpack." While Brittney retrieved her book, Sydney turned off the television and settled herself on the couch. Brittney sat on Chantel's other side and they began to read.

"When's Daddy going to get here?" Sydney asked when Chantel had finished two chapters.

"I'm sure he's on his way." Chantel looked at their sweet

faces. *How lucky Dillon is,* she thought. Being a part-time parent was certainly better than not having any children. Like her. "Why don't you go and take a bath for school tomorrow? Afterward, you can each put on one of my T-shirts and lie in my bed and watch TV until your dad comes."

"Cool!" Brittney shouted.

Sydney stood up and clapped her hands. "Cool!" she echoed.

As the girls headed down the hall, Chantel checked her watch again. Dillon was an hour and a half late. Where was he?

She found the business card he'd given her when she'd rear-ended him and called his cell phone, but got only his voice mail.

"Dillon, this is Chantel. I'm getting a little worried about you. Stacy said you'd be here at six-thirty to pick up the girls. They're fine, just so you know, and I'm okay with having them. It's just that they keep asking about you, and I don't want them to worry. Give me a call when you get this message, okay?"

Twirling her hair around one finger, Chantel hung up. Was he all right? Had he gotten into another accident or something?

Please let him be safe, she prayed, trying to will away the apprehension that knotted her stomach. Then she went in to get the girls settled in her bed.

DILLON SAT on the couch, glancing at the clock every few minutes while Stacy cleared away the dishes after the candlelight dinner she'd just fed him. He'd tried to help her clean up, but she'd pressed another glass of wine in his hand and insisted he relax.

He would rather have helped. He already felt bad enough,

letting her baby-sit and now eating her food. He didn't want to add to the list of favors. Besides, he needed some way to keep himself engaged while he tried to work out how he was going to get through the evening without hurting her feelings.

"Do you know when the movie started?" he called to her.

Stacy's voice came from the kitchen. "Chantel didn't say."

"I still can't understand why she'd whisk the girls off to a movie without asking me if it's okay," he repeated for the third time. "I had other plans tonight, and they have school in the morning."

"I told you—Chantel's like that. She's not very practical. She thought a movie might take their minds off their mother and asked me if they could go. Neither of us thought you'd mind. As a matter of fact, I thought it might be nice for you and me to have a little time alone. The cabin was so crowded, you know?"

"Yeah." *Crowded with memories of Chantel.* "Do you mind if I try Chantel's house once more?"

Stacy appeared at the doorway from the kitchen, drying her hands on a dish towel. "I've already left her three messages. She'll call us as soon as they get home."

He set his empty glass on the coffee table in front of him. Stacy's house was far more utilitarian than Chantel's. Chantel surrounded herself with warm jewel tones, lots of textures and art, and it all said, "Welcome home." Stacy's place had functional furniture—vinyl, instead of leather, polyester, instead of silk—and everything was arranged in very symmetrical configurations.

Dillon itched to remodel the twenty-year-old tract house. It needed more light and a fresh coat of white paint. But he felt that way about many of the buildings he entered. He figured it was natural for an architect. Only Chantel's place had felt just right, at least on the inside, and he wasn't sure if that was because of the design, the decor or simply her presence. He suspected the last.

Stacy disappeared, then came back carrying her own drink and a newly opened bottle of wine. "More?" she asked, filling his glass nearly to the brim without waiting for his answer.

"I've probably had enough," he said. She'd served him a couple of glasses of good scotch before dinner, and he'd had quite a bit of wine since. But Stacy was sliding closer, and he didn't know what to do with his hands. So he picked up his glass and began to drink again.

"Are you always this uptight after work?" she asked.

"Am I uptight?" He took another sip.

"You're acting a little jumpy. I'm sorry you're upset about the movie."

"It's not that. It's been a long day."

"Come sit here on the floor. I'll loosen up your shoulders. A friend of mine is a massage therapist. She's taught me a few tricks."

Dillon polished off his drink, then refilled his glass. "Actually I feel fine," he lied. "The chardonnay's great, by the way."

He looked at the half-empty bottle—their second—and realized he'd drunk most of it. He'd probably have a hangover in the morning, but that became the least of his concerns when Stacy slipped her hand beneath his elbow and threaded her fingers through his.

"What ideas do you have about the buildings you're going to design for downtown?" she asked, referring to the new project he and his partner had landed today.

"Something with a lot of glass. We want twin towers that look modern, open. We may have an atrium in the lobby and on the first three floors of each building, or maybe something in the middle that links them. It would break up the space, bring nature back into the concrete world of the city."

How much longer could the movie last? he wondered. Had Chantel done this to him on purpose? Had she known about the candlelight dinner?

"How's the baby doing? The one who was born last month with the heart condition?" he asked.

"She's hanging in there, but she needs more surgery. She's got a fifty-fifty chance, at least. Ten years ago, she probably wouldn't have survived this long."

"I hope she pulls through."

"So do I." Stacy laid her head on his shoulder and began to snuggle closer, wrapping one arm around his waist.

Dillon loosened his collar by another button and used the excuse of pouring more wine to pull away. "Want some?"

"I've never seen you drink so much," she said. "If you go on like this, you won't be able to drive home." She gave him a meaningful smile. "But I guess we could ask Chantel to keep the girls overnight."

"They're going through a really hard time right now. I don't think that would be wise." He read disappointment in her eyes and felt worse than he had a few minutes ago. Why had he ever asked Stacy out in the first place?

Because they'd known each other for two years, and things were easy, comfortable. She had a lot of qualities he'd liked—still liked. And he'd had no idea their relationship would become so one-sided.

"I'd better get going," he said, standing. "I'll stop by Chantel's later and pick up the girls. I need to hit the mall while it's still open and buy a few things for them to wear. They came to me with very little."

"Want me to go with you?"

"No, it won't be any fun for you. It's just going to be a quick trip. Thanks for dinner."

Dillon retrieved his suit coat and headed out to his car, but he'd gone only a block before he knew Stacy was right—he shouldn't be driving. He'd had too much to drink, and he didn't want to endanger his life or anyone else's. Pulling over to the curb, he used his cell phone to call a cab.

By the time the cab arrived, the alcohol had hit Dillon's blood stream full force, but he managed to remember Chantel's address. He repeated it to the driver.

The cabby blinked, no doubt hearing the slur in his words. "You sure, buddy?"

He didn't care that she wasn't home yet. He'd wait. "I'm sure. Just take me to her."

CHAPTER NINE

THE TELEPHONE startled Chantel awake. She blinked and looked around, confused. She was on the couch and the television was still on, its sound turned low. How late was it?

The chime of her pendulum clock told her the time before she could get her eyes working well enough to check. Nine-thirty. Jeez, it was still early. She must have nodded off as soon as she put the girls to bed half an hour ago.

Shoving herself into a sitting position, Chantel answered the phone.

"Hello?"

"Chantel, it's Stace."

"Hi. How's work?"

"I'm not at work. They ended up not needing me, after all, so I made dinner for Dillon. He's on his way to get the girls. I'm sorry he's so late."

Chantel absorbed this information, wondering why neither Stacy nor Dillon had called her. Maybe they'd been having too much fun.

The thought wounded something inside her, even though she told herself it shouldn't. "No problem. I enjoyed the girls." Which was the truth. If she couldn't have children of her own, Chantel wished Stacy would get married and provide her with some nieces and nephews to spoil.

Maybe that's exactly what'll happen—with Dillon.

"You were really great to baby-sit. I admit I took advantage of you, but Dillon and I haven't had any time alone for a couple of weeks. You understand, don't you?''

''Of course.''

''Great. I owe you one, Chantel. Oh, and one more thing…''

''What?''

''Would you mind telling him you were planning to take the girls to a movie but changed your mind?''

''What?''

''I know it sounds silly, but I didn't want him to worry about Brittney and Sydney, so I told him you'd taken them to a movie. I'd appreciate it if you'd play along.'' She paused. ''I really like him, Chantel.''

So do I. But giving him up was part of her penance, wasn't it? ''What are sisters for?''

''Thanks.''

Stacy hung up, and Chantel let the receiver dangle in her lap as she rubbed her eyes. Dillon and Stacy had spent the evening together while she'd been watching the clock, worrying about him. Stacy should have called her.

Someone banged on her door. Dillon. Already. Chantel put the phone on its cradle, straightened her T-shirt and cut-off sweats, and went to answer it.

He was standing outside, his suit coat slung over one arm, his tie and shirt collar loosened. He looked like he was coming home to her after a long day, and for the briefest moment she felt the impulse to pull him into her arms and bury her face in his neck.

''It appears you've had quite a night,'' she said, instead.

He nodded. ''How are the girls?'' His voice was just a little too loud.

''They're fine. They're asleep in my bed.'' She moved aside to let him in, smelling alcohol mingled with a hint of cologne as he passed. ''How much have you had to drink?''

"Too much." He dropped his coat on the chair by the closet. "Your sister made me a candlelight dinner—steak and potatoes and cheesecake, soft music playing in the background."

Chantel thought of the spaghetti she'd made him, which was a far cry from steak and potatoes and candlelight. "Did you enjoy yourself?"

He cocked one eyebrow at her. "That's what you wanted me to do, wasn't it? Enjoy myself? Fall in love with your sister? You took the girls to a movie so Stacy could create this romantic evening. Would you have been happy if we'd made love?"

Chantel flinched. "If that's what you wanted."

His gaze grew pointed. "Bullshit. You know what I want. I haven't been keeping any secrets."

Rubbing her arms, Chantel walked across the room and settled back on the couch, covering her legs with the blanket she'd brought out from her room. "Did you guys have a talk about your relationship?"

He sat down in the chair opposite her and stretched his legs in front of him, crossing them at the ankle. "What did you think I should say? You won't let me tell her how I feel about you."

"How you feel about me doesn't matter. It's how you feel about her that counts."

"You want me to tell her I feel like she's in the way?"

Chantel decided to change the subject. "I hope you didn't drive here," she said.

"I took a cab."

"Where's your car?"

"Not far from Stacy's."

"Is the cab waiting?"

He crossed his arms over his chest, an act of belligerence. "I sent it away."

Uh-oh. Chantel swallowed, trying to ignore the fact that they were alone. Yes, his daughters were here, but they were asleep down the hall. So she and Dillon had all night—if they wanted it.

Dillon stood and closed the distance between them, sinking onto the couch next to her. Chantel slid over to allow him more room, but the arm of the couch and his large body boxed her in. "Tell me again why we can't be together," he said. "It's crazy, but sometimes I forget."

Chantel closed her eyes. There were times when she forgot, too, or at least wanted to. She could feel the heat of his arm through their clothes and remembered the way his body had warmed her, the smooth supple feel of his skin with nothing between them. She remembered hearing him groan her name when he was too lost in passion to even know he'd spoken. How many times had they made love that night? A lot. Too many times to ever forget.

"Don't make this harder than it already is, Dillon. You've had too much to drink, and you're not thinking straight. I'll wake the girls and drive everyone back to your place."

"Because of Stacy?"

"Because of Stacy. I wish things could be different, but they're not, and there's nothing we can do about that."

"I don't believe it. There's always something that can be done."

"For a price."

He shoved a hand through his hair. "I think it's more than Stacy that's bugging you. I think you're scared."

Chantel took a deep breath. "I *am* scared. I have to believe I've changed. That I'd never hurt my sister again, disappoint my family the way I did when I was nineteen."

"We all make mistakes, Chantel."

"Not this kind of mistake."

"Were you that much in love with Wade?"

Chantel let her rigid control slip a little, felt the support of Dillon's body next to her. "I'm not sure what I felt at first."

"Then what was the attraction?"

"I was awed by him, I guess. Stacy had brought home other boyfriends who sometimes came on to me. But none of them were like Wade. When he was around, the sun shone a little brighter, you know?" She chuckled bitterly. "He was charismatic and charming...and persistent. Even though I'd been teased as a child and still felt quite insecure, I'd been thinking about modeling, and Wade encouraged me, shared that ambition with me. He was always so certain of everything—who we were, where we were going, what we should do next. I let him lead me, and I shouldn't have."

"What about Stacy?"

"He insisted he was going to call the wedding off, anyway, that it had nothing to do with me. But I shouldn't have let him wear me down."

"Did you ever tell Stacy about the things he was saying to you?"

Chantel remembered trying to approach her sister. She'd hinted at it along the way, hoping Stacy would give her the opportunity to be completely honest. But every time she broached the subject of Wade, her sister clammed up and brushed her off. "A few times," she admitted. "But Stacy didn't want to hear it."

"So deep down she knew."

"Probably. I don't know how she could have missed his interest in me, but she wanted the wedding so badly she ignored it. She seemed to care more about catching someone like him, someone other women found attractive, than in marrying the man he truly was. I knew he was too ambitious and spoiled and even selfish, but I was stupid enough to think I could change him."

Dillon put an arm around her and pulled her head down on his shoulder. Chantel tried to resist, but the quiet ticking of the clock in the background and the low hum of the television had a hypnotic effect. She didn't want to think. She just wanted to enjoy Dillon's presence.

"Did you tell your family what you were going to do?"

Chantel shook her head. "Wade insisted it would be less painful for everyone if we simply left." She closed her eyes against the overwhelming regret. "How could I have done such a thing?" she whispered. "When I finally called home, my father told me I wasn't the person he thought I was. He told me never to contact him again."

Chantel felt Dillon gently rubbing her arm, but she was cold inside. So cold she feared she'd never be warm again. She'd betrayed her sister, her father. And now her father was gone. She could never apologize or make it up to him. She often visited his grave on Sundays to say the things she wished she'd said, but she knew it wouldn't change a thing.

"And when you and Wade started having problems? What did your father say then?" Dillon asked.

"Are you kidding? My family never knew. I'd made my bed—I was determined to lie in it. They didn't want anything to do with me. And I didn't deserve their love and support."

"So what *did* you do?"

"Nothing."

"Except nearly starve yourself to death. A self-inflicted punishment."

She rolled her eyes. "That sounds pathetic."

"My father's a psychiatrist. There was a time I wanted to be one, too."

"What changed your mind?"

"A friend who was interested in architecture. He's my partner now. That, and the fact that my father never seems to practice what he preaches. Once he and Mom split, he paid child support, but that was it. I hardly ever saw him. When I did, it felt uncomfortable. And after all these years we're still strangers. Fortunately he lives in Washington D.C. with his second wife and their grown kids, so I only hear from him at Christmastime.''

''Are you glad you're an architect, instead of a psychiatrist?''

''Yeah.'' He smoothed the hair out of her eyes. ''Have you ever seen anyone for counseling, Chantel?''

She laughed weakly. ''Are you suggesting I'm crazy?''

''No. I just think it might be a good idea to talk to someone who could help you come to terms with all this.''

''I've never wanted to tell anyone. I don't know why I told you now.''

''Could it be that you were hoping I'd decide you were a bad person, someone I couldn't possibly love?''

The way he tilted her chin to look into her eyes made Chantel fear he was going to kiss her. But he didn't. He just stroked her jaw with the pad of his thumb until she wished she could feel his lips on hers again, feel the completeness they'd experienced once.

''Let's get some sleep,'' he said. Standing, he turned off the television and the lights. Then he pulled her down beside him on the couch, her body cradled by his, and covered them both with the blanket.

STACY STOOD in front of the mirror wearing her black lace bra and garter belt. What had gone wrong? The meal had been perfect, the wine superb, the music and lighting soft and relaxing. So why had Dillon rushed off?

Taking another sip of wine, the last of the bottle, she sank to the floor. If she looked as good as Chantel did, he wouldn't have left without so much as a peck on the cheek, she thought dejectedly. It was just that she reminded men of their sister or their mother. As a result, they were always friendly but practical. Uninterested in romance.

The telephone rang, and Stacy gulped the rest of her wine before she crossed to the nightstand to answer it. "Hello?"

"You sound odd. Were you asleep?"

Wade. Stacy glanced at her empty glass and wished for more. "No."

"Good. Then you don't mind talking?"

"For a minute." She knew she should tell him to go to hell, but the sound of his voice still stirred something in her. She hadn't been able to hang up on him when he'd called her yesterday, either.

"Did you speak to Chantel?"

"Yeah. She's not going back to you."

There was a long pause. "Why not? Is it that other guy?"

"What other guy?"

"I don't know. Some guy came to the house while I was there."

Stacy considered that for a minute. Chantel had only been in town for a few weeks. Stacy was pretty sure she wasn't seeing anyone yet. "Must be her neighbor or something. She hasn't been dating that I know of."

"He seemed pretty damn possessive for a neighbor."

She couldn't picture Chantel's neighbors. Had she met any of them? She wasn't sure. She'd have to think about it again in the morning. "I don't know who he is. I'll ask her later."

"You do that."

"How long are you in town?"

She heard him sigh. "As long as it takes."

"I don't think hanging around will do you any good. You're not going to change Chantel's mind."

"She's always come back to me in the past."

"She's left you before?"

"Just for a day or two, here and there. No relationship is perfect."

Something else suddenly occurred to Stacy. "She said she was sick while she was in New York."

"Naw, she had it good in New York. She's a fool to walk away."

"Oh."

Silence fell between them, and Stacy fiddled with the ribbons on her corset, wondering what her life would have been like if she'd married Wade. Had he changed much? Did he still have any feelings for her? "Are you staying with your parents?" she asked.

"Yeah."

"Are you comfortable there?"

Another long pause. "You offering to let me stay at your place?"

"Maybe."

"'Maybe' doesn't tell me whether or not to make the drive."

Stacy wavered for a minute, indecisive. Part of her was thrilled at the thought of being with Wade again, at the prospect of possibly stealing him back. Maybe then she could finally assuage her wounded ego and forgive Chantel.

She moved close to the mirror again and stared at her reflection. Maybe her new lingerie *would* come in handy, after all.

"Do you want me to come over or not?" he persisted.

Stacy sucked in her stomach and turned sideways to see her profile. She looked great, she decided. Maybe he'd be sorry he left her.

His regret would feel wonderful. She knew it would. "If you want to," she said, and hung up.

"IT'S LATE. Where are you going?" Wade's father asked, looking away from the television long enough to frown at him.

"A friend's," Wade answered indifferently, searching the keys dangling from a rack of little brass hooks on the wall.

"Chantel's? She taking you back?"

"That's not where I'm going, but she'll take me back. It's just a matter of time."

Henry mumbled something about Chantel and good sense, but Wade wasn't listening. His parents' disapproval of him and his life-style wasn't anything new. "Can I take the Cadillac?"

"You gonna fill it up?"

"Come on, Henry, you know I don't have any money."

His father shook his head, his face revealing disgust. "I'm not likely to forget, not when it's me who paid the rent on your fancy New York apartment for three months before you lost it. But I'll tell ya, I'm getting mighty sick of helping out. You're thirty-three years old, Wade, too old to be depending on us. You said you wanted to come out here and look for a job, so I bought you a plane ticket, but I haven't seen any job search going on."

"My agent called. He thinks he has something lined up for me, something that'll pay me more for one shoot than you've ever made in a year."

"Great!" his father exclaimed, nearly jumping out of his recliner. "Then make more money than me, get another apartment and pay your own damn bills! That's exactly what I want you to do!"

"Henry." Wade's mother's quiet rebuke came from the kitchen, where she was busy cleaning the refrigerator or dishing out ice cream or doing something domestic, as always. "Let's not have words. Wade's just had a run of hard luck lately. Ever since Chantel left, he's been too upset to work—"

"And when she was around, he was doing too well to bother with us. We heard from him maybe once a year."

"They were busy, dear. You know how it must have been with all those photo shoots. You've seen the covers."

"I've seen Chantel on the covers."

Wade's restraint nearly snapped. Who was his father, Mr. Middle America, to criticize *him?* The sum total of his father's working career had given his parents nothing more than twenty-year-old tract house, a modest pension, a 1988 Cadillac and a 1996 Buick.

"If he'd stayed home and gotten an education like his brothers, he'd have a steady income," his father was saying, but Wade had finally spotted the keys to the Cadillac. Scooping them off the kitchen table, he strode from the house, leaving his parents to argue without him. He'd heard everything he wanted to hear from them. The story was always the same. They didn't understand that he was destined for bigger things, that he'd settle for nothing short of the fast-track life he'd enjoyed for the past ten years. He'd had it all until Chantel left him. Then things had gone downhill. But as soon as he got her back, they'd take New York by storm.

Fortunately for him, Stacy had just provided him with the perfect way to get her attention. And possibly a little revenge.

WHERE WAS HE?

Still wearing the lingerie she'd purchased at the mall, Stacy pulled on a silky robe, belted it and poured herself another glass of scotch. Maybe he wasn't coming. She was probably crazy for even inviting him. After Dillon left, she should have gone straight to bed. Instead, she'd gotten herself drunk.

For a moment she considered calling Wade back and telling him not to come. But it was probably too late. He'd be here any second. Besides, she wasn't sure she *didn't* want to see him. She wasn't sure of anything.

Crossing her legs, she admired the way her high heels accentuated the muscles in her calves, then rested her head back on the couch, feeling the gentle burn of the liquor. At first she'd been nervous, almost panicky, at the thought of seeing Wade again. But the more she drank the less she worried. Ten years ago she'd worn his ring, planned to become his wife, warmed his bed, and he'd run off with her sister. Why hold it against him?

Giggling at that, she took another sip of her drink. No big deal, she told herself. She just wanted to see him again. He hadn't been the most giving lover she'd ever had, but he'd possessed the kind of charisma that made whoever he was with feel special. Unless that had changed, along with everything else.

If it had, maybe she *didn't* want to see him again. She couldn't decide. But even that didn't seem to make much difference, not in her current frame of mind.

The doorbell rang and Stacy got up to answer it. ''Knock, knock…who's there?'' she chirped, suppressing another giggle.

When she opened the door, she found Wade leaning against the railing, wearing a pair of blue jeans, a short-sleeved shirt and a maroon sweater vest. Except for the bleach in his hair and the short cropped cut, he looked very much the way she remembered him, as handsome as ever. Golden skin, well-defined arm muscles, a knowing grin. The earring he wore in one ear glinted in the porch light. She remembered the night she'd met him at a dance club. He'd dazzled her at first sight, made her feel breathless—and he did the same to her now.

Or maybe that was the liquor.

"Come in," she said, holding the door open and trying not to sway on her feet.

He moved past, smelling like expensive hair products and too much cologne, and surveyed her living room. "You own this place?" he asked.

She nodded. "Can I get you a drink?"

His gaze cut to the bottle of scotch on the coffee table, then to the glass she still held in her hand, and his smile widened. "Sure. Looks like you've got a head start on me, though."

"I've had a few." Stacy had already brought an extra glass from the kitchen. She bent to pour him a liberal amount, but he took the bottle from her unsteady hands and filled the glass himself.

"It's been a long time," he said, watching her. "I like the changes."

"Yeah?" She smiled and struck what she hoped was an appealing pose.

"You look good."

"But not as good as Chantel?"

He cocked an eyebrow at her. "Not many women look as good as Chantel," he said simply.

"Is that why you left me for her?"

Downing his scotch in one gulp, he set the glass on the coffee table. "Did you invite me over so you can bitch and moan about what happened ten years ago?"

Stacy chuckled softly. He had no idea what he'd put her through and he didn't care. Well, neither did she, not right now, anyway. "Don't you think you deserve it?"

"Let's just say that's not why I came here. We could have talked on the phone." Reaching out, he loosened the top of her robe and gazed inside it. "And I doubt you wear that little number to bed on a regular basis. I wouldn't want to waste it."

She laughed, feeling attractive, wanton in her sexy lingerie. "Aren't you even going to ask me how I've been before you start taking off my clothes?"

He shrugged, letting his fingers glide back and forth over the curve of one breast. "Okay, how've you been?"

She watched the movement of his hand. "Busy. I'm a nurse, you know."

"Great," he said, pulling her roughly to him. "Let's play doctor."

"DADDY, I'M HUNGRY."

Dillon opened his eyes, and Sydney's face came slowly into focus. He still held Chantel, could smell the scent of her shampoo and feel her arms over his own, as if she was afraid he might let go. He wanted to nuzzle the soft skin beneath her ear, but he didn't. There was no need to confuse Sydney. Or chase Chantel farther away from him.

"You up already, sweetheart?" he asked his daughter, disentangling himself.

Chantel stirred, and he eased out from behind her. As anticipated, he had a splitting headache, and his mouth felt like cotton.

"Can we have sugar cereal today, Daddy?"

Sydney's words seemed to stomp through his head. He winced at the noise, then wondered where Chantel stored her aspirin. "What time is it?" he asked.

"Time to get up," she replied.

He chuckled, but that hurt his head even more. If ever he'd longed for a box of Fruity Pebbles, it was now. He wanted to pour Sydney a bowl of it, then sink into a chair where he could sit quietly until the pain lessened.

"Dillon?" Chantel was awake now, gazing up at him with her long hair mussed and one side of her face imprinted with the pattern of the couch pillows.

And still she looked beautiful to him.

"Sydney's up and she's hungry. Mind if I look for some cereal?"

"There's some Wheaties and All-Bran above the stove."

Sydney wrinkled her nose. "Yuck."

Dillon didn't bother to chastise his daughter for her poor manners; his head hurt too badly. "I don't suppose you have any Fruity Pebbles, do you?"

"You let your girls eat that stuff?"

He would have chuckled again, but didn't dare. "Oatmeal didn't go over too well yesterday. And today I just want to keep the racket down."

She stretched and smiled. "Oh, yeah. Last night." She eyed Sydney without saying more, and Dillon appreciated her discretion. He hadn't had a hangover in years, not since he'd quit partying with the college crowd—except for that first Christmas without Amanda and the kids.

"What happened last night, Daddy?" Sydney asked.

"I had to work late," he replied. "How 'bout we fix up that All-Bran with some honey?"

"Or strawberries," Chantel suggested. "There's some in the fridge."

"Strawberries?" Brittney stood at the end of the hall. "That sounds good."

"On *bran* cereal," Sydney muttered.

"Oh, I get it now."

This time Dillon gave them a warning look. "Hey, when you're a guest at someone's house—"

"—you eat whatever they put in front of you," Brittney finished.

"With a smile," Dillon added.

"They don't have to act like guests around me," Chantel said, throwing off the blanket and getting up. "Here, you guys sit down. You, too, Dillon, and I'll get something for your headache and see what I can come up with for breakfast."

"Just a little cold cereal will be fine," Dillon insisted. "We don't want to put you out. Or we can call a cab and eat back at our own place."

"You won't be talking about eating at your place when you smell my pancakes," Chantel said.

Dillon admired the long lines of her legs as she moved about the kitchen. He wanted to repeat everything they'd done that night in the storm—wanted to make love to her again and again. Only, she wouldn't let him close, and he knew he'd break the fragile person sheltering inside her if he pushed.

Noticing the clean plate and cup she was clearing from the table, he guessed she'd been planning to feed him dinner last night. But that didn't make sense. "What movie did you guys go see?" he asked, pulling Sydney onto his lap. Even though she was getting a little too big to sit there comfortably, he knew it was still her favorite spot.

"We didn't go to a movie," Brittney said. "Chantel helped us finish our homework and read *Charlotte's Web* to us. Then we had our baths, and she dried our hair while we sang to the radio. It was fun."

"And we ate meatballs," Sydney said.

"With sausage," Brittney added.

He kissed Sydney's cheek, picturing the domesticity of the scene and wishing he'd been with them, instead of guzzling scotch and wine at Stacy's. "I'm sorry I missed it."

"No one makes spaghetti like Chantel."

"I'm not much of a cook," Chantel admitted, "but I can make a good pot of spaghetti."

"If I'd known you weren't at the movies, I would've been here. Why didn't you answer the phone?"

"Because it didn't ring," Sydney said.

Dillon's gaze clashed with Chantel's. "Wait a second. It was a set-up, wasn't it?"

Chantel didn't answer.

"Just tell me one thing," he persisted, the anger he'd felt last night returning. "Was it your idea? Were you in on it?"

She paused, spatula in hand. "Would you believe me if I said no?"

He considered the sincerity in her voice and his anger eased, replaced by a glimmer of hope. "If things had gone the way Stacy planned, would you have been happy about it?"

"Please," she murmured. "Don't ask me that."

But the look on her face was all the answer he needed.

CHAPTER TEN

DILLON UNLOCKED the Taurus, which he'd parked near Stacy's house, and got his girls strapped in, then thanked Chantel for the ride—and for the huge breakfast she'd made. Pancakes, eggs and orange juice. A big improvement on cereal, as far as his daughters were concerned. But now they needed to hurry or Chantel would be late for work and the girls would be late for school. Dillon had already called his receptionist to say he'd be taking the morning off.

"Any chance you'd let me thank you for helping with the girls by making you dinner this weekend?" he asked Chantel, bending to see inside the window of her Jag. "Just as friends?"

She started to shake her head, then seemed to think better of it. "Just as friends?" she repeated.

Dillon smiled. "You can't have too many friends."

"Especially when you're new in town." She glanced quickly toward Brittney and Sydney and waved. "I really like your girls, Dillon."

"They like you, too. They want to see you again."

She sighed. "Okay. When?"

"Friday at six-thirty work for you?"

"As long as you invite Stacy, too."

Dillon scowled. "Are you sure you want all three of us to be together?"

"That's the only way I can see you. I won't go behind her back."

He thought for a moment. It would be awkward, but there was certainly merit to doing things as a threesome. Stacy would probably be less aggressive. Chantel might relax enough that he could get to know her better. And neither of them would have to deal with any guilt.

"Okay, you win. I'll ask her today. You'd better get going."

She flashed him a grin, waved to the girls again and drove off.

He watched until the taillights of her car disappeared around the corner, then blew out a long sigh. What was he going to do? He had a missing ex-wife, a friend who wanted to be his lover and a lover who wanted to be his friend. Would there ever be a time when life became less complicated?

Sliding behind the wheel of the Taurus, he started the engine, then remembered that he'd meant to stop by Stacy's. He'd forgotten his pager at her place last night, and Sydney had left something she'd made at school.

He glanced down at his wrinkled shirt. Would Stacy assume he hadn't been home if she saw him? He had yet to shave, and his hair was uncombed, but it would be so much easier to stop there now, instead of driving all the way back later in the day.

"What's wrong, Daddy? Why are we sitting here?"

Dillon looked over at Brittney. "I was just thinking, honey. Sydney wanted me to pick up the puppet she made in school yesterday, which she left at Stacy's. But I think I'd better get you girls off to school first."

She frowned. "I have band today and my clarinet's at Mom's. What am I going to tell the teacher?"

"What time do you need it?"

"At noon."

"Then I'll rent one and bring it to the school, okay? No

worries.'' He squeezed her hand, hoping to coax a smile out of her, but her brows drew together.

''Does that mean Mom isn't coming home?''

With a click from behind, Sydney released her seat belt and leaned through the crack in the bucket seats. ''She's probably coming back today, right, Dad?''

What did he say? Either their mother was too badly hurt to call or find her way home, or she'd abandoned them.

He didn't want his girls to hear either explanation. He didn't want his girls to live with either possibility. ''We don't know yet,'' he said. ''I haven't heard from her. But I'm sure I will.''

''Why can't we go look for her?'' Sydney asked, and it was while he was gazing into her troubled eyes that he realized he couldn't let the mystery last forever, regardless of the ugly truth that might be uncovered.

''Because we don't know where to look,'' he told her. ''But I know of someone who might be able to help us.''

''Who?''

''He's called a private investigator.''

BY THE TIME he'd gotten the girls off to school, then showered and shaved, Dillon felt like a new man. He had a long list of errands, but his secretary had managed to clear his schedule, and he was determined to use the morning as productively as possible.

First on his list was retrieving his pager from Stacy's, so his office could get hold of him even if his cell-phone battery gave out. As he turned down the same street where he'd parked his car the night before, he thought of the barbecue he'd mentioned to Chantel and made a mental note to invite Stacy. Repaying her for the dinner she'd made him might even the score a little and make him feel less like a traitor.

An old brown Cadillac sat in the middle of Stacy's driveway. He wondered briefly who could be visiting so early, but Stacy had a lot of friends. He assumed it meant she was up and headed to the front door.

But it wasn't Stacy who answered his knock. Wade stood there staring out at him, wearing nothing but a pair of pants that weren't buttoned all the way up. They blinked at each other, then Wade started to laugh.

"Stacy, you've got a visitor," he said. "Let's hope you don't have him throw me out like Chantel did. This is starting to get pretty repetitive."

"What?" Stacy appeared at Wade's side, wearing a silky robe and carrying a cup of coffee. When she saw him on the stoop, her eyes widened and her jaw dropped. "Dillon! What are you doing here?"

Dillon wished he'd decided to do without his pager or had simply bought a new one. "I'm sorry. I didn't realize—"

Stacy's blush climbed from her neck to the roots of her sleep-tousled hair. "Um, it…it's not what you think," she said. "Wade and I used to be engaged, but…actually, he and Chantel are, um, involved now. Not us."

"He knows who I am," Wade volunteered. "We met at Chantel's, didn't we, buddy?"

Stacy's cheeks retained their flush, but the expression in her eyes altered. "You what?"

"This is the guy I was telling you about last night. The one who showed up at Chantel's while I was there," Wade explained.

Stacy looked dazed. "Is that true?"

Dillon didn't know how to answer. He just knew it was imperative she not find Chantel at fault. "I stopped by, but your sister basically told me to get lost."

Wade splayed his hands on his hips. "Oh, yeah? I guess

that was after I left, because I specifically remember her inviting you in.''

Dillon's hand itched to smash Wade in the face. This pretty boy had carelessly cost Chantel her family ten years ago, and he obviously wasn't about to stop causing trouble now. ''As I remember, you were making quite a nuisance of yourself, and we had to handle first things first,'' he said.

''What were you doing at my sister's?'' Stacy asked him. The color had drained from her face, and Dillon could only imagine what she was going to say to Chantel.

''I asked her if she'd be willing to go out with me,'' he admitted.

''And?'' Stacy's voice was barely a whisper.

''She said no.''

''Because she's still in love with me,'' Wade interjected.

Dillon looked him in the eye, then turned back to Stacy. ''No. Because she loves *you*,'' he told her. Then he walked away, leaving behind his pager, his daughter's puppet and the damage he'd wreaked. But not the memory of the pain in Stacy's eyes or the sickening knowledge that Chantel would pay the price.

And it was his fault.

STACY THOUGHT she might throw up. Waking to find Wade in her bed had been bad enough. She'd hoped, until she actually opened her eyes, that last night had been nothing but a bad dream and simply wanted to forget the whole thing. She'd made a mistake. That was all. A big mistake that left her feeling worthless and dirty and used.

But it was nothing compared to the humiliation of Dillon's catching her with Wade. What must he think? Wade had answered the door only half-dressed! And she was sure that her weak attempt to cover for what had happened between them had done nothing to convince Dillon. The truth had been staring him right in the face.

Except that it didn't matter. Dillon didn't care about her, anyway. He wanted Chantel, just as she'd feared from the beginning. It was all happening again. She'd talked herself out of believing Dillon had any interest in Chantel; she'd told herself to have some self-confidence. But he *had* been interested in her sister. Was probably *still* interested in her.

Wade was looking at her oddly. "Are you going to pass out or something? What's wrong?"

What's wrong? she wanted to shout. *What's always wrong—Chantel, of course. And you. And my own stupidity.*

Without another word she fled to her room. She needed to be alone. She needed to shower and wash every trace of Wade from her body, and wished she could wash away the memories just as easily. The thought of his touch sickened her.

But he followed her down the hall and held her door open so she couldn't shut him out. "What's gotten into you?" he asked. "Who was that guy?"

"I *thought* he was my boyfriend," she muttered, glaring up at him.

"And Chantel's been seeing him?"

Stacy didn't know how to answer that. Dillon had said Chantel turned him down, but how was she to know whether or not that was true?

"Stacy?" She felt Wade touch her arm, remembered his hands elsewhere on her body, and swallowed against a rising bout of nausea. She'd wanted to seduce Dillon last night. She'd served him a candlelight dinner and hinted that she'd serve him more. And instead, she'd taken her one-time fiancé into her bed.

Ugh! It was too awful to bear thinking about!

"So what are you going to do?" Wade asked, his brows knitting as he watched her.

"I'm going to talk to my sister, like I should have when I first noticed you panting around her skirts," she said. "Now let go of me and get out. And don't ever come back."

"WHERE DID I PUT that?" Chantel murmured to herself, searching her desk for the form letter she was supposed to send to any of the senator's constituents who were concerned about attaining a "wild and scenic" designation for the South Fork of the Yuba River.

"Did you say something?" Maureen called from her own desk.

"No, nothing." Chantel ducked behind the divider that separated her from Maureen and dug her nails into her palms. Her mind wasn't on her work today. It was on a pair of strong arms holding her through the night, and the thought of seeing that same man again this weekend. But she couldn't afford to daydream about Dillon. She had to focus; she'd made too many mistakes this morning. Chantel knew she still had to prove herself—especially since the senator had hired her despite the fact that his top aide had recommended someone else.

Slowly releasing her breath, she tried to calm down and remember. Then she laughed when her eyes lighted on the letter she needed. It was sitting, plain as day, on the tray where she kept the employees' messages.

The telephone rang and she picked it up.

"Senator Johnson's office."

"Hi, Chantel. This is Tim."

The senator. Tim Johnson. She'd only seen him once since he'd interviewed her. Chantel felt a nervous flutter in her chest. "Good morning, Senator," she said.

"How are you?"

"Fine, thank you."

"Good. Listen, we're going to be having a staff meeting tomorrow morning, so I want you to remind everyone to come in an hour early. Afterward, I'll be seeing a couple of people in my office. Will you make sure we've got doughnuts or something I can offer them? And some decent coffee?"

"Of course."

"Also, tell all the aides I'll be expecting their reports for last month. No excuses."

"Of course." She jotted it down.

"Thanks."

The other line rang, but Chantel waved for Maureen to answer it.

"I'm doing a fund-raiser with the governor, a barbecue," the senator continued. "Will you check with the campaign-committee chair and make sure the invitations went out? I have a new man running things, and I don't want any screw-ups on this."

"I'll take care of it."

"Great. You're welcome to come to the fund-raiser, too, you know. And feel free to bring a friend."

Chantel thought of Stacy and wondered if her sister would like to meet the governor.

"Line two is for you," Maureen called to her. Chantel nodded, her attention still on the senator, who was thanking her and saying goodbye.

"Could you put me through to Layne?" he asked when he'd finished.

"Of course."

Chantel punched the "hold" button, then panicked when she couldn't remember how to transfer the call.

"Star 89," Maureen reminded her, and Chantel breathed

a sigh of relief when she heard Layne's voice boom out from behind his door, "Hello, Senator."

Seeing the flashing light on line two, Chantel picked up, expecting to hear Stacy's voice. Her sister was the only one who'd ever phoned her at the office.

"Stace?"

"It's Dillon."

"Oh, hi. Did you get the girls off to school okay?"

"I did. Then I rented a clarinet for Brittney and brought it by the school so she wouldn't miss band and I ran some other errands." He cleared his throat. "Listen, Chantel, I'm afraid I have some bad news."

"Did you find your wife?"

"Not yet. It's not that kind of bad news, but I wish it was. Then it would be my bad news and not yours."

Chantel felt a chill climb up her spine. "What is it?"

"I went to Stacy's this morning to get my pager. I accidentally left it there last night."

"And you wanted to get Sydney's puppet. I remember you said something about it at breakfast."

"Well, you'll never guess who answered the door."

Chantel couldn't even imagine. Stacy didn't have a roommate. Another man? But why would that be bad news? "You got me. I don't have a clue."

"Wade."

She chewed on the end of her pencil, trying to imagine Wade at her sister's house. "What was he doing there?"

There was a slight hesitation. "I'm not sure. He wasn't wearing much. I think he might have stayed the night."

Chantel expected the thought of that to bother her. But it didn't. Although she was concerned about Stacy. "I hope she's not stupid enough to get involved with him again, Dillon. He'll chew her up and spit her out without a second thought."

"There's more."

"What?"

"He recognized me. And he told Stacy I'd been to your house."

Chantel squeezed her eyes shut. *Please, God, not when she was trying so hard to do the right thing. Poor Stacy!*

"Chantel?"

"I'm here."

"I just wanted to warn you, in case..."

In case Stacy's upset. And of course she will be.

"Thanks for letting me know," she said at last.

"I told her I went to your place to ask you out, but you refused. At this point, I think the truth is our safest bet."

"But not the whole truth, Dillon. Not about that night in the storm. I'm afraid...I'm afraid that would be the last straw."

Dillon remembered the look on Stacy's face and hoped they hadn't reached that point already.

"I won't say any more."

"Okay."

"I'm sorry, Chantel."

"I know."

She hung up and sat staring at the phone, and all the work piled up on her desk around it.

What was she going to do now?

THE INTERCOM buzzed, interrupting Dillon's efforts to fit ten window offices and a reception area into two thousand square feet of garden-style office space on his computer-assisted design program. He generally liked doing tenant improvements. For the most part, they were quick and easy, the bread and butter of his business, but he was having a hard time concentrating on anything this afternoon. He kept seeing Wade, barely dressed, at Stacy's, and wondering what it could mean, in the end, for all of them. And his secretary had interrupted him several times already.

"What is it, Kim?" he asked, buzzing her back.

"There's a Stacy Miller here to see you."

Stacy. She'd come on to him last night, then slept with her ex-fiancé, but knowing her the way he did, he doubted she was proud of it. "Send her in."

Turning off his computer, Dillon pushed back his chair and stood as Stacy stepped into his office, wearing a pair of black slacks and a crisp white shirt, and looking painfully self-conscious.

"Hi, Dillon," she said.

"Hi, Stace. You want to sit down?" He propped himself on the corner of his desk and motioned to one of the chairs close by.

She moved forward and took a seat, but she couldn't seem to meet his eyes. "I came to apologize for last night."

Dillon studied her face, noting the fresh blush that tinged her cheeks. "You don't owe me any apologies, Stacy. We've never had any commitments between us."

"I know, but it couldn't have looked very good, what you saw this morning."

"Are you telling me Wade didn't spend the night?" For her sake, Dillon hoped so.

She squirmed for a moment, but finally shook her head. "No."

He wondered what he could say to make her feel better. She was obviously miserable. "Are you sure you want to start seeing Wade again?" he asked.

"I don't want anything to do with him. Last night I'd had too much to drink, and he and I still had some unresolved issues, and..." She shook her head again. "I don't know. I was stupid and I did something I sincerely regret."

"We all make mistakes."

"I guess. There's a lot of history behind what happened with Wade last night, but that's no excuse."

Dillon smiled. "My advice is to forget it and move on, and to stay away from him in the future. I don't like that guy."

Stacy's eyes searched his face. "That sounds like you care. But it doesn't sound like you're jealous."

Dillon couldn't miss the bitterness in her voice. "I don't want to lose our friendship," he said.

She blinked rapidly, and Dillon suspected she was on the verge of tears. "That's a line I've heard before. 'Hey, I just want to be friends.'"

"It's not a line. You're a great—"

"Stop." She raised a hand. "I don't want any consolation prizes."

He continued, anyway. "I'm being sincere, Stacy. You're a great person, with a lot to offer a man."

She chuckled sarcastically. "Another man."

He didn't answer.

"Are you doing this because of what I did with Wade last night or because of Chantel?" she asked.

Dillon thought about putting an arm around her and trying to comfort her, but she was too close to tears. He wanted to help her salvage what pride she had left, not throw her over the edge. "What I said this morning is true. I'd like to date Chantel, but she won't see me."

"God!" Stacy squeezed her eyes shut as two tears streaked down her face.

"I'm sorry, Stacy," he said softly.

She waved his words away. "Don't be. I made it easy for you with my behavior last night."

"How I feel has nothing to do with last night. I know you can't be glad about any of it—"

She made a sound of utter disgust.

"—and I'm sure this seems trite, but you'll find the right man someday."

"And what do I do then?" she asked. "Just hope he never meets my sister?" She got quickly to her feet and left.

"YOU WEREN'T GOING to tell me?"

Stacy had let herself into the condo and was waiting for Chantel when she got home from work. Chantel had had five hours to prepare herself for a confrontation, had seen her sister's car in the parking lot, but the knot in her stomach wouldn't go away. Ever since she'd spoken with Dillon, she'd been trying to figure out what she could say. There was just one thing: She wouldn't let a man come between her and her sister again. She wouldn't repeat the mistakes that had cost them both so much.

If Stacy could only understand that, could only believe in her…

But Chantel hardly dared to believe in herself, so it was a thin thread to hang her hopes on. How could Stacy ever trust her after Wade? Especially when Dillon was twice the man and held twice the appeal?

"There wasn't anything to tell you," she said, trying to read the level of her sister's emotion as she set her purse and keys on the counter. "Dillon asked me out. I said no. That's all that happened."

Stacy bowed her head. "Why? Why do they all want you?"

Chantel's heart twisted. She hated to see her sister suffer, to know *she* was the cause. "Wade didn't really want me. He wanted the dream of New York and becoming a supermodel. I was his security blanket, his second chance at success should he fail. Except, he didn't anticipate hating me for the attention I received. I've often wondered what would have happened if neither of us had done well, or if he'd climbed to the top, instead of me. Probably the same thing. We would have split eventually.''

''And Dillon?''

Chantel took a deep breath, hating the lies. But some things were too precious to risk. Her sister was one of them. ''With Dillon it's just a passing whim. He doesn't really know me,'' she said.

''So it's all about looks? Looks mean everything?''

''You know better than that.''

''Then why does this happen over and over, Chantel? Why can't I feel good about me when I'm around you?''

''Maybe because you compare us too often, and most of the time you use the wrong measuring stick.''

Stacy stared at her. ''What do you mean?''

Chantel softened her voice. ''That you're a wonderful woman and if whoever you're dating can't see that, then he's not worthy of you.''

Stacy shook her head. ''If I'm so wonderful, why do my boyfriends all go after my sister?''

''I don't know. Maybe they just don't take the time to get to know you well enough.''

''Because they only care about what they see.''

Chantel bit her lip. When she was young, she'd been teased because she was so tall and skinny and gawky. Now, she was treated as though she had nothing except her looks. Couldn't her sister understand that her life wasn't ideal, either? ''We're different, Stacy. We look different. We have different talents. That's okay. But until we agree to accept our differences, we can never be friends.''

''That's easy for you to say. You're the supermodel. You're the one who has it all, including the only two men I've ever loved!''

Chantel rubbed her temples. Stacy was too upset to be rational. Or maybe she just didn't want to see that their problems went far deeper than Dillon and Wade. "I've never purposely tried to hurt you, Stacy. I made a mistake with Wade. I know I can't fix that, but I've tried to apologize—"

"*I'm sorry?* That should make it better?"

"Maybe not, but some things aren't worth worrying about, not in the long run."

"Like?"

"Like which one of us is prettier or garners more male attention."

"I don't believe this! You're basically telling me to lump it and move on. And I don't think you have the right!" Stacy grabbed her purse and headed to the door.

Chantel's temper threatened to snap, but the memory of ten long years without her sister kept her cautious. "Stacy, forget what I said. If Dillon's all you care about, I'll make you a promise. I'll stay away from him. I won't return his calls if he contacts me, won't open the door to him if he comes by. I'll tell him I never want to see him again. Will that make you happy?"

Stacy didn't answer, but the slamming of the door echoed in Chantel's head for several long minutes after she'd left.

"Will that make him marry you?" she asked the now-silent house. And then the tears came.

CHAPTER ELEVEN

"So you've hired a private investigator?" Helen asked.

Dillon propped the portable phone on his shoulder and flipped the burgers he was barbecuing for dinner, talking over the loud sizzle of the meat. Chantel had called and canceled, so the night didn't look as promising as it once had, but he was trying to make the most of it. "Signed the contract this morning."

"Does he think he can find her?"

"He holds to the theory that people don't simply disappear."

"I guess he's never watched *America's Most Wanted*." That was exactly what Dillon had thought as he'd sat in Mr. Curtis Trumbull's office. At the same time, the man's confidence had been reassuring. He'd matched the television stereotype: dogged manner, cheap suit, old desk, messy office. Although Dillon doubted he had a bottle of booze stashed away in his drawer. And there'd been no blond bombshell sitting out front to answer phones and greet visitors. Trumbull was a one-man show. "He thinks he can learn something before the weekend's out."

"It's already Friday night."

"His job isn't nine-to-five, weekdays only."

Helen breathed out, and he pictured her smoking another of her cigarettes. She had one in her hand most of the time. "What about the girls? Are they adjusting okay?"

"Can't you hear them giggling?" Just beyond the back

porch, where Dillon monitored the progress of their dinner, the girls were jumping on the trampoline he'd bought them this week, which sat right next to the swing set he'd designed and built for them a year ago. "They're doing great. A van picks them up after school and takes them to Children's World, where they do arts and crafts or play outside for a couple of hours. On Thursdays I take off early to get Sydney to her gymnastics class and Brittney to karate."

"Oh, good." A hacking cough interrupted her. "I think it's important to keep their lives as normal as possible."

"So far, my biggest problem has been getting them to eat healthy food, but a mother at the school gave me some kid-friendly recipes we're going to try."

"Amanda used to be so careful about what they ate."

Certainly not recently, Dillon wanted to add, but he held his tongue. Her voice sounded more gravelly than normal, and he suspected she was crying again. "Trumbull will find her, Helen. Regardless of the outcome, at least we'll be able to get some closure. I think that's important for the girls, too."

Helen cleared her throat but didn't answer.

"Do you still want us to come over on Sunday?" he asked.

"I'd like to take them for the weekend, like I usually do."

All those weekends I was supposed to have them, and you and Amanda forced me to fight for my legal rights. "No, I want to spend some time with them. It's been a crazy, stressful week for all of us. We need a chance to relax and play and simply feel okay together."

The telephone beeped, letting him know another call was coming in. "I've got to go, Helen. We'll see you on Sunday."

She said goodbye, and he switched to the other line.

"Dillon? It's Mom. What's happened? When Lyle and I got home from our honeymoon, we had three messages from you."

"I didn't realize you'd be gone so long."

"I told you we wouldn't be back until the seventh of April. We're actually a few days early."

She probably had told him, but he hadn't paid any attention. That was his way of blocking out her irresponsible behavior. She was on her fifth marriage, her fourth honeymoon—she claimed his father had never taken her on one—and he didn't like this latest husband. Lyle had no profession or money to speak of, and Dillon suspected he'd married Karen for the free ride. But his mother seemed crazy about him. At least for the time being.

He removed the burgers from the grill, wishing again that Chantel hadn't canceled, and told her about Amanda.

"That girl is no good. I don't know why you married her."

"Because she wasn't always like this. She said she wanted the same things I did, but she grew dissatisfied fast. She didn't want to be a stay-at-home mom. But she didn't want to work, either."

"I'll bet she's run off with this guy," Karen said. "How could a woman do that to her own children?"

In a way Karen had done the same thing to Dillon. She'd stuck around, but she'd been gone in spirit ever since her divorce from his father, getting involved with one man after the other. Dillon wasn't sure anymore why he'd wanted to talk to her, except that she lived only a few miles away and it seemed natural to turn to his family during a crisis that concerned his children. At least his mother was more receptive than his father.

"Did you see Dave while you were in New England?" he asked.

Dillon listened to his mother marvel at the beauty of Dave's farm and how little Reva had changed. Then he heard about the rest of her trip across America in the new motor home she'd bought, including her visit to his other uncle, who lived in Indiana.

"I wish they'd both move back to California," she finished, "so we could live closer as a family."

Dillon was glad that Dave, at least, had lived close by most of the years he was growing up. Otherwise he might never have righted his rebellious ways. "You've got Janet and Monica," he reminded her. His sisters.

"When they have the time."

His mother was retired. He and his sisters had families and careers; none of them had that much time. "Our dinner's getting cold, Mom. I'd better go," he said at last. "I'm glad the two of you had fun."

"Do you need me to take the girls so you can go out tonight?" she asked out of the blue. She'd never been much of a baby-sitter. He wondered what prompted the offer now.

"Go out with whom?"

"What about that nice young woman Stacy?"

"We're not seeing each other anymore."

"You've broken up already?"

"We were just friends."

"Well, now that you've got your daughters back, you should start thinking about settling down again."

Dillon squirted ketchup on the buns he had waiting on the picnic table. "I am settled. I like my home. I'm busy with my job. That'll have to be good enough for now."

"But those girls are going to need a mother."

"They've lived without one for the past few weeks and probably much longer," he muttered. "Listen, I've got to go, Mom, or I'm going to have to reheat these burgers."

"Are they done, Daddy?" Brittney yelled, and he waved her over.

"Just tell me you'll start looking for the right woman," his mother said, persistent as ever.

Dillon thought of Chantel and winced. He'd found someone he wanted to be with, but pursuing her would only cause her pain. "I suppose it'll happen when the time's right."

"I hope so. Marriage is so wonderful."

Some smooching sounds came over the phone, and Dillon realized Lyle and his mother were kissing like a couple of teenagers. The mental picture nauseated him a little. He wanted his mother to be happy. He didn't necessarily want her to return to her youth.

"You can still say that after five?" he asked.

"Sometimes it takes a few tries to get it right."

Tries? Dillon shook his head. Getting married wasn't like trying on a pair of shoes. A divorce hurt like hell. When he got married again, he promised himself it would be forever.

CHANTEL SAT in the back row of the movie theater, holding a soda and a large bucket of popcorn. She knew she probably wouldn't eat more than a few kernels. But the smell was nice.

"Is anyone sitting here?"

A young woman stood in the aisle, holding the hand of a dark-haired young man. They both looked about eighteen. "No, I'm alone."

The couple smiled and sat down, then opened a box of mints and talked and laughed and ate. Their companionship contrasted so sharply with Chantel's solitude she felt it like a physical pain in her chest. Stacy hadn't called her all week. Chantel had considered contacting her and apologizing again, but she doubted Stacy was ready to let go of the past, no matter how many times she said she was sorry.

Words could only do so much.

The lights went down and the movie screen flickered to life. The trailers started, but Chantel wasn't really interested. She'd come hoping to distract herself from the knowledge that Dillon had invited her to a barbecue tonight, that she could be with him right now, having as much fun as the teenagers to her right. But nothing could distract her, not even the action-and-suspense movie she'd purposely chosen.

For a brief moment she considered leaving the theater and driving over to his house. Why deny herself? Stacy had shut her out again and might never come around. Tonight's sacrifice hardly seemed worth it. But there was that little matter of the kind of person she wanted to be. And she *didn't* want to be the kind of person that turning to Dillon would make her.

"AMANDA MARRIED John Heath."

The investigator's scratchy voice came over the phone the following Wednesday evening while Dillon was putting away groceries. "When?" he asked, losing interest in his task.

"The weekend they arrived in Vegas."

Dillon glanced through the open kitchen into the living room and thanked heaven that Brittney and Sidney were still engrossed in a Mary Kate and Ashley Olsen movie. "Where are they now?"

"I traced them to Utah. I have their address if you want it."

"Just a minute." Dillon retrieved his day-planner and jotted down an address in Salt Lake City. "Do you have their phone number?"

"Yeah. It's not listed, but they weren't smart enough to know that it can be found other ways."

"Like?"

"They made it easy for me. They gave it to the neighborhood video store."

Privacy certainly wasn't what it used to be, Dillon mused. Not that he planned to contact the happy couple. He already knew what he'd wanted to know. Amanda wasn't lying dead on the side of the road somewhere. She'd left the girls of her own free will, though why she hadn't simply given them to him, he had no idea. Maybe because she knew he would have demanded she sign a custody agreement. This way, she probably believed she could come back any time she changed her mind.

That thought didn't sit well with him, but it certainly wasn't Curtis Trumbull's problem.

"Do you want me to do anything else?" the investigator asked.

"No, that's it. Do I owe you anything more?"

"There's a small balance on your account. I'll bill you."

"Thanks."

The phone clicked as Trumbull hung up, but Dillon continued to stare at the handset, wondering what he was going to do now. He needed to tell the girls right away, needed to relieve their anxiety. But how did a father face his children with such news? And what about Amanda's mother, who'd always stood by her, defended her, assisted her?

Amanda had betrayed them all. For John Heath, whoever *he* was.

The phone started beeping from being off the hook and Dillon finally hung up. He squeezed the back of his neck, where the muscles were so tight they were giving him a headache. Then he heard Brittney giggle as she turned off the television set, and he knew their movie was over. Shoving his hands in his pockets, he headed into the living room.

"Sydney, Brittney, come sit down on the couch with me. I have something I need to talk to you about."

WADE STALKED into his bedroom, barely resisting the urge to slam the door. His father was at him again. When was he going to get a real job? When was he going to grow up and act like a man? When was he going to take responsibility for himself, be more like his brothers?

Slumping onto his bed, he picked up the phone and dialed his agent in New York.

"How's that job coming?" he asked the moment Steve's voice came over the line.

"Wade? It's two o'clock in the morning here. What the hell are you doing calling me at home this time of night?"

"I haven't heard from you in weeks, man. I need that job. Is it coming through or not?"

There was a deep sigh on the other end. "It's not. I would have called you if it was. I told you when I talked to you that it was a long shot."

"So that's it? You don't have anything for me? What the hell do you expect me to live on?"

"I'm doing what I can, but the competition's stiff right now. There's nothing that really pays, you know what I'm saying? I could probably scrounge up some odd jobs here and there, but they're for amateurs. You're way beyond them, and they don't pay squat. They're nothing you could live on."

Wade ground his teeth. It was the same damn story. He'd always gotten these kinds of answers and nothing but chicken-shit jobs, while Chantel had been vaulted to fame and fortune. And *he* was the professional! He was the one who could withstand the pressure. Look what had happened to her!

"It doesn't have to be the cover of *GQ,* all right, Steve?" he said, getting desperate. Something had to break. Henry's patience wouldn't last much longer. His father would cut him off, and then where would he be?

"I told you," Steve said, "the male market is tough. But I've got some work here for Chantel that could pull you guys through. Some big stuff. You still bringing her back?"

Wade had tried and tried to talk to Chantel, but she screened her calls and wouldn't return his. If he visited her condo, she refused to answer the door. When she'd left him in New York, he'd thought she'd come back to him eventually. He'd never dreamed she could survive without him. Her world had revolved around him since she was nineteen.

But he was beginning to fear he'd been wrong.

"Yeah, she's coming back with me," he said with more confidence than he felt.

"Then call me as soon as you're in town. These people don't wait long, you know what I'm saying? She's already missed several golden opportunities. But her look is in. We can still play with the big boys if you guys don't take forever."

"Tell everyone to hold on to their hats. We won't take forever," Wade promised, and hung up.

What now? He had to reach Chantel. She was blowing it, blowing it for both of them. And he was running out of time. If he didn't do something quick, he'd be shit out of luck and working nine-to-five like every other nobody.

He dialed her number. After the third ring her answering machine kicked in. Dammit! He knew she was home. Where else would she be at eleven o'clock at night?

Stacy. She could tell him what was going on—if he could get her to talk to him. He'd tried to call her several times since their night together, but she always hung up on him.

It took almost six rings for her to finally answer. "Hello?"

"Stacy, don't hang up."

"You woke me," she said. "What do you want?"

"I want to know what's happening with Chantel. I mean, is she seeing that Dillon guy or what?"

A long pause. Wade assumed she wasn't going to answer, but then her voice came back across the line. "Not that I know of. I haven't talked to her for weeks."

"Will you call her? Find out why she won't let me in?"

"You're kidding, right? You expect *me* to help *you?*"

"Why not? We're friends, aren't we?"

"No. As far as I'm concerned, you can go to hell."

Wade felt a muscle in his cheek start to twitch. "So that's the way you want to play it, huh? Then maybe I should mention to Chantel how you invited me over to see your pretty lingerie."

She laughed. "You do that, Wade. I doubt she'll be very impressed with the part you played that night, either." Then the phone clicked and the dial tone hummed in his ear.

"Bitch," he muttered.

WHEN HER ALARM went off, Chantel groaned and pulled the pillow over her head. She was still tired, and she felt nauseated. For some reason, she couldn't seem to shake the flu that had plagued her for almost a week. But she couldn't call in sick again. She'd missed two days already and wasn't about to miss the staff meeting with the senator this morning.

She just hoped she didn't throw up on the conference table.

Dragging herself out of bed, she went to the kitchen where she had a fresh supply of 7-Up and crackers, which seemed to be the only food her body could tolerate. As a result she'd already lost weight.

Just what she needed after fighting so hard to get back to normal, she thought.

Taking her makeshift breakfast with her, she headed into the bathroom to get showered.

Almost an hour later, she was wearing her blue pinstripe suit and gathering her keys. Another wave of nausea hit as she hurried to her car, but she forced it back, through sheer will, and unlocked the Jag. Setting her purse and briefcase inside, she was about to get behind the wheel when a hand on her arm nearly cost her the small amount of breakfast she'd managed to get down.

"Wade! What are you doing here?" she cried. "You nearly scared me to death!"

Letting go, he jammed his hands in the pockets of his cargo pants. "What else was I supposed to do? You screen your calls, you won't let me in at the door. I need to talk to you."

He didn't look good. His clothes were wrinkled, as if he'd slept in them, and he badly needed a haircut and a shave.

"What's wrong with you? You look like I feel," she said.

"I can't eat or sleep anymore. I never dreamed you'd really walk out on me."

Wade had walked out on her almost every time she'd ever really needed him, in one way or another, but she wasn't about to go into all of that again. "What we had died a long time ago," she said simply.

"I don't believe that. You still love me. You'll always love me."

"Whatever. I'm not coming back, Wade. I can't say it any plainer than that."

"But you're nothing without me. Look at you, heading off to your little secretary's job."

"There's nothing wrong with my job. I'm glad I've got it."

"But you could be on the cover of *Vogue!* I just talked to Steve a few days ago. He said it's not too late."

"Wade—"

"What's gotten into you, dammit? Doesn't your career mean anything to you anymore? Don't *I* mean anything?"

Chantel stared at him, dumbfounded. Where was all this emotion coming from? He'd left her in the hospital for months with no more than an occasional visit. "I don't want another cover, Wade. I want a family."

He ran a hand through his already mussed hair. "I'm ready to go that route, Chantel. I've been thinking about it a lot."

She was too sick and weak to hide the pain his words caused her. "It's too late, Wade. You know that." Her voice broke. "I can't have children."

She got into her car and tried to shut the door, but he held it. "Then we'll adopt, okay?"

"I'm going to be late."

"Wait, you know that counseling you were always talking about? We'll go there. We'll get some help and make our relationship work. Why throw away ten years, babe? This is me, the man you love, right?"

Chantel pinched the bridge of her nose. Why now? "This is quite a reversal, Wade, and I really don't have time to deal with it."

"Can I come over tonight, then? Just to talk?"

She pictured the senator and Maureen and all the field reps gathered around the conference table and knew she had to leave now or risk walking in after they'd started. "Okay," she said. "Come at six."

"CHANTEL, DID YOU FINISH that summary of legislation I gave you to type?" Lee asked, stopping at her desk.

Chantel cringed inside. Lee had been asking her the same question every day for a week. She should have finished the summary days ago, but she had a list of other priorities, and she just wasn't running at top speed. It was all she could do to answer the phones and do a little bit of scheduling. "Um, not quite," she admitted. "I've been pretty busy. When do you need it?"

"Last week," he said pointedly, and walked away.

Chantel set the constituent case she'd been working on aside and pulled out the file that held Lee's handwritten notes. She'd get his typing done now, she decided, but the nausea she'd felt all day reasserted itself, and she couldn't do anything but lay her head on her desk.

"What's wrong?" Maureen asked. "Are you ill?"

"No!" Chantel jerked her head up and forced a smile. She couldn't go home sick, not again. They'd be sorry they hired her.

"You look pale."

"I'm a little tired, that's all."

"Do you want to take an early lunch?"

Yes! Please, yes! But Chantel knew she couldn't take *any* lunch. She was running too far behind. "Maybe I'll grab something after I finish this for Lee," she said.

"You're sure?"

Chantel pumped more life into her smile. "I'm sure."

"Okay." Maureen seemed hesitant, but after another searching look, went back to her own desk and Chantel let herself slump. How was she going to succeed here? She wasn't used to the pressure of an office situation, still had a lot to learn. And she felt so sick....

Buck up, she ordered herself. She had to perform or she'd lose her job, and she couldn't afford that. She doubted she could face the failure. Besides, she had very little savings left. She'd spent what money she'd salvaged from Wade's reckless life-style on her condo and had to have a salary to survive.

Unless... She thought of Wade and what he'd said this

morning. Had he been sincere about marriage and children? She'd fought so hard to escape him and New York, but it felt as if they were both waiting for her to admit defeat and come back.

Unlike this job, modeling was easy for her. And the lifestyle in New York was comfortingly familiar. Why fight it anymore? She'd come home to California for Stacy, but Stacy didn't want a relationship with her, not after what had happened with Dillon.

Dillon... Chantel felt a lump rise in her throat. She could have loved him. She knew she could. He was everything a man should be—

Give up, Wade whispered. *Look at you. You can't even hold down a simple job. Why would Dillon want you? You belong with me. We belong together.*

But the anorexia was there, waiting for her, too.

She was slipping, slipping away, and she was too sick to stop it. "Help me," she prayed, breaking into a cold sweat, and finally her father's voice rose above the confusion in her mind.

You're my little girl, Chantel. You can do anything....

SOMEHOW SHE SURVIVED the day. Chantel didn't know how, but she managed to complete at least some of her work. Then she drove home, hurried into the condo and collapsed on the couch. She knew she should try to eat something so she could get her strength back. But she couldn't stand the thought of throwing up. It was easier not to eat. She was good at starving herself.

Sleep came quickly, enveloping her in a dark shroud that eased the nausea. But it felt as if she'd barely closed her eyes when someone started banging on the door.

"Chantel? Are you there? It's Maureen."

She'd been expecting Wade. What was her boss doing here?''

Clambering to her feet, Chantel fumbled with the lock and swung the door open, then leaned on it for support.

''Are you all right?'' Maureen asked, concern etched on her face.

Chantel nodded. ''I'm fine. It's just the flu. I guess I'm not quite over it yet.''

''Why didn't you tell me?''

''I didn't want to go home sick again. I was afraid—'' she drew a ragged breath ''—I was afraid I'd lose my job. But I don't think I'm going to make it in tomorrow.''

''Of course you're not working tomorrow. You need to stay home and get well. I guessed something was wrong. That's why I decided to stop by on my way home from work, but I had trouble finding your address.''

''I'm sorry, Maureen.'' Chantel raised a hand to her aching head. ''If I weren't sick, I could do the job. But I can't seem to get well. Maybe you should replace me.''

Maureen took her arm and helped her back to the couch. ''That's a little premature, I'd say. Anyone can come down with the flu.''

''But you need someone you can depend on—''

''Chantel?'' Wade stood at the open door, gazing in at them. ''What's wrong?'' he asked.

Maureen answered him. ''We don't know. It might be the flu.''

''Or some kind of backlash from the anorexia,'' he added.

Chantel wished he was close enough to pinch. She didn't want anyone at work to know about her anorexia.

Maureen turned back to her. ''Sounds to me like we should call a doctor.''

''No!'' Chantel protested. ''I've had enough of doctors and hospitals. It's the flu. I just need to get into bed.'' She made a feeble attempt to stand, but Wade had to half lift her.

"I knew this would happen if she didn't have someone to take care of her," Wade said, helping her down the hall.

"I don't need anyone to take care of me," Chantel muttered, but Wade's implications were the least of her problems. The room was spinning, and she was afraid she might faint, until she felt the softness of her mattress beneath her.

"Let me help you out of your suit," he said.

"No. I don't care about the suit." She pulled her goose-down comforter up to her chin, resenting Wade for playing the part of concerned husband. But she didn't have the strength to argue with him. And Maureen was there.

Her manager introduced herself to Wade, then put a hand on Chantel's forehead. "She doesn't have a fever. Aren't you supposed to have a fever with the flu?"

"I don't know, but I know someone who does," Wade said, and a moment later, Chantel heard him talking on the phone. "I think you should take a look at her. She's really sick... Seems she's lost some weight... She might need a doctor."

"Do you have to see a specific doctor for insurance purposes?" he asked her, gently shaking her shoulder.

Chantel didn't answer. She just wanted to sleep so she could shut out the nausea. But Maureen took her hand and persisted until she gave them her doctor's name and insurance information, which Wade repeated into the phone.

"We'll be waiting," he said, and hung up.

And finally it was quiet enough for Chantel to sleep.

CHAPTER TWELVE

STACY DASHED OUTSIDE just as the sun began to set on what had been a breezy May day and started her car, then ran back inside when she realized she'd forgotten her purse. She should have called Chantel as soon as her anger had died away. Instead, pride had prolonged her stupid stubborn silence. If Wade hadn't called just minutes ago, she might have let the weeks turn into months with no contact between them. Who knew how long Chantel would have continued feeling sick before she broke down and asked for help? What if Wade hadn't gone over there?

In the face of real illness, Stacy and Chantel's differences seemed minor. Especially when Stacy considered the possibility of losing the last member of her family for good.

Wade had said it might be the flu, she told herself. Healthy young women didn't die from the flu, right? But the guilt she felt about her part in their estrangement nagged at her. Chantel's genetic makeup wasn't her fault. Maybe Stacy would have done the same thing at nineteen, if their roles had been reversed. Only weeks ago she'd slept with Wade simply to bolster her ego.

With a grimace Stacy wished she could blot out that night. She gunned her Honda, and when she reached the freeway, immediately merged into the fast lane. A voice in the back of her head warned her about getting a ticket, but she pressed the accelerator closer to the floor, anyway.

When she arrived, Wade was sitting in a chair by Chantel's bed, staring at her in the dim light filtering through the window. A heavyset woman Stacy recognized as Chantel's manger from the office, Maureen something, sat on the corner of the bed.

"Is she okay?" Stacy directed her question to the woman. It was the first time she'd seen Wade since their night together, and she would rather have avoided speaking to him again, but it was Wade who answered.

"She fell asleep almost the minute I hung up with you."

Stacy gazed down at her sister's face. Despite the poor lighting, she immediately noticed the dark circles beneath Chantel's eyes and the paleness of her skin. "I called her doctor before I left home. It's after office hours, but he said he'd wait, that we could bring her right in."

"I'll carry her out," Wade volunteered.

Stacy looked at Maureen. "Listen, you can go. I'll take care of her from here."

Maureen nodded, glanced worriedly at Chantel and handed Stacy her card. "Call and let me know how she is, okay?"

Stacy agreed, and Maureen left just as Wade slipped one arm beneath Chantel's knees and one under her shoulders, to lift her from the bed.

Chantel groaned. "Where are we going?" she asked. "I don't feel well."

"Chantel, it's me." Stacy touched her arm, and her sister went completely still. "Everything's going to be okay. We're taking you to see a doctor."

"I can walk."

"There's no need. Wade's here. He may as well carry you."

Chantel sighed, but settled into his arms as though grateful she didn't have to prove her words. "You guys are making too big a deal of this. I just have the flu."

"Then I hope you don't mind letting us get a second opinion," Stacy told her. "You look a bit ravaged for just having the flu."

"Evidently you haven't had the flu for a while," she murmured. "But if we have to go, then let's hurry before I throw up again."

Stacy chuckled. "Hang on to your lunch, it won't be long now."

They got to the doctor's office fifteen minutes later. All the nurses had gone home except one, who was kind enough to show Chantel to a room right away. Stacy sat in the empty waiting area across from Wade, staring blankly at the magazines on the coffee table nearby and marveling at what an unlikely threesome they made. "Thanks for calling me," she said at last.

He looked up from an issue of *Mademoiselle*. Stacy couldn't remember ever seeing another man choose that particular magazine. "She could be on here again, you know," he said. "She was once, about five years ago."

"She doesn't seem to want that anymore." Stacy didn't understand what had chased Chantel away from New York, but she did recognize a flicker of hope in herself. If her sister wasn't going to run after fame and fortune again, if she was actually going to stick around, maybe they could rebuild their relationship, after all.

"Ever since she got sick, over a year ago, she hasn't been the same," he murmured, almost to himself.

Stacy pinned him with a hard gaze. "What are you talking about? You said she never got sick in New York, that she had it good there."

He set the magazine aside, and for the first time, Stacy noticed how bloodshot his eyes were. "She was sick," he admitted, hunching down in his seat.

"How sick?"

"She spent months in the hospital."

"*What?*" Stacy nearly leaped out of her seat. "Why didn't you call us?"

"She said she needed to pay the price for her own dumb decisions." He gave her a twisted smile. "I guess that meant me. I wasn't about to call up and announce to everyone that she regretted coming to New York with me."

Stacy felt a cold unease creep over her heart. "What kind of illness keeps you in the hospital for months?" she asked. "Cancer?"

He shook his head. "Anorexia. When she went in, she weighed only ninety pounds."

"What? She's six feet tall!" Stacy felt the sting of tears and squeezed her eyes shut. She couldn't avoid the mental picture of her sister lying in the sterile atmosphere of a hospital for months, believing her family didn't care about her. Chantel couldn't have believed anything else. Her own father had told her not to contact them again. At the time Stacy had thought it a just punishment. Now she realized just how much her playing the martyr had manipulated him into casting his own daughter aside. "And here I thought she was living the high life," she whispered. "Miss Cover Model on the front of every magazine."

"She nearly died."

"But you were there for her, right?" Stacy asked hopefully. "I mean, she didn't have to fight that battle alone."

He grimaced. "Oh, like you would have been there for her, had you known. She tried to reach you several times during our first year together, but you wouldn't accept her calls. You could have contacted her once in a while, you know. You could have forgiven her."

Stacy winced at the memory of hanging up on Chantel the one time she did get through. Her father had died and she'd missed the funeral. Chantel had insisted she'd received Stacy's message too late, that she'd been on location at a shoot, but Stacy had chosen to believe she hadn't cared enough to make the trip. "You were my fiancé, Wade, and she—"

"You knew I didn't really love you, that I let it go as far as I did out of a sense of obligation. I remember trying to tell you how I felt about Chantel, but you shut it out and did nothing."

"I was young and stupid."

He sneered at her. "She was younger than you."

DILLON SAT at the exit to the grocery-store parking lot, letting his engine idle. Helen was at home with Brittney and Sydney. She'd stopped by to visit and had joined them for dinner, then he'd gone to pick up a few things for the girls' lunches. He was finished shopping, and home was to the left, but he wanted to go in the other direction—to Chantel's condo.

Another car came up behind him, so he flipped on his signal and made a right-hand turn. It had been weeks since he'd talked to Chantel. He'd called her once to see how Stacy was treating her, but she'd been distant, and he'd known better than to call again. Pressing her would only chase her further away. He'd hoped she'd get in touch with him, but she hadn't, and he was beginning to think she never would. So he'd told himself to forget her and go on.

But it wasn't that easy. She crept into his thoughts at the most inopportune moments—in the middle of giving a presentation on an industrial park, while making dinner for the girls, even while talking to Dave on the phone. He'd been thinking of Dave and Reva's relationship and wondering if he'd ever find a woman he'd want to spend so many years with, and Chantel had just popped into his mind.

She was driving him crazy. He had to see her. He had to

know, without a doubt, that what they'd shared couldn't grow into anything more lasting.

The night was cool and breezy and smelled like rain. Dillon rolled down his window and let the wind ruffle his hair as he drove, and fifteen minutes later, the redbrick walls of her condominium complex appeared on his left. He turned into the drive, telling himself he'd only stay for a few minutes, just long enough to see how she was doing. But before he could even pull into a parking space, he saw something that made his blood run cold: the same brown Cadillac he'd seen in Stacy's drive.

Wade. Had Chantel gone back to him? The thought turned Dillon's stomach, but he knew how easy it could be to fall back into an old relationship. How many times had he wished he could work things out with Amanda? It had to do with knowing a person so well, remembering what had attracted you in the first place, hoping that whatever hadn't worked could change. And there was always the lure of New York. That was something Dillon couldn't offer her, ever.

Damn. He was a fool to have come. Shoving the car into Reverse, Dillon backed out of the drive and peeled away. He was better off without Chantel, he told himself. Where could it go, anyway? He had his girls to think of now. He had no time to build a relationship with a woman. It was just as well.

But he didn't care how logical it all sounded. The idea of Wade with Chantel made him want to bust Pretty Boy's jaw.

CHANTEL COULDN'T get rid of her unlikely caregivers.

At home in her own bed, she rolled over and covered her ears to block out another of Wade and Stacy's many arguments, wishing they'd leave her in peace—but wishing it only halfheartedly. If she was honest with herself, she had to admit she'd never felt better emotionally. Stacy had been more open and giving over the past three days than Chantel ever remembered her being, and she was thrilled by the prospect of what was starting to grow between them. Wade was another story, but his father had kicked him out, so she was letting him stay until he found some kind of work. And she was doing her best to be patient with him.

Now, if she could only get well enough to lead a normal life again.

What was wrong with her? The doctor hadn't been able to tell her yet. He didn't think it was the flu. He didn't think it was any kind of allergy, to her home or to microscopic particles or whatever. He thought her anorexia might be reasserting itself, but was skeptical even there. And all the tests he'd run had shown nothing. They were waiting for a few more—the results of several blood tests—before they had to start all over again.

"Why leave it on the counter?" Wade asked, his voice rising as it came from the kitchen. "Then the food dries on, and the dishwasher's no good. At least rinse it off!"

"And then leave it in the sink like you? Since I'm the one who's been doing all the housework, anyway, what does it matter?" Stacy yelled back. "You know I'll take care of it."

Were they fighting about the dishes? Last time it was who had what section of the newspaper. They were at each others' throats constantly.

"The question is when. Besides, I did some vacuuming yesterday."

"Ooh, big deal—"

"Stop it!" Chantel cried weakly. "I can't take you guys arguing anymore."

There was a momentary silence. "Now look what you've done. You woke her up," Wade said.

"I'm not the one who started ranting about dishes!"

"I wasn't ranting. You make me sound like a fishwife."

"If the shoe fits…"

Their voices came closer, along with the sound of their footsteps, until they both appeared at Chantel's door and tried to fit through it at the same time. With an irritated look at Wade, Stacy squeezed through first.

"What's wrong?" she demanded.

Chantel let out a long-suffering sigh. "Do you guys think you could go a couple of hours without bickering?"

"We weren't bickering!" Wade said. "Bickering's what women do."

Stacy gave him a jaunty toss of her head. "Like I said, if the shoe fits…"

Chantel covered her ears again. "Stop!"

Her sister pointed an accusing finger at Wade. "It's his fault. I can't believe you're letting him stay here."

"So I'm a bit of a neat freak," he admitted, smiling proudly. "At least I'm not a total slob."

Stacy bristled. "Are you calling me a slob? The one who's been cleaning up after you for the past three days?"

Wade shrugged. "I've done my part. Who do you think took care of Chantel last night while you were at work?"

"And left a sinkful of dishes for me to load when I got back."

"At least they'd all been rinsed off."

"That's enough!" Chantel sent them both a reproving glare and shoved her pillows against the backboard so she could sit up. "Are you trying to drive me out of my own home?"

They exchanged quick hate-filled looks but didn't say anything.

"Anyway, I'm feeling a little better today," Chantel went on.

"Really?" Stacy crossed to sit on the end of her bed, and Wade, not to be outdone, joined her. "No nausea?"

Chantel shook her head. "Not right now."

"You think you could eat something?" Wade asked. They'd been force-feeding her almost every time she woke up, then holding her head over the toilet when what went down came back up.

"I'm not sure I want to go through all that again."

"The doctor said you need to eat, Chantel," Wade reminded her.

"But it doesn't do me any good if I can't keep it down."

That worried expression Stacy had been wearing on and off came on again, and Chantel relented just to see her sister's puckered brow relax. "Okay, I'll try."

Stacy looked at Wade. "Make her some pancakes, Wade. You need to do something to earn your keep around here."

He pulled a face at Stacy but spoke to Chantel. "Do pancakes sound all right?"

Nothing sounded worse. Except perhaps eggs, bacon, oatmeal, doughnuts, any kind of cold cereal, any lunch item... Chantel forced a smile. "Sounds great."

Wade left to start the pancakes, and Stacy edged closer. "You're really giving us a scare here, you know that? Everyone's worried about you. Maureen calls all the time to check on you."

Chantel didn't even want to think about work. She'd just missed another three days. "They're going to have to let me go if I don't get better soon." She fought the lump rising in her throat. "I mean, what else can they do?"

"The senator's being pretty good about it." Stacy waved to the large bouquet of flowers the office had sent, along with a card each of her co-workers had signed.

Chantel knew that sending flowers probably wasn't the senator's idea—more likely Maureen's—but she was pleased, anyway. "It's just that this is my first chance to really prove myself. I can't stand the thought of failing."

"You can't help being sick. Let's handle first things first, then we'll worry about your job, okay? Speaking of work, I have to leave for the hospital in a few minutes, but I'm sure Wade will be here." She sneered. "As long as there's free room and board, I doubt he'll be going anywhere soon."

"Is he still talking about moving back to New York?" Chantel whispered.

"When he first got here, he was talking like he had a string of jobs lined up, but he hasn't mentioned them lately."

"You don't think he's still expecting me to go back with him, do you?"

"I don't see how he could. You're not well enough to go anywhere."

"I can't believe his dad kicked him out," Chantel said. "It's the last thing I need."

"You're too nice. I'd kick him out, too."

Ever since Stacy had spent the night with Wade, she claimed she couldn't stand the sight of him. Chantel guessed it was her poor judgment she couldn't stand. Wade just reminded her of it. To a point, she felt the same way, but they'd been together too long for her not to help him out now. "How did you get the day shift?" she asked, changing the subject. "It's not even noon."

"I think the nurse who does the scheduling is losing her mind," Stacy joked. "She gives me completely different hours every week. But I have to run." She checked her watch. "I'll see you later."

Stacy rushed out, leaving Chantel to contemplate the

change in her sister's attitude these past few days. There were still some things they couldn't talk about—like Dillon—but Stacy was treating her more warmly than she had since they were kids. Chantel suspected her night with Wade had humbled her a little, taught her that people don't always use their best judgment and that she was no exception.

The telephone rang. Wade answered it in the kitchen before Chantel could slide far enough toward the nightstand to grab it herself. A moment later, he called out, "It's the doctor, Chantel."

Chantel picked up the phone and waited for the click that told her Wade had hung up. If the news was bad, she wanted to hear it in privacy. "Hello?"

"Ms. Miller? This is Dr. Campbell. Your blood tests are back, and I wanted to ask you a few questions."

"Okay."

"When was the date of your last period?"

For nearly a year she hadn't menstruated at all. But in the past six months, she'd had a couple of brief periods, if you could call them that. Since the anorexia nothing had been the same. "I'm not sure," she said. "There really wasn't any reason to make a special note of it."

"Just hazard a guess."

"Let's see, it's been…jeez, I don't know, at least three months."

Wade came to stand in the doorway again, but Chantel didn't acknowledge him beyond a quick glance. "What do you think's wrong with me, doctor?"

"I don't think anything is *wrong* with you, Ms. Miller. According to your blood tests and what you've just told me, I think you're pregnant."

Chantel dropped the phone, then scrambled to pick it up. "But that's not possible," she said, feeling her hands, her arms, her whole body start to shake. Because Wade was watching her closely, Chantel tried to control her shock so she wouldn't give anything away, but she felt as if the doctor had landed her a hard blow to the head. *He's made a mistake. That's all there is to it.*

"It wasn't probable," Dr. Campbell corrected her. "But anything is possible. Now, I'm not sure if this comes as good news or bad. Perhaps it's something we should talk about. After all you've been through with the anorexia, your body is ill equipped to support another life. If you choose to keep the baby, you'll be facing a high-risk pregnancy."

If you choose to keep the baby... The words reverberated through her head. A baby was all she'd ever wanted. She'd never do anything to endanger it; she'd go through hell to have it. But she still felt as though this must be someone's idea of a cruel joke. "Are you sure that I'm...you know?"

"I'm fairly certain you're pregnant. I'm not very optimistic that you'll be able to carry the baby to term. I want to be honest with you about that right up front."

Tears streamed down Chantel's face, and she was powerless to stop them. Wade hurried into the room and took her hand, curiosity and concern showing in his expression. "What is it?" he murmured.

Chantel shook her head and tried to absorb all the ramifications of the pregnancy at once. If her body could only manage for another seven or so months, she'd have a baby. Better yet, it would be *Dillon's* baby. He'd been the one to give her this gift, and the knowledge that she carried part of him inside her nearly made her burst with joy. Until she remembered Stacy.

"Oh, no," she said, closing her eyes. What was she going to tell her sister? She and Dillon had already told Stacy that he'd asked her out, nothing more.

"Are you okay, Ms. Miller?"

"Fine," she managed. *One step at a time.* There was no

reason to go rushing into any confessions. She might not even be able to carry the baby. She could lose it tomorrow.

Her mind rebelled against that thought, and she wrapped an arm around her abdomen in a protective gesture.

"I need you to see a gynecologist/obstetrician right away, and I have an excellent one I'd like to recommend. Her name is Dr. Bradley."

"Is it serious?" Wade asked.

Chantel ignored the question. "Find me something to write with," she whispered, instead.

He shuffled through the nightstand and came up with a pen and a magazine. Chantel flipped to the inside cover and jotted down Dr. Bradley's name and number.

"I'm sure she'll want you to come in right away so she can do an ultrasound. I'll call her myself, and tell her to expect to hear from you."

"Thanks Dr. Campbell. I'm so…grateful."

He chuckled. "I'm glad you're pleased with the news, and I wish you the best of luck."

Chantel hung up, then stared at the number for Dr. Bradley's office.

"So?" Wade prompted, and Chantel felt a flicker of unease. If she *was* pregnant, it would be a difficult secret to keep with Wade around. But she couldn't let him know, at least not until she decided what to do.

"The doctor thinks I'm okay." She searched for a lie he might believe and drew a blank. "He, uh, just wants to run one more test."

Wade looked skeptical. "You're obviously not okay. You can't even get off the bed."

"The doctor thinks this…will pass."

"So it is the flu?"

Chantel grasped the lie he unwittingly offered her. "Yeah, just like we thought."

"Then you're going to get better."

She nodded.

"And meanwhile?"

"Meanwhile I'll eat whatever you put in front of me," she said, unable to hold back the dazzling smile that was dying to come out. Amid the hope, the fear, the confusion and the guilt, she felt a ray of pure joy at the thought of having a baby, and she couldn't deny it. Especially Dillon's baby. His gift to her. Something to love of her very own.

Wade raised his brows in surprise. "Wow, you really seem better all of a sudden." He surprised her by bending down and kissing her forehead, as he might have done when they were together in New York, and Chantel realized he still didn't believe things were over between them. Oh, well, she had more important concerns right now. "I'm glad it's nothing serious," he said.

Chantel rubbed her stomach, consciously willing her baby to survive. If Wade only knew how serious it was…

CHAPTER THIRTEEN

STACY STOOD in the glass-walled nursery and cooed to the newborn she held in her arms, trying to get him to take some glucose water. His mother wouldn't have milk for a day or two, so an occasional bottle of water was supposed to tide him over.

"How's he doing?" Leslie, the other nurse working maternity, rolled a silver gurney holding an empty plastic cradle to the side and came over to get a better look at him.

"He's a little fussy, but he likes it when I hold him tight."

"Is his mother sleeping?"

"Probably not yet. I just took him in for a feeding. Unfortunately colostrum isn't very filling." Stacy bent closer to the infant and breathed in his fresh sweet smell. Would she ever hold a child of her own?

First comes love, then comes marriage. Then comes Stacy with a baby carriage.

Love. She couldn't even complete the first step of that silly rhyme. She couldn't make a man she wanted fall in love with her. Dillon had called a couple of times to be sure she was okay after that awkward scene in his office, but she knew he was only being kind. It had been almost a month since she'd last heard from him. The more days that passed, the less likely it was he'd call again. She supposed she could contact him and try to salvage their friendship, at least, but her feelings were still too raw for that.

"What are you doing after work?" Leslie asked, interrupting her thoughts.

She'd been planning to go back to Chantel's, but she hated the idea of seeing Wade. The man made her skin crawl. She couldn't imagine what she'd seen in him all those years ago, what had possessed her that night several weeks ago. He was selfish and shallow and lazy. Nothing like Dillon. She shrugged. "Not much. What do you have in mind?"

"Want to come over to my place and order a pizza tonight? We could rent a couple of movies and kick back," Leslie suggested. Her husband was out of town on a business trip, and she'd already admitted she hated to be alone.

"Sure," Stacy replied with more enthusiasm than she felt. Now that she knew Chantel was going to be okay, there was really no point in putting her life on hold any longer. And she certainly wasn't eager to spend more time with Wade. "I just need to call and check on my sister."

Returning to the nurse's station, Stacy dialed Chantel, then grimaced when Wade answered. *Sponge,* she muttered to herself. "Let me talk to Chantel."

"She's asleep."

Stacy tapped the telephone with one long nail. "Did she hear anything about her tests today?"

Wade's voice wasn't any warmer than hers. But he answered. "They say it's the flu. She has another doctor's appointment in the morning."

"If they know it's the flu, what does she have to go back for?"

"How the hell should I know?"

"Oh, forgive me. I thought you were there with her. You're not likely to stray very far from a free ride, right?"

"What's the matter, Stacy? You jealous?"

"Hardly. I thought you were going back to New York, anyway."

"We will. When Chantel's well."

Stacy almost told him Chantel wasn't going back, but she wasn't completely sure. *Would* her sister leave with Wade in the end? "So what's this doctor's appointment tomorrow?"

"Campbell referred her to a Dr. Bradley for one more test."

"Bradley! Are you sure? Bradley's an obstetrician who delivers here at the hospital."

"That's the name Chantel wrote down."

"But that doesn't make sense. The flu is a virus."

"Who knows? She's always had trouble with that female stuff. Maybe it's all tied in. Or maybe they're checking something to do with the anorexia."

"Did she say what kind of test they plan to run?"

"I didn't ask. It's just some precautionary measure. I'm sure she'll be fine."

Bradley. Stacy twisted the phone cord around her finger, then let go. "Yeah. Well, I'm going out with a friend. Tell Chantel I'll see her tomorrow."

"Breaking out the black nightwear, Stace?" he taunted.

"Screw you."

"You've already done that."

"Oh, yeah? I guess you weren't good enough to remember," she said, and hung up.

CHANTEL GLANCED around her dark room, made darker by the lined chintz curtains she'd asked Wade to close before the sun went down. What had woken her? Slivers of moonlight peaked through a few cracks near the sill, and everything looked normal.

She glanced at the clock on her nightstand. Normal for

one in the morning, anyway. She didn't know what had disturbed her sleep. Possibly a bad dream or simply that she'd spent too many days in bed.

Sitting up, Chantel paused long enough to overcome her dizziness before she scooted to the edge of the mattress and headed to the bathroom. Fortunately she felt a little stronger than she had. The nausea wasn't so bad. She suffered only from a slight headache.

When she finished in the bathroom, she washed her hands and shuffled out to the kitchen for a drink, expecting the door to the guest room, where Stacy slept, to be closed and to find Wade on the couch. But Stacy's door stood open, revealing a perfectly made bed. And Wade wasn't in the living room.

Where were they? Wade hadn't mentioned going anywhere when he'd brought her some chicken from a fast-food outlet for dinner, and the last she'd heard from Stacy was that she'd be back when she got off work at eight.

Maybe, now that they believed she only had the flu, they'd tired of their vigil and gone out for some fun. It certainly wasn't typical of Wade to play nursemaid to anyone. He liked things fast and loose and was probably dying for a little excitement. And for her, Chantel reveled in the thought of some time alone.

"I'm going to have a baby," she whispered, suddenly remembering and trying to absorb, again, what the doctor had told her that afternoon. She'd been saying the same thing to herself over and over every time she woke up, but Wade had been around, and she couldn't say it aloud. Now she wanted to shout her good news to the world. "I'm going to have a baby!" she exclaimed. "Dillon's baby!"

A yearning to tell him, to feel his arms around her, swept over her, and she considered calling him. How would he take the news? She'd asked him not to contact her, and he'd called only once since the big blowup with Stacy. Did that mean he'd moved on? That he didn't care? Stacy hadn't mentioned his name or said what had happened between them, and Chantel had been too afraid to ask. For all she knew, they were still dating.

The thought of Dillon and Stacy seeing each other made Chantel feel weak. Her problems with her sister were bad enough already. How was she going to tell either one of them, or even Wade, about the baby?

The moon glinted off the telephone near the couch, and Chantel sat down next to it. She knew Dillon's number by heart, had memorized it from that scrap of paper he'd left on her counter once, simply because she'd looked at it so often.

He'll be sleeping, and he has his girls now. I shouldn't wake him, she thought, but she had to talk to him, if only for a few minutes. The sound of his voice would make the fact that they were having a baby together seem more real.

She picked up the receiver and dialed, her breath growing shallow with nervousness. It occurred to her to use the pretense of asking if his truck was out of the shop, but she knew that would sound pretty silly at one o'clock in the morning. The accident had happened almost two months ago. Of course his truck was fixed.

"Hello?" His voice was filled with sleep, as she knew it would be.

"Dillon? It's Chantel."

Hearing her name seemed to instantly clear away the cobwebs. "Are you all right?"

"I'm fine."

There was a long pause, and Chantel realized she didn't have anything to say. She just longed for him so much it had become a physical ache.

"Did you, uh, have something you wanted to tell me?" he asked.

I'm going to have your baby. "No, I...I don't know why I called."

She heard some rustling in the background and pictured him sitting up in his bed.

"Listen, I'm sorry I woke you," she said, feeling like an idiot. She hadn't even had the ultrasound yet. She could lose the baby at any time. And until she decided what to do about Stacy, she couldn't tell Dillon, anyway. "I'd better go—"

"Chantel?"

"What?"

"Come and see me."

"I can't. It's one in the morning."

"I don't care what time it is."

"I haven't been feeling very well."

"What's wrong? Don't tell me it's the anorexia—"

"No." She swallowed hard and curled her fingernails into her palms. "I think it's just the flu. You wouldn't want to get it."

"Let me worry about that. Come over so I can take care of you. I'd go to your place, but I've got the girls here."

"I know."

"Can you make it to my house?"

Chantel knew she could. And without Wade and Stacy here to stop her, she felt herself giving in. Was it so wrong to want to be with the father of her baby?

Dillon must have sensed her weakness, because he allowed her no chance to argue. He gave her directions, then said, "I'll be waiting for you," and hung up so she couldn't refuse.

DILLON'S ADDRESS was in a woodsy, hilly neighborhood. The lots were large, with a great deal of natural landscaping between homes that were all different. Some had a Mediterranean appearance. Others were California ranch-style. Dillon's looked as if it belonged on the side of a lake. It was relatively new, with a green steep-pitched roof and a front porch that wrapped almost all the way around. A hammock hung between two large trees off to the side, and the large stretch of front lawn had just been cut. Chantel could smell the grass clippings as she got out of her car, could hear the delicate tinkle of wind chimes.

The porch light was already on, a welcoming beacon, but still she felt a moment's hesitation. She'd promised Stacy she wouldn't see Dillon. She'd left her sister and Wade a note, in case they came home, but it said merely that she couldn't sleep and had gone for a drive—hardly enough to keep them from worrying about her should they return while she was gone. There were a thousand reasons she shouldn't have come. But somehow, as the door opened and Dillon walked out of the house to wait for her on the porch, she couldn't remember any of them. He wore only a baseball cap and a pair of faded jeans.

The muscles in his powerful arms flexed as he leaned on the railing, watching her, his face inscrutable. She remembered running her fingers over his ribs and pressing her palms to his chest as she'd sat on top of him, feeling him deep inside her….

He didn't say anything as she approached, and Chantel wondered what he was thinking. She'd showered and blow-dried her hair, but she hadn't bothered with any makeup. The bulky sweater she'd chosen hung loosely on her and did little to enhance her figure. She'd actually been hoping that it would camouflage the evidence of her recent weight loss.

''Aren't you going to say anything?'' she asked, feeling

breathless and weak from the effort it had taken to get ready and drive across town.

"Only whatever's necessary to get you back in my arms," he murmured, but the next moment she was there without his having to say another word. He drew her to him as soon as she was within reach, and she did nothing to stop him. He nuzzled her neck, groaned, then ran his hands all the way down her back as though he longed to consume every inch of her. "I've missed you."

Chantel closed her eyes and clung to him. "I shouldn't be here," she whispered.

"I thought it was over. What made you call me?"

"How did I stop myself until now?"

He chuckled into her hair. "Come in before you get cold. You're shaking."

He scooped her into his arms and carried her in. As he was about to set her down on the couch, she tightened her arms around his neck and shook her head. "No. Take me to your room."

He hesitated, then kissed her forehead, her cheeks, the tip of her nose. "What's going on, Chantel? You've lost weight, you don't look well, and after telling me to forget it more than six weeks ago, you show up at my house and want me to take you straight to bed."

The kitchen light was on. It spilled into the area where they stood, throwing Dillon's face into shadow and making it difficult for Chantel to read his expression. "You don't want to?"

His laugh was hoarse. "That's not the problem."

"Then what?"

"What about Stacy? You'd feel guilty and you'd hate me in the morning."

She sighed and turned her face into the hollow of his shoulder. He was right, and she knew it. Besides, the short burst of energy she'd experienced earlier was gone, and in its place was the old fatigue and nausea.

"Tell me why you've lost weight," he said.

Chantel hated to lie to him again. To avoid that, she said, "I don't want to talk about it."

"I think we should."

He placed her on his leather couch, then switched on a lamp that revealed a whole wall of built-in cabinetry, hardwood floors and a round area rug. Sitting across from her on a chest that served as a coffee table, Dillon turned her hands palms up and began lightly tracing her lifelines with the pads of his thumbs. "You haven't been at work."

"How do you know?"

A sheepish smile curved his lips. "I called a couple of times just to hear your voice. Maureen finally told me you've been out for a week."

"You called?" That felt good, knowing he couldn't walk away from her as easily as he'd made it appear. "Maureen didn't pass on the message."

"I didn't leave one." He suddenly looked vulnerable, almost boyish. "What do we have between us, Chantel? Anything?"

Chantel bit her lip. She couldn't tell him about the pregnancy until after the doctor's appointment. She needed final confirmation before facing all the difficult decisions she would have to make. And she needed time. She also wished she knew, in advance, how he'd react to the news.

Or maybe it would be smarter—safer—not to tell him at all. He had enough to worry about with his missing ex-wife and his two daughters. The last thing he needed was this kind of surprise. She'd gotten her life in order again and would now have a child. Did she really want to risk it all on what Dillon's reaction might be?

"I don't know," she said. "If you hadn't kept searching for me in the snowstorm—"

"What?" Dropping her hands, he stood, a scowl marring his handsome face. "Is that all you feel? Well, I don't want your gratitude."

Chantel shook her head, growing weaker by the moment. She shouldn't have come. She doubted she had the strength to make it back home. "I can't answer your questions right now, Dillon. I can't explain anything or promise anything. I just...I just wanted to see you. But I don't feel so good...."

"What's wrong?" Concern replaced his earlier frustration. "None of this makes sense, Chantel."

"I'm sick," she said, because she didn't have the energy to debate with herself any longer. "It comes and goes. Just give me a minute."

Cupping her chin with his hand, he tilted her face toward the lamp on her left and studied it. "You're scaring me."

She took a deep breath, trying to settle her stomach. "I'm okay."

"Like hell you are." Bending, he slipped one arm beneath her knees and the other around her back and easily gathered her in his arms again. "I should take you to the hospital."

"No. I have a doctor's appointment in the morning. I can make it till then."

"When is it?"

"Nine o'clock."

"Fine. I'll make sure you're there on time."

"Where are you taking me now?"

Dillon carried her to a set of stairs that rose into blackness. "To bed."

DILLON AWOKE to the familiar squawk of his alarm and quickly shut off the noise before it could wake Chantel.

Then he wrapped one arm around her middle and pulled her back into the cradle of his body, wanting to hold her for a few minutes more.

She groaned and began to stir, eventually rolling over to face him. He watched her wake up, noting the dark circles beneath her eyes, the gauntness of her face.

She blinked, her magnificent amber eyes finally opening wide as she offered him a shy smile. "Good morning."

"Good morning," he said, content just to look at her. He was still bare-chested, but before he'd gotten into bed with her last night, he'd traded his blue jeans for pajama bottoms. Chantel wore a pair of his sweats, and even with her blond hair in a tangled mess, she was beautiful. What he liked most was the sweetness that showed in her eyes and in her smile. "How do you feel?"

"A little better."

He watched her glance around the room, taking in the ceiling which was made mostly of glass and now revealed the purplish predawn sky, the large bathroom behind him, and the French doors that opened onto a balcony overlooking the backyard.

"This is incredible, Dillon," she breathed.

He smiled, feeling a sense of pride. "I designed it myself."

"For Sydney and Brittney's mother?"

"No. I bought this place after the divorce, and I've been remodeling it a little at a time. You're the first woman I've brought up here."

She blushed, and Dillon wanted to reach out and trace the curve of her breasts, pull off her sweatshirt and hold them in his palms. But if Chantel was indeed feeling better, it wasn't by much. And there was always Stacy standing between them.

Inhaling deeply he decided it was time for a cold shower. "Don't wake up," he said, allowing himself a chaste kiss on her temple before getting out of bed. "I'll drive the girls to school and then bring you something to eat."

"I have to leave."

"No. You're not well enough to go anywhere by yourself. I'll take you to the doctor's this morning. Do you need to stop by your place first?"

The thought of showing up at the condo with Dillon and finding Wade or Stacy waiting for her made Chantel bolt upright—an action she instantly regretted when her head began to swim. With a groan she fell back. "I should. Stacy and Wade are probably frantic by now," she said weakly.

He paused at the side of the bed, his jaw tightening. "Wade again. He was at your house the other night."

"It's a long story," she said, "but he and Stacy have been taking care of me."

"So are you thinking of going back?"

"To New York?"

"To Wade."

Chantel recalled how good Wade had been to her in the past few weeks, how he'd asked her for another chance and promised they could have a family. She had to admit that sometimes she did think of returning to him. It was difficult to give up on a relationship in which she'd already invested ten years of her life. And Wade had changed. He needed her.

But looking at Dillon, she knew, with startling clarity, that every time Wade took her in his arms, she'd be thinking of someone else—a man with dark hair and blue eyes, an architect whose bedroom ceiling was made entirely of skylights. She'd be thinking of Dillon Broderick.

And if she *was* pregnant with his child...

"No," she said. "I'm not going back to him."

He propped his hands on his hips. "Chantel, I don't know what, exactly, there is between us, or where it might be headed. But I have to be honest with you. While I was married to Amanda, I became too well acquainted with jealousy. I'm not interested in experiencing those feelings again."

"I was always faithful to Wade."

"That's partially what I'm worried about. Are you still in love with him?"

"No."

"Does that mean you're going to give us a chance? That you'll talk to Stacy? And get rid of Wade?"

"I can't talk to Stacy. At least not yet."

"When?"

Chantel thought of her impending doctor's appointment. "Give me a few days."

He seemed impatient but relieved. "Okay. Then I think we should both sit down with her."

"And if she cuts me off again?"

The look in his eyes grew haunted. "You'd still have me."

And you'd come with what guarantee? she wanted to ask. She'd tried to console herself with Wade, too, but the self-respect she'd lost was too high a price to pay, even for love. "Dillon, what if we tell Stacy we want to see each other and she refuses to speak to me again? And then—" feeling a surge of illness, Chantel took a moment to catch her breath "—two months down the road, we decide we're not meant for each other, after all?"

He studied her for a moment. "I can't answer that. I've never been much good at fortune-telling."

"Neither have I. All I have is the benefit of past experience."

"What happened in the past doesn't have to repeat itself."

Chantel closed her eyes. "Just give me a few days," she said again. "And let me go to the doctor's by myself."

He frowned. "Why don't you want me to take you?"

"It's not that I don't want you to take me." She flailed around for some excuse that might distract him, send him toward an alternative course of action. "It's just that I'm sure you're probably busy this morning. And there's no need to miss work, especially when I'm actually feeling better." She smiled, despite a rising bout of nausea, and wished at the same time that she could force some color back into her cheeks.

He arched a brow at her. "Let me worry about my schedule, okay?"

She gulped, hoping he understood that gynecologists did more than deliver babies. Otherwise he might guess her condition right away. "But what am I going to wear?"

"Just wear what you wore here last night."

Chantel looked at the sweater and jeans that were draped across the arm of an overstuffed chair. They were still clean. She'd only worn them for an hour or so the night before.

"Do you want to give Stacy a call?" he asked, running a hand through his hair, which only made him look sexier. "Just so she doesn't worry?"

"And tell her what?" Chantel groaned.

"That you have a ride to the doctor."

The only thing she could tell Stacy was that she'd gone out for a drive and was planning on getting herself to the doctor. It was a lame reason for being gone all night, and she knew it, but she certainly wasn't prepared to tell her sister anything about Dillon. Not yet, and not when there would be so much to say later.

Dillon rounded the bed and handed her a cordless phone.

She dialed her own number and waited, but on the fifth ring, the answering machine picked up. She left a short message saying she was feeling fine and would soon be on her way to the doctor's, without bothering to explain anything else. Then she dialed Stacy's number.

Again she reached only an answering machine, and she left the same message, then hung up and slumped back onto the pillows.

"Dillon?" she called. The door to the bathroom was now closed, the shower running. He couldn't hear her. "How would you feel about having more children?" she asked.

CHAPTER FOURTEEN

"YOU HAVE TO SEE a gynecologist?" Dillon asked, staring at the gold lettering on Dr. Bradley's door.

Chantel had tried to persuade Dillon to run a few errands or get a cup of coffee at the coffee shop down the street while she visited Dr. Bradley on her own, but he'd insisted on accompanying her. And now she was facing the very thing she'd dreaded, trying to keep him from guessing the truth before she was ready to tell him.

"My doctor referred me here. He thought my, er, sickness might have something to do with my reproductive system." At least that wasn't a total lie. Her sickness did have to do with her reproductive system, just not in the way he'd think.

Dillon nodded and opened the door. "What do they suspect the problem is?"

That question was a little more difficult to handle. Chantel chose evasion. "I'm not sure yet. I should learn something today."

The nurse behind the front desk glanced up as they approached, and Chantel gave her name. "It'll be just a minute, Ms. Miller, but first we need you to complete some paperwork."

She accepted a clipboard that held several forms asking about her medical history. Chantel filled them out, then returned them to the front desk. Shortly after, an assistant called her back.

Another nurse weighed her and guided her into a small

examination room, where she took her blood pressure. Handing her a paper lap cover, she told her to strip from the waist down.

"The doctor will be with you shortly."

Chantel mumbled a thank-you, but felt too ill to move at first. Occasionally she felt like her old self, but those times didn't last.

Resting her head on her forearms, she tried to talk herself out of the nervousness that only added to her nausea. Somehow it would all work out. But that seemed a hollow and forlorn hope when she thought of her sister's anger and the possibility of having a baby all on her own. Besides her problems with Stacy, she'd assured Dillon that she couldn't have children. What if her pregnancy made him angry? What if he didn't want anything to do with her or the baby?

Wouldn't it actually be better to pretend the baby was entirely her own?

Coward. Hiding the baby's paternity wouldn't be fair to the child or to Dillon. And who was she trying to kid? The truth would come out eventually. It always did. Wasn't her pregnancy proof of that?

Letting her breath go in a hiss, she raked a hand through her hair and began to undress. She'd just finished when a soft knock sounded at the door.

"Come in."

The doctor entered, wearing a white coat and a warm smile. "Hi, I'm Dr. Bradley." She picked up the chart the nurse had left and studied the information. "I see you've already had a blood test. Dr. Campbell had the results forwarded to me. Are you happy about the baby?"

"I am. I'm just afraid of what might happen. Dr. Campbell had some concerns."

Dr. Bradley nodded. "I can see why, but we're going to

do everything we can to make sure your baby arrives safely, Ms. Miller. I see here that you're not married.''

Chantel nodded, feeling a twinge of guilt. She wanted to explain how it was that night in the Landcruiser, when they'd believed they might not get out alive. She sighed. This certainly wasn't how she'd always pictured starting a family. She'd hoped to do things the right way, the way she'd been taught. But nothing in her life had really gone as planned. Her only solace now was that the doctor probably wasn't thinking about the moral implications. She was just doing her job.

''You haven't written down the baby's father's name. Does that mean you don't know who he is?'' she asked.

''No, he's with me today. I just…I must have missed that question,'' Chantel responded, unwilling to explain why she hadn't been free to divulge that information at the time she filled in the form.

''What's his name?''

''Dillon Broderick.''

Dr. Bradley's pen made a scratching sound. ''Okay, fine. Let's get started. I'd like to check your cervix, make sure it's closed and everything else is fine. Then I'll send you to the lab for the ultrasound.''

A few minutes later Chantel was dressed again and carrying a slip of paper to the lab across the hall from Dr. Bradley's office. As she passed Dillon in the reception area, she smiled and said, ''They need to do a couple of lab tests. I'll be right back.''

''Where's the lab?''

''Just over there.'' She pointed. ''You go ahead and read.''

''No, I'll come.'' He set his magazine aside and followed her.

When they reached the other office, Chantel waited until

Dillon had found a chair before she presented herself at the window.

"Thank you, Ms. Miller. We'll call you as soon as the technician's ready," the woman told her.

Chantel sat next to Dillon and tried to distract herself by watching the exotic-looking fish in a large aquarium against the far wall, but the pending ultrasound—the thought of actually seeing her baby—kept her too anxious to relax. Could this really be happening? To her?

Dillon took her hand, startling her out of her preoccupation. "What's wrong?"

"Nothing." She considered telling him right then and there, and inviting him to come with her to see their baby. But at the moment, she couldn't think straight, and too much hinged on this decision. She had to decide what she was going to do, make a plan. The doctor had told her chances were good she'd be feeling better in a few weeks. She'd probably even be able to go back to work, provided she didn't develop any serious complications, like toxemia.

"You look worried."

"No. I'll just be glad when this is over."

"What are they going to do? Draw blood?"

The nurse called her name, saving her from answering. "I won't be long," she said.

This time Chantel didn't have to strip. She merely had to lie down and raise her baggy sweater so the technician could move a silver instrument lathered with gel across her stomach. Staring up at a small screen overhead, she waited as the woman adjusted a few dials on the machine next to her. Then the sound of static erupted over a speaker and a mostly black picture flickered to life.

"Let's see if we can find that little guy," the technician murmured, moving the wandlike instrument just below her navel before homing in on something that looked completely unfamiliar to Chantel.

"Ah, there he is."

"He?" Chantel croaked.

The technician laughed. "It could just as easily be a girl. You're not very far along. It's too early to determine the sex with any accuracy. I just prefer to say he or she, instead of it."

Chantel nodded, still trying to make out the shape of a baby. "What part of him is that?"

"His foot. See?" Reaching up to the monitor, she traced the white form against the black picture and Chantel finally recognized it as something that looked human.

"Omigosh. There *is* a baby in there!"

"You bet there is. Here, let's get a heartbeat."

The technician moved the wand some more, showing different parts of the baby, the curve of his head, the spine, what seemed to be a fist. Then a rapid heartbeat came across the speakers, and Chantel could see a white flutter keeping time with the sound.

She was awestruck. Just when she'd finally accepted that she'd never have a child of her own, here she was seeing inside her womb, watching her baby, hearing his heartbeat.

Dillon. His name popped into her mind, and she wanted him at her side. He'd given this to her. *He has to see it,* she thought, and knew then that she could never keep the fact of this baby from him. She only hoped he'd be as happy as she was.

And that someday Stacy would understand.

The technician started to move the sensor away, but Chantel quickly stopped her. "Just another minute or two," she pleaded.

The woman smiled and settled the microphone over the

baby again, and Chantel closed her eyes and listened—to a miracle.

WHERE WAS SHE? Wade paced the floor, wondering what could have happened to Chantel. After Stacy's call the night before, he couldn't face another night of watching television. He'd phoned an old friend and they'd gone bar-hopping, but he'd come home at three to find a note from Chantel saying she'd gone for a drive. Only she hadn't come back. He'd been out searching for her all morning.

He called Stacy's again, wishing he could get hold of her, then cursed when her answering machine came on. Wait! Didn't Chantel have a doctor's appointment this morning? She was supposed to see a Dr. Bradley. A gynecologist, according to Stacy.

Jogging down the hall and into Chantel's bedroom, he rummaged through her nightstand for the magazine she'd written on when Dr. Campbell called, but he couldn't find anything. She must have taken it with her. Picking up the phone, he punched in 411 and asked for Dr. Bradley's number.

"A Woman's Place," the receptionist answered when he'd dialed it.

"This is Wade Bennett. Do you have a patient there by the name of Chantel Miller? I think she had an appointment this morning."

"I'm sorry. We're not allowed to divulge that information, Mr. Bennett."

"But I'm her boyfriend. She hasn't been feeling very well and—"

"I'm sorry. We respect our patients' right to privacy."

Damn! Wade cursed and hung up. He'd have to drive over there.

DILLON BEGAN TO TAP his foot, growing anxious. How long could it take to draw some blood? He'd cleared his morning of any appointments, but he had a lot of drawings to do and several sets of plans that needed to go out by overnight courier. Now that he had the girls living with him, he no longer had the time he used to, and his work was quickly falling behind. Not that he'd change anything. He just needed to make more efficient use of the hours they were in school and day care.

Standing, he crossed to the receptionist's desk. "Do you know how much longer it'll be?"

A petite woman with dark hair pulled severely off her face glanced up from a stack of folders. "You're with Chantel Miller, right?"

He nodded.

"I'll check." She disappeared for several seconds, then returned wearing a much warmer smile. "Your wife is doing fine, Mr. Miller. They're just about finished with the ultrasound now."

Dillon was too stunned to correct her on the husband-wife issue. "The what?"

"The ultrasound. The baby looks fine, by the way. Its heartbeat is coming through loud and strong."

Dillon blinked. Then he cleared his throat. "Are you sure we're talking about the right woman? Chantel just went back to have some blood drawn."

"Oh, no, we take the blood right here." She waved to four chairs arranged in an open area to her left. "And your wife is the only ultrasound we have scheduled this morn—" Evidently the look on his face alerted her to his total surprise, because her words suddenly dropped off and a red flush crept up her cheeks. "You brought her here. This isn't some kind of secret, right?"

Evidently it was. And the thought of how he'd sat stupidly in the waiting room, completely unsuspecting, rankled. What was Chantel trying to prove?

"Aren't you the father?" she finished weakly.

Dillon didn't know. Chantel had told him she couldn't have children. They'd been together only one night. Of course he'd made love to her several times while they were in his truck—he hadn't been able to get enough of her, still longed for more—but Wade had been hanging around a lot since then. What if…

He refused to even think it. Chantel couldn't be pregnant with Wade's baby. She had the flu. That was what she'd told him.

But denial did little to stop the anger that began to course hotly through his blood. Without another word, he stalked out of the lobby and back to Dr. Bradley's office, where he approached the front desk. "Chantel Miller is still across at the lab, but she wanted to ask the doctor what her due date is." He pasted a pleasant smile on his face to hide the clenching of his jaw. "I guess she forgot it already."

The nurse's brows drew together. "But that's exactly why we sent her to get the ultrasound. We can't give her a due date until we see how far along she is."

"Can't you hazard a guess?"

"Just a minute." The nurse disappeared and returned with a manila folder. "Can I get your name, please?'

"Dillon Broderick."

She glanced at some notes inside, then said, "With her history, it's hard to say, Mr. Broderick. But according to the approximate size of her uterus, the doctor is guessing she's somewhere between seven and nine weeks. We'll know more when we get the results of the ultrasound."

Seven to nine weeks. Tahoe fell right in the middle of that range. But Wade's appearance did, too. "Right. I'll tell her,'' he said, but as he turned to leave, the door opened and Chantel stood there.

"Ready?'' she asked, her eyes unreadable.

Dillon nodded curtly and strode past her without waiting. When they reached his truck, he left the passenger door standing open for her and came around to his own side. He stuck the key in the ignition as he slid behind the wheel but didn't start the car.

She didn't get in as he'd expected. "Would you like me to find another ride home?'' she asked, hovering at the door.

He propped his hands on the steering wheel. "You weren't going to tell me?''

"I wasn't even sure, until today.''

Please tell me the baby's not Wade's. He knew he couldn't ask, simply because the answer meant too much to him. He wasn't ready for the truth. Not yet... "When did you first suspect?''

"I never suspected. I thought I had the flu.''

"And?''

She clutched her purse tightly, like a shield against his hostility. "When I didn't get well the way I should have, Wade insisted I see a doctor.''

Wade again. Dammit! Dillon wanted to pound the man. He'd mistreated Chantel and left her alone for months in a hospital while she was suffering with anorexia. He didn't deserve her.

"Dr. Campbell called yesterday to let me know the blood tests were back,'' she went on, "and that there wasn't anything wrong with me—at least nothing that nine months wouldn't cure.'' She gave him a hesitant smile.

He sighed. "I thought you couldn't have children.''

"That's what they told me at the hospital before I was released.''

"But it happened, anyway.''

She nodded.

"Get in."

"I don't want to get in if…if you're angry about this."

He stared at her. "How am I supposed to feel? How do you feel?"

"I've always wanted a baby. I'm scared, but I'm excited, too." She glanced down at her toes. "And I was hoping you'd be happy about it."

Then tell me the baby's mine! The emotional impact of that thought nearly stole Dillon's breath away. What if the baby *was* his? He had two little girls already. He'd promised himself he'd be true to them, never give them any competition for his time and attention, at least until they were considerably older. But a new baby was definitely competition. Chantel was competition. Especially when he couldn't stop thinking about her and felt as though his heart was being torn from his chest at the prospect of losing her to Wade.

"I'm not angry," he said softly, struggling to control his emotions. "Get in."

She complied, but she was blinking rapidly, and obviously fighting tears.

"If you're so happy about this, why are you about to cry?" he asked, feeling some of his anger subside.

"Because what I just saw was so incredible, so perfect. I wanted you to be there with me, but I didn't want you to know yet, not until I decide how to tell Wade and Stacy."

Dillon took a deep breath to prepare himself. "Tell Wade what?"

She stared at him as though he'd lost his mind. "About the baby."

"*His* baby?" he asked, the words finally tumbling out, almost of their own accord.

As Chantel continued to stare at him, he felt more vulnerable than he ever had in his life. Amanda would have exploited it, kept him guessing. But Chantel took his hand and kissed the very center of his palm, then nuzzled it with her cheek. "You may not believe this, but I've only slept with two men my whole life. And Wade and I haven't been together for over a year. This baby is yours," she whispered.

CHAPTER FIFTEEN

WADE SAT in the parking lot of the medical complex, wondering which building housed Dr. Bradley's office. The receptionist had given him an address when he'd called back, but he hadn't thought to ask her for specific directions once he found the property. He hadn't expected the complex to be so large and sprawling.

He nicked the paint of the neighboring car getting out of his father's boatlike Cadillac. But it wasn't his fault most of the lot had been built for compact cars. What was he supposed to do? Park on the road just because his dad owned a gas-guzzling hog?

Striding to the marquis placed in the middle of a patch of green grass surrounded by marigolds, petunias and some little pink flowers he didn't know the name of, he glanced up at the five high-rise medical buildings towering over him, then began to search the directory for Dr. Bradley's office.

Second building. Third floor. He turned and squinted against the sun, gazing out over the sea of cars in the lot, looking for Chantel's Jag. But he couldn't see it. Turning again, he made his way down the winding sidewalk to a metal-and-glass structure labeled Building 2.

"Excuse me." A young woman dodged around him as he entered, making him miss the elevator. Cursing her, as well as the parking lot, he pushed the button and waited, glancing through the lobby windows. Suddenly he saw a woman who resembled Chantel sitting in a white Land-cruiser parked close to the building.

He did a double take and realized it had to be her. How many other women sat so tall? But who was she with? He took a few steps in her direction, then his stomach sank and his blood pressure rose. Dillon! She was with Dillon. Was that where she'd spent the night, too?

He slipped through the silent swinging doors and stood in the dark shade of the building, watching them, but he could have been doing cartwheels across the lawn for all they noticed. They were deep in conversation. Dillon was touching Chantel's face. And she was closing her eyes as though he was reaching her very soul.

CHANTEL'S HEART pounded as Dillon ran his fingers down the side of her face. "We're going to have a baby?" he asked reverently.

She nodded. "If I can carry it long enough."

His hand continued its downward course, trailing over one breast before he flattened his palm against her stomach, looking dazed.

"You should've seen the ultrasound, Dillon," she told him. "I saw his tiny foot and his hand, and his little heart beating so fast—"

"His?"

Chantel noted the wonder on his face and smiled. "I don't know the sex yet."

"But I could be having a son."

"Or you could be having another daughter."

He grinned. "Maybe she'll look just like you."

Chantel chuckled. "Only please let her be short."

"What do you mean?" he demanded with a scowl. "I love tall women."

Does that mean you love me? Chantel squelched the hope

that someday he might. She didn't deserve Dillon. She'd come back to California to pay penance for what she'd done to Stacy, not to fall madly in love. And she feared that was exactly what would happen if she let Dillon any closer. "It's not fun to be called names and to be stared at all the time," she reminded him.

"We'll teach her to be proud."

We'll teach her... Chantel felt her heart melt, partly because of his words and partly because of the magic of his touch. Hooking one hand behind her neck, he leaned forward and gently brought his lips to hers, as if savoring the taste and feel of her. Her eyes closed as he deepened the kiss, and she remembered the magical way it had been that night when they'd made their baby. "This Landcruiser must work as some kind of aphrodisiac or something," she joked.

He chuckled and she inhaled the spearmint on his breath. "Best make-out car I ever bought. But this time, I'd rather go home to celebrate. How are you feeling, babe?"

"Better."

"Can I interest you in testing out my new bed?"

"We slept in it last night, remember?"

"Oh, I already know it's comfortable enough. I just want to be sure it doesn't creak too loudly." He kissed her again, his lips moving purposefully over hers, rousing more memories of what it felt like to be loved by Dillon, along with a dose of fresh undiluted desire. She thought of the skylights in his room and imagined lying on her back, his muscular form poised above her, the sun shining all around, and wanted to agree.

But losing herself in Dillon's arms still felt too much like betrayal. She had to talk to Stacy first, tell her the truth. Although Chantel doubted that honesty would eradicate her guilt, at least she wouldn't be doing anything in secret.

"Stacy and Wade are probably waiting for me, wondering what the doctor said."

He sat back and looked at her. "And I think it's time to tell them."

Chantel wasn't so sure. What if she miscarried? She would have hurt her sister for nothing.

For nothing, or for a chance at happiness with Dillon?

Would she never conquer the selfishness that kept her seeking what *she* wanted over her sister's best interests? As soon as Stacy learned Chantel was carrying Dillon's child, she'd feel like sloppy leftovers. Her self-esteem would plummet.

And Chantel couldn't be the cause of that again. Not after all her good intentions. Not after all the promises to herself that if Stacy would only give her another chance, she'd move heaven and earth to prove herself worthy.

"You look miserable," Dillon said, slinging one arm over the steering wheel.

"I'm just trying to decide what to do. How can I tell Stacy I'm pregnant with your child?"

He rested his head on one fist. "It won't be easy. But what's the alternative? In seven months, the baby will be here. That's not something we can hide."

"Unless I tell her the baby belongs to someone else."

Dillon stiffened and the blue of his eyes darkened. "Hell, no! The baby's mine, and I don't want anyone thinking it isn't. Especially Wade."

Chantel had known, even as she said it, that claiming the baby belonged to someone else wasn't really a possibility. She couldn't do that to Dillon or their child. She was just searching for a way, any way, to salvage her sister's feelings. And to save herself from having to break the news.

"I'll need a few days."

His scowl grew fiercer. "I don't want to push you into

saying something until you're ready. But you do realize it's not going to get any easier, don't you?''

A lump swelled in Chantel's throat, and as hard as she tried to swallow it, it wouldn't go away. ''I just need a little more time with her before…before she's gone.''

The look on Dillon's face softened, and he reached across the seat to squeeze her hand. ''Maybe she'll surprise us both. Unlike Wade, I never promised her anything. We weren't engaged. We only dated a few times and kissed once.''

''You kissed her?'' Chantel groaned. Considering how much she hated the thought of that, she could guess how terrible Stacy was going to feel when she learned about their night in Tahoe.

''I kissed her goodnight. I didn't see fireworks. That was it.''

''Evidently she saw fireworks. She told me she was in love with you, Dillon, and you guys have been friends long enough for her to know.''

''It was a crush, nothing more.''

''You'd like to believe that because then it's easier to think Stacy won't be seriously hurt by all this. I wish I had that luxury.''

His brows drew together. ''I'm not sure. Maybe you're right, but I was being honest with you when I said Stacy and I were never that close.''

''It's possible to love someone who doesn't return your feelings.''

''I know,'' he said, and Chantel wondered if he was thinking of his ex-wife. How could Amanda have loved Dillon and still have done the things she did?

Chantel hesitated, then voiced the concern that kept flitting across her mind. ''What if *we* don't become that close,

Dillon? We haven't spent a great deal of time together. Heck, you know Stacy better than you know me.''

''Not in the biblical sense.'' He grinned, probably trying to ease the tension, but she was too wound up to let his humor relax her.

''There's more to a relationship than sex,'' she said.

''Do you think you're talking to a man whose sole purpose is to get a good lay? I have two kids already, remember? I think I know what it takes to make a relationship work, or at least I know what can screw it up beyond repair.''

Chantel sighed, realizing she and Dillon were arguing because she was trying to wheedle something out of him he wasn't willing to give, some sort of commitment that would make the coming confrontation with Stacy a little easier. But it was too early in their relationship for that. And it was a cowardly thing to do, anyway—to let go of one hand only after she was hanging on securely to another.

She had to let go of everyone—Stacy, Dillon and Wade— and stand on her own two feet and be strong for her baby. Her meeting Dillon was an accident, a twist of fate, nothing more. If Stacy wouldn't forgive her, Chantel would have to deal with that. And if Dillon didn't end up loving her, she'd have to forge ahead on her own. That was the only way to garner any self-respect. ''Let's go,'' she said calmly.

He turned the key in the ignition, but before putting the truck into drive, he glanced over at her. ''What have you decided?''

''That I've got to do this my way. And that I'll do it when I'm ready.''

Wariness clouded his eyes. ''That sounds suspiciously like you're shutting me out.''

Chantel chuckled humorlessly. ''No, I'm doing the only fair thing. I'm giving us room to get to know each other, room to decide where we want to go from here and room to breathe.''

DILLON WASN'T SURE he wanted room to breathe.

Then again, he wasn't sure he didn't.

Since that night in Tahoe, he'd thought a lot about Chantel, had wanted to spend time with her. Her quiet strength, so at odds with her vulnerability, had struck a chord in him. But he hadn't thought beyond that to anything more serious. Commitment, children, marriage—those things typically took care of themselves as a relationship developed. He didn't think about them much in advance.

But he and Chantel were having a baby together, and Dillon wasn't exactly sure what he should or shouldn't do about it.

Pulling out of the medical building's parking lot, he turned left and stopped at the first traffic light. He knew he didn't want anyone to think the baby belonged to someone else. He took care of his own. He also knew he desired Chantel, felt protective of her. To a certain extent, that meant he already claimed her, too.

What about Brittney and Sydney? He'd sworn he'd never force them into a stepparent situation, at least not while they were so young. He hated the thought of another adult coming into their lives and their home with the power to make or break their happiness. *Chantel* hardly fit the image of a wicked stepmother, but he'd never—until now—even considered making an exception.

Signaling, he turned left at the next light and moved into the far right lane before merging onto the interstate. He thought briefly of the work that awaited him at the office, but it no loner seemed so urgent. Because he had bigger things to worry about. He was going to be the father of a new baby.

How had this happened? And how could he ever sort out his feelings about it?

Dillon gunned the accelerator and shot over into the fast lane. It suddenly felt as if he was leading two very different lives—the responsible loving father of two young girls, and the lonely divorced man who'd just gotten a beautiful ex-model pregnant. How the hell did he integrate the two?

Chantel stared out the window, less emotional now, almost serene. Instead of calming Dillon, however, her attitude only increased his own anxiety. Most women in her situation would be demanding to know how he felt about them and whether he was going to support the baby. She acted as though she didn't expect anything from him. As though she'd raise the child on her own as easily as accept his help.

If he'd been a different kind of man, that would have given him freedom, he supposed. But he couldn't walk away, didn't want to, even if she'd let him. He just felt a certain panic at knowing they'd come face-to-face with the life-changing consequences of one reckless night.

He shot her a glance and bristled at her composure. Didn't she care whether or not he was part of her life? Whether or not he took an interest in their baby? She'd seemed to at first. But that was before they'd addressed the issue of Stacy.

"Thanks for the ride," Chantel said as soon as they pulled up to his house.

Knowing he couldn't talk her into coming inside with him, Dillon caught her arm as she started to get out of the truck. "Call me if you need me."

She nodded. "Thanks."

He watched her climb into her own car, which was still sitting in his drive, then let his head rest on the steering wheel.

Ready or not, they were going to have a baby.

CHANTEL BRACED HERSELF before opening the door to her condominium. She hadn't seen either Stacy's car or Wade's in the parking lot, but she had no idea what might be waiting for her inside. It seemed like an eternity since she'd been home, and if, by chance, Wade was there—if his parents had taken back their car or something—she knew he'd barrage her with a million questions she'd find difficult to answer. What could she tell him? Now that the baby was real, now that she'd seen its little heart beating and *believed,* she had to reveal the truth.

But dread weighted her movements. Slowly she let herself into the house, then blinked in surprise when she found everything just as she'd left it the night before. At least, she thought it was the same. She hadn't really paid much attention.

"Stacy? Wade? Is anyone home?"

No answer. Chantel did a quick turn through the rooms, confirming that she was indeed alone, then sank gratefully into one of the wing chairs in her living room. She was physically exhausted, emotionally drained.

Drawing a lap blanket up over her legs, she decided that whoever controlled fate sure had a morbid sense of humor. She'd been struggling with her promise to stay away from Dillon Broderick; adding his baby into the mix made that virtually impossible. Her feelings were confused and contradictory. Joy at the thought of having a child, the secret thrill of knowing she now had an unimpeachable excuse to keep in contact with Dillon—and pain and regret that her happiness about these things came at her sister's expense.

Right now the pain won out. Tears trickled down her cheeks as she stared at the blank television set. Outside, the clouds passed over the sun, darkening the room and making it feel more like evening than noon. She should call Maureen at work and give her an update. She should force herself to eat something for lunch. The baby was going to need much more than the samples of prenatal vitamins the doctor had given her. But she couldn't move. She simply sat there and worried about what she'd say to Stacy, without coming any closer to a decision.

The telephone rang just as Chantel started to drift into an uneasy sleep. Jerking back to full awareness, she stood and rounded the coffee table, hurrying toward the phone.

"Hello?"

"Chantel?"

It was Stacy. Talons of anxiety clawed at Chantel's stomach, and she was glad she hadn't eaten, after all. "Hi, Stace. Where are you?"

"I'm at home, getting ready for work. Wade left several messages on my recorder saying he couldn't find you. Are you okay?"

"I'm fine. I've had a good morning." Which meant she hadn't thrown up, despite the nausea. "Why didn't you come back here last night?"

"A friend of mine from work wanted me to do something with her."

"Good, I'm glad you got out. Was it fun?"

"It was okay. How'd it go at the doctor's? You made it there safely, didn't you?"

Chantel tried to take a deep breath, but her chest was too tight to let in much air. "Yeah. It went fine."

"What did they say?"

That I'm due in about seven months. "They said everything's going to be okay. I should be feeling better in a few weeks."

"Weeks! Gee, Chantel. You caught one ugly flu."

Tell her, Chantel's mind urged. But she couldn't, not yet. She needed a little more time before their relationship reverted to the hostility of just a few weeks ago. Besides, she wanted to sit down alone with her sister and explain what had happened in person; anything else was cowardly.

Stacy filled in the silence when Chantel didn't respond. "What about work?"

"I'm going to do as much as I can from home, then go back in when I feel better. I talked to Maureen yesterday, and she insists they can wait."

"That's nice of her."

"I'm sure she's had to battle several of the field reps on that. They want their stuff and they want it right away, which means she's having to pull more than her own weight. I really owe her."

"Well, she seems really nice."

Chantel chewed on her lower lip. "What time do you get off work, Stace?"

"Eight."

"Do you think you could come by? I need to talk to you."

"Sure. What about?"

"I'll tell you when you get here," she said, her hand gripping the receiver so hard her knuckles turned white.

"Okay. No problem."

Stacy hung up, and Chantel let the breath she'd been holding seep out. But none of her fear went with it.

CHAPTER SIXTEEN

DILLON WATCHED his two girls hurry across the schoolyard toward the Landcruiser and waved at them. He hadn't stopped thinking, even for a minute, about Chantel and their baby. Sydney and Brittney had no idea he'd been seeing the woman who'd baby-sat them that one night. And after all the recent changes and upsets in their lives, he hated the idea of surprising them.

Taking a deep breath, he smiled as they climbed in. "Hey, kiddos. How're my girls?"

"What are you doing here, Daddy?" Sydney asked.

"How come we don't have to go to Children's World?" Brittney chimed in.

A gust of cool wind ruffled his hair before the doors thudded shut.

"I got off a little early today." He didn't add that the couple of hours he'd spent at work had been wasted. Unable to focus on anything except the startling news he'd received that morning, he'd scrapped several sets of plans and started over, again and again.

"I got a hundred on my spelling test today," Brittney announced.

Yesterday afternoon Dillon had invested a good hour in drilling her on the words. "Way to go! I think that calls for ice cream. What do you think, Sydney?"

Both girls excitedly agreed. "Then can Suzie come over?" Brittney asked.

Dillon had started making some inroads with the other parents—mostly mothers—getting to know them so they'd feel comfortable letting their daughters come to play at his house, but he hadn't heard of Suzie before. "Have you made a new friend?"

"She just moved here."

"Well, maybe tomorrow. Today I thought we'd do something else. Remember Chantel? She had you over at her house a while ago."

"Yeah, she was really nice," Brittney said.

Dillon glanced into the backseat to gauge Sydney's reaction.

"And pretty," his younger daughter added, struggling to close her seat belt.

"Maybe we could go visit her if she's home. That okay with you?"

They nodded, and Dillon dialed Chantel's number on his car phone, then pulled away from the curb. He didn't dare drop by in case Stacy was there, but he couldn't help wanting to see Chantel and his girls together, to get a sense of how they'd do if they ever became a family.

Was Chantel really carrying his child? He still couldn't believe it.

"Hello?" She sounded as if she'd been sleeping.

"It's Dillon. Did I wake you?"

"I was just resting, but I have to get up, anyway. I have some stuff to do for Maureen. She's coming by later to pick it up."

Dillon slowed for a speed bump as he drove out of the neat middle-class neighborhood where the school was located. "Have you talked to Stacy?"

"She's coming over tonight after work."

"When's that?"

"She gets off at eight."

"So she's at the hospital now?"

"Yeah."

"Does that mean the girls and I can stop by for a few minutes?"

"I'm not sure. I haven't seen Wade all day. I don't know where he is and—"

"You're not going to tell me no because of *Wade?*"

Silence, then, "That's not the only reason, Dillon. I realize this is more my fault than yours. When we were together that night, I told you I couldn't get pregnant—"

"You didn't know."

"True, but you don't deserve to have any more responsibilities right now. You've got your children to take care of, and I'm perfectly capable of handling this on my own."

She was showing him the door again, letting him know it stood wide open. Dammit! Why was she trying to make it so easy for him to walk away? Didn't she care about him?

Dillon looked over at Brittney. She was digging through her backpack, pulling out completed assignments, apparently looking for her spelling test. "I want to be part of this," he said, and it surprised him how much he meant it. Even with all the risks and pitfalls, he couldn't leave Chantel to go through the pregnancy alone. "I can't…" He let the last of the sentence dangle so Brittney and Sydney wouldn't clue in.

"You can't turn your back on your own child, and that's admirable. I just want you to know we don't come as a package deal. I'll be supportive of your relationship and won't ever try to stop you from seeing the baby or being part of his life. You believe me, don't you?"

"Yeah." *Until you want to move somewhere or marry someone else or…* "But what's best for *you?*"

"What's best for me doesn't matter."

"I don't think my taking a hike is best for any of us, though."

"She wants you to go hiking, Daddy?" Brittney asked.

Dillon shook his head at his daughter and gripped the phone more tightly, waiting for Chantel's response.

"You're not listening. I didn't suggest you take a hike. I want you to be part of the baby's life. What more do you want?"

Marry me. Where had that come from? He'd only known her two months. He couldn't marry her, couldn't put his girls at risk. "I don't know yet. Can't we figure it out as we go along?"

"Okay."

"So can we come by?"

There was a short pause. "Sure."

THE DOORBELL RANG just as Chantel finished applying a little makeup. She was feeling surprisingly well, considering how sick she'd been the past couple of weeks. Maybe she was living on adrenaline. Or maybe, as the doctor had said, there was simply no rhyme or reason to morning sickness. Regardless, she was grateful for the reprieve.

Pulling on a clean cotton-knit top, she went to answer the door. Dillon stood there, flanked by his girls. She tried to picture the four—or rather, five—of them becoming a family someday and couldn't imagine it. Things like that happened to other people, not to an ex-model who'd stolen her sister's fiancé and deserved to live out her life alone.

Chantel stepped back so they could enter. Dillon brushed against her shoulder as he moved past, and she had the urge to run her fingers down his arm and hope his large hand closed over her own.

With an effort she kept her hands to herself. "How was school?" she asked, giving the girls a warm smile.

"Great! Brittney got a hundred on her spelling test," Sydney said.

"We got ice cream to celebrate," her sister added.

"Congratulations, Brittney! I'm glad you decided to visit. Would you guys like to stay for dinner? We could order a pizza."

Dillon caught her eye. "Are you feeling well enough to have us here that long?"

"I'm doing better, actually."

He smiled, drawing her attention to his lips, which were soft yet firm. He could kiss more wickedly than the devil, she thought, remembering—and wanting to press her lips to his.

She turned away quickly because she knew that if her eyes revealed half of what she felt, they'd make a beggar out of her.

"Want to sit down and do your homework, girls? If we get it over with now, we won't have to worry about it later," she suggested.

As Dillon's daughters hauled their backpacks to her kitchen table, Dillon came to stand behind Chantel. When he spoke, his voice hummed in her ear and his breath teased the back of her neck. "Why am I sensing a little extra energy here?" he asked.

Chantel slanted him a glance. Noting his cocky grin, she realized that her eyes—or some other body language—had given her away, after all. "I think your receptors are screwed up."

"Where's my math homework?" Brittney asked, sorting through a stack of notebooks.

"Maybe you forgot it," Sydney told her.

Dillon obviously wasn't listening. The girls were preoccupied and so was he. "I think they're working fine," he whispered. "I think you're sending me these signals because, considering our present company, you feel safe."

She arched a brow at him. "I am safe."

"Not for long," he said.

THAT NIGHT Dillon whistled as he shepherded his girls out of Chantel's condominium and toward his truck. Dusk had fallen and the temperature had dropped into the sixties, but none of them were eager to leave. They'd had an enjoyable evening together, the four of them—so enjoyable it had been all he could do not to stake a very personal claim on Chantel, one his girls could see. Through willpower alone, he'd managed to escape without touching her, but only by promising himself that what *he* wanted would come later. He needed to take things slowly, let the girls get used to the idea that there might be another woman in his life.

For the first time he felt hopeful, excited by the prospect of a more permanent relationship. The girls liked Chantel. She was kind and easy to be around. He was beginning to believe she could actually be an asset in his daughters' lives, instead of a detriment. And for all of Chantel's talk about her and their baby not coming as a package, she still wanted him. He could feel the raw physical power of it whenever she looked at him.

"It's not over till it's over," he muttered.

"What, Daddy?" Brittney looked up at him, her brow wrinkling.

"Nothing." He chuckled. "I'm just talking to myself."

"You really like Chantel, don't you?" Sydney asked.

He scowled. Was he that transparent? He had to admit his attraction was difficult to hide. An invisible magnetic force seemed to pull him and Chantel together, causing them to brush against each other every time they passed, to touch at the smallest opportunity. Unfortunately such brief contact appeased nothing, only made him hunger for more.

If she was his wife, he wouldn't have to leave her now...

"Yeah, I like her," he admitted. "Do you?"

The furrow in Brittney's brow deepened. "She's okay." She fell silent for a moment, then murmured, "What if you fall in love with her?"

He cleared his throat to hide his surprise and nearly asked, "What if I already have?" Instead, he said, "What if I do?"

"Then you'll run away and marry her, like Mom did with that guy, right?"

Sydney reached up for his hand. He gave it a squeeze and placed his other hand reassuringly on Brittney's neck. "I'd never run away from either one of you. Are you kidding? We're together forever now. A team of wild horses couldn't drag us apart. All five Power Rangers couldn't separate us. Even King Kong—"

Sydney giggled and Brittney rolled her eyes, but a dimple dotted her cheek. "Okay, Dad. We get the picture."

"Nothing, *nothing* could keep us apart," he promised. But then his cellular phone chirped and when he heard the caller's voice, he realized he might have spoken too soon. There was one thing that could stand in their way. One person.

Amanda.

THE COOL NIGHT WIND came in short gusts, carrying a spattering of rain. Folding her arms across her uniform, Stacy ducked her head and hurried from beneath the hospital's portico to her car. She hoped to climb inside before the light sprinkle turned into a real shower, but Wade rolled down the window of his brown Cadillac idling in another row and waved to get her attention.

"Stacy!"

"What are you doing here?" she asked, leaving her own car to approach his window. Just the fact that he was there made her wary, but her unease grew when she saw the look on his face.

"What's wrong?"

"We need to talk."

"I'm supposed to head over to Chantel's. Why don't you follow me?"

He grimaced. "I'd rather talk here if you can spare a minute."

Stacy hesitated. What on earth could he want? He seemed so serious. "Okay."

"Get in."

The power door locks clicked as she rounded the old Cadillac. She got inside to the sweltering blast of the heater, then leaned her back against the door. "Your hair's a mess. That means something catastrophic has happened. What is it?"

"Cute," he said, but her glib remark did nothing to ease the tension of his jaw. Evidently something serious *had* happened.

"Did you get bad news from your agent?" she asked.

"That bad news came a long time ago," he admitted. "I'm not going back to New York. I no longer have a career there."

Stacy had suspected as much. "Is that really so bad? You already knew you couldn't model forever. And New York's a long way from California. Your whole family lives out here—"

"I don't care where my family lives," he interrupted. "We've never been close, and I doubt that's going to change anytime soon."

"Well, your folks did lend you this car, didn't they? They can't be all bad."

"I'm not here to talk about my family." He pinned her with an unswerving gaze. "Chantel is seeing Dillon Broderick."

Stacy blinked, then swallowed hard. "I don't want to hear this," she said, and started to open the door, but his hand shot out to stop her.

"You may not want to hear it, but it's true. I saw them together in the parking lot at the doctor's office this morning, acting like lovebirds."

"You're just trying to hurt me. You're vicious and mean, and I don't know what I ever saw in you. I'm going over to Chantel's," she said.

"Then you might want to call first."

Stacy turned back, letting her door gape open despite the rain. "What's that supposed to mean?"

"He's there now. I saw his car. And I'll tell you something else. I don't think she's sick."

"What?"

"I think she's pregnant."

Four words. Only four small words, but they hit Stacy like an ax slamming into a tree. "That can't be true," she whispered. "Chantel can't have kids. The doctors told her—"

"The doctors could be wrong. Why else would Dillon be taking her to an obstetrician? You were puzzled by that yourself, remember? Think about it."

"Then it's your baby," she insisted. "Or someone else's. Dillon and Chantel barely met at the cabin. I introduced them."

"I guess lover boy didn't waste any time, because the baby can't be mine. I haven't had sex with Chantel in almost a year."

Stacy stared at the wet shiny blacktop without seeing anything. "It can't be," she said to herself more than Wade. "She's just sick. It's the anorexia."

"I don't think so, Stacy." Suddenly Wade looked tired, like a two-year-old who's spent himself on a tantrum and had no energy left. "What I saw made certain things apparent."

Stacy shook her head, refusing to believe. Dillon. She'd been trying to forget him, get over him, but the thought that he'd been sleeping with Chantel brought back all her old feelings—along with a few new ones, the most prominent of which were jealousy and rage.

She got out, heedless of the rain that now fell in great fat drops. "I can't believe it. She's my sister!"

"Yeah." Wade laughed. "Well, I guess now we know what kind of sister she is, huh?"

CHAPTER SEVENTEEN

IT WAS GETTING LATE. Chantel frowned at the clock on her living-room wall and picked up the phone to call Stacy again. Her sister should have arrived more than an hour ago. A nurse at the hospital had confirmed that she'd left at eight, and no one answered at Stacy's house, so where was she?

The answering machine came on again, but Chantel didn't leave a message. She'd already left two. Fearing that her sister might have had an accident, she tried the highway patrol. Was her number anywhere in Stacy's purse? Would anyone think to call her?

In a distant professional voice, the police dispatcher informed her that there'd been no accident involving a blue Honda.

Thank God! Chantel released her breath and sank onto the couch. Maureen had stopped by, but it had been difficult to concentrate when her mind whirred with what needed to be said to Stacy. After Maureen had left, she'd vacuumed, just to keep busy. But she'd forced herself to quit after doing the living room. This was the longest she'd been up since getting sick and the first day she'd felt anywhere close to human. She didn't want to end up back in bed tomorrow because she'd done too much too fast.

Outside, the storm worsened. Rain beat a steady rhythm as the wind manipulated the trees like marionettes, making their branches sway, clacking them against the windows.

Except for the pink azaleas blooming profusely along the fence of her side yard, it felt more like December than May.

Dropping her head in her hands, she rubbed her face. Stacy would get here, she promised herself. But she found it strange that she hadn't seen Wade. Had he left for good? She hoped he had, but she couldn't believe that. Not when his stuff was still at her house.

Had he come home to find Dillon's car in the lot, somehow recognized it and gone to tell Stacy?

That was a stretch, but possible. Even if he'd recognized Dillon's car, though, wouldn't he have confronted her?

For the next fifteen minutes she put her faith in the belief that he would have. Then she dialed his parents' number.

Wade's father answered the phone.

"Henry, it's Chantel." This man used to be "Dad" to her. She'd visited his house every year at Christmas and felt a moment's awkwardness at reverting to his given name but didn't know what else to call him now that she and Wade had broken up. "I'm sorry to bother you at bedtime, but I was hoping to catch Wade."

"You can call here anytime, Chantel. You'll always be part of the family, even though Wade was fool enough to lose you. You know, Ronnie still hasn't married. You should go for him."

Chantel chuckled. Ronnie was one of Wade's younger brothers and the apple of his father's eye. "Ron's only twenty-three."

"But he's got his head on straight. No wild ideas about runnin' off to New York. He stayed home like he should and now he's nearly finished school. Going to be an engineer."

"Wade mentioned it. I'm happy for him. But I'm sure he has enough women knocking down his door."

"None who can compare with you."

Tears stung Chantel's eyes. She missed Wade's family. They'd never been very close, mostly because Wade and his parents disagreed about everything and argued all the time. But it felt good to know they'd approved of her, if not her decision to become a model. "You were always nice to me."

"As nice as our no-account son would let us be. I tell you, I don't know what's gonna become of him. I wish he was here so the two of you could talk, but I don't know where he is. He took the Caddy a couple weeks ago, and we haven't seen him since."

So they hadn't kicked him out. Wade had lied to her again. She should have known. "I'm sure he'll show up sometime," she said.

"Is everything okay?"

"Fine."

"Well, don't be a stranger. Come see us once in a while now that you're living in the area."

"I will," she promised, then hung up. She tried to picture herself knocking on their door several months pregnant. Somehow she couldn't imagine it.

Tapping her fingernail on the lamp table, Chantel tried to decide what to do next. Should she drive over to Stacy's? What good would that do if Stacy wasn't home? Maybe her sister had simply forgotten their appointment and gone out with a friend.

She picked up the phone and called Dillon, just because she needed to talk.

"Am I interrupting anything?" she asked when his deep voice came on the line.

"Just *The New Adventures of Mary Kate and Ashley Olsen.*"

"Is that a movie?"

"A book."

"Sounds like fun."

"Not the third time around. At this point I think I'd prefer to read the labels on vitamin bottles."

Chantel smiled, picturing his girls all snug in their beds with Dillon sitting next to them, reading. "It's one of the girls' favorites, huh?"

"Yeah, they love it. I need to go out and buy them some more books." He lowered his voice. "How'd it go with Stacy?"

"She never came over here."

"Have you tried calling her?"

"Only a dozen times." The telephone beeped, indicating that she had an incoming call. Chantel's stomach tensed. "Someone's trying to get through," she said. "I'd better go."

"Chantel?"

"Yeah?"

"I need to talk to you. Call me later, okay?"

"That sounds ominous."

"It's about Amanda. Just something we should discuss…in addition to everything else."

Chantel bit her lip, wondering if she was ever going to pull out of the emotional tailspin that had started when she realized Dillon was her sister's boyfriend. "Okay," she agreed.

DRIPPING WET, Stacy propped her head against the cool metal of the pay phone and listened to her sister's voice. "Hello? Hello? Wade, is that you?"

The pain that radiated through her heart grew more severe, despite the hour she'd just spent walking in the rain, trying to get some control of her emotions. "What Wade says—is it true?" she finally asked without preamble.

"Stacy, thank heaven it's you. I've been so worried. Please come over so we can talk—"

"Just tell me if you're seeing Dillon."

"I haven't been seeing him."

"Then you're not pregnant."

There was a brief pause, as if Chantel didn't know what to say, then, "Wade had no right to do this to us, Stacy. Don't let him. He's just trying to hurt me."

"Well, he's done a pretty good job of hurting me, too. He came to the hospital tonight to tell me you're pregnant with Dillon's child. I don't want to believe it, but deep down I know even Wade wouldn't lie about something like that."

"Don't underestimate him. I've made that mistake one too many times myself." Chantel sounded tired, defeated.

"That's not an answer."

"Please come over. I hate this, Stacy. I don't want to lose you again."

Stacy could hear the sincerity in her sister's voice, but it did little to combat the vision of Dillon and Chantel meeting secretly while she stupidly trusted her sister's word. Remembering the candlelight dinner she'd made him and the black teddy she'd bought to wear for him—and what had happened afterward—she flinched, feeling utterly humiliated. They'd both probably laughed at her pathetic attempts to interest Dillon, then laughed again at her stupidity for letting Wade come over. "Tell me it's not true."

Silence.

"Chantel, tell me it isn't true!"

"I can't."

Stacy squeezed her eyes shut and rubbed her forehead. "You promised me," she whispered, feeling the warmth of tears on her face. "I cared about him. Why do you have to have them all?"

"It's not like that—" Chantel started, but Stacy had heard

enough excuses ten years ago, when the same thing had happened with Wade. Dashing a hand across her wet cheeks, she hung up the phone, saying a silent goodbye to her sister—forever.

CHANTEL SCOOPED her keys off the counter and hurried outside. The air was damp and chilly, but she didn't care about the wet or the cold and didn't bother to go back for a jacket. She needed to talk to Stacy. She couldn't leave things as they were—not after the way their telephone conversation had gone.

Wade wasn't going to win this round, she vowed.

She got into her car and pulled out of the parking lot. Somehow she had to convince Stacy that what had happened with Dillon was an accident.

The drive to Stacy's house seemed more like forty minutes than the usual fifteen, but according to the digital clock glowing in her car, Chantel made good time. She turned into the driveway shortly before eleven, cut the engine and headed up the walk.

"Stacy, it's me!" The door was locked, but she banged on it, then looked under the mat for the spare key her sister kept there. It was gone. Using one hand to cut the glare of the moon, she peered through the living-room window to see that the entire house was dark. She could make out the shadows of Stacy's furniture, but no sound or movement.

"Stacy? Are you there?" She knocked again before going to the garage, where she stood on tiptoe, trying to see if Stacy's car was parked inside.

No luck. She was tall, but not tall enough. She walked around the side yard and through the gate to check the back door, but it was locked, too. And all the rooms were as dark as those in front, including Stacy's bedroom.

Where was she? Chantel folded her arms against the wind

and rain and made her way back to her car. She figured her sister had to come home sooner or later. And when she did, Chantel would be waiting for her.

Climbing into her car, which still had a crumpled front bumper because she couldn't afford the insurance deductible, she shivered. She was wet to the skin after walking around the house. She could only pray that Stacy would be home soon.

The minutes ticked away, turning into an hour, then almost two. Chantel's teeth chattered as she rubbed her arms for warmth, wishing she'd brought a coat. She should go home, she told herself, and wait until Stacy was ready to talk to her. But somehow she feared that day would never come. She had to see Stacy *tonight*…

If only she wasn't so darn tired. She started the car and cranked up the heater, which quickly dispelled the chill. But the warmth did little to ease the aching of her head and back, and slowly, she became aware of another kind of discomfort—cramps.

DAMMIT, WHERE WAS SHE? Dillon slammed down the phone after his tenth attempt to reach Chantel. She'd told him she'd call. Why hadn't he heard from her? What had happened with Stacy?

He could only guess things hadn't gone well. When his worry escalated as the minutes passed, he risked calling Stacy's house, but there was no answer there, either. He had to drive over to Chantel's and see what was going on.

Running an impatient hand through his hair, he walked down the hall and peeked in at his girls. They were sound asleep, but they were too young to leave alone, and it was after midnight. Who could he call to come sit with them?

He went into the living room and stared at the phone. His mother. Hadn't she just told him he needed to find himself another wife? Well, he wasn't sure he'd found a wife, but he knew he was having another baby. Not that he thought *that* situation would please her.

"Hello?"

Dillon felt a twinge of remorse for waking her this late. He knew she went to bed early. Now that she was older, her life had finally settled into a routine. She and her new husband had dinner, watched *Jeopardy,* played a board game and retired.

"Dillon? What is it? Are the girls okay?"

"They're fine, Mom."

"Are you hurt?"

"No."

"But it's the middle of the night." He could hear her moving in bed, trying to wake up. "Why else would you be calling?"

"I've got a personal emergency. I need you to come over and sit with the girls."

"A personal emergency? What's that supposed to mean? You said you weren't hurt."

"I'm not." Dillon swallowed his pride and braced himself for a response that would be full of irritation, at best, and a flat refusal, at worst. "I'm worried about a friend. I need to check on her."

"A friend?"

"She's been sick and I can't get hold of her."

"She's probably sleeping!"

"I don't think so. Look, Mom, I know this is putting you out and I'm sorry, but it's not like I've ever bothered you in the middle of the night before."

"When you were in high school, I could never get you to come home on time. You woke me up plenty of—"

"Mom, can we discuss my past sins later? I'm dying to get out of here."

She sighed. "Oh, all right. I'll be over in fifteen minutes."

"Thanks." He hung up and dialed Chantel's again, then Stacy's. Still no answer at either place.

DILLON GRABBED his keys from the top of the refrigerator as soon as his mother arrived. "I owe you one, Mom," he said, pausing long enough to kiss her cheek.

To his surprise, she smiled and embraced him, smelling of rain and the perfume she always wore. "You have a good heart, Dillon. I don't know if I've ever told you that."

She hadn't. She'd been too immersed in her own rocky love life, but he didn't hold it against her. He knew she'd be there if he really needed her. She'd grumble, but she'd come through, the way she had tonight. That was more than he could say for his father, who'd always done just the opposite.

He told her he loved her and strode out as she was removing the plastic hood that protected her permed hair from the rain.

The windshield wipers squeaked and the heater hummed as he drove to Chantel's condo. The roads were still wet, and a light fog was starting to replace the rain. He fiddled with the radio, settled for an old rock station, then cursed when he had to stop for yet another traffic light.

Finally he turned into the lot at Chantel's condo, only to find her parking space empty. It was one o'clock and she'd been ill. Where was she?

He thought briefly of Wade and how badly he might have taken the news of the pregnancy. Could he have become violent? God, he hoped not. In Chantel's current condition, she'd be no match for him...

"Don't borrow trouble," he told himself aloud. Odds

were she was with Stacy. He sat idling, wondering whether or not to go to Stacy's when his cell phone rang.

"Chantel?"

"No. It's Stacy." Her voice sounded odd, strained.

"Are you okay?" he asked.

"I am, but I'm not so sure about Chantel—or the baby."

Dillon's stomach knotted painfully, and his throat constricted until he could hardly breathe, let alone speak. Fortunately Stacy needed no prompting.

"I think maybe you should meet us here."

"Where?" he managed.

"At the emergency room."

STACY GREETED Dillon almost as soon as he entered the hospital. Mascara streaked her face, testifying to earlier tears, but her eyes were dry now.

"What happened?" he asked.

"When I got home, I found her backing out of my drive. She looked terrible. She was shaking and crying about the baby."

"Is she going to be okay?"

Stacy took a deep breath and nodded.

"And the baby?"

"She's cramping and spotting. They don't expect the baby to make it."

Dillon felt dazed. He stared down at Stacy without really seeing her, thinking about the baby Chantel wanted so badly.

"If she miscarries, she may never get pregnant again," he said, stating the obvious.

Stacy pushed the hair out of her eyes. "Probably not."

Don't let her lose it, he prayed.

"She's been asking for you." Her expression was unreadable. Had Chantel had a chance to talk to her about what had happened that night in the Landcruiser? Clearly Stacy knew he was the father of Chantel's child or she wouldn't have called him. But from her attitude, he couldn't tell how she'd reacted to the news.

Only two other people waited in the lobby, a man holding a bloody cloth over one arm and an old woman who sat with her purse at her feet, hands folded primly in her lap. Both were staring at the television bolted to the ceiling.

He and Stacy passed through a door across from the street entrance and hurried down a short hall that led into a large examination room, separated into compartments by blue cloth dividers. A baby cried at the far end. Two doctors conferred near a desk up front. He followed Stacy to the second cubicle on the left.

Chantel was lying on a table, curled on her side and facing away from the door. At first he thought she was sleeping, but at the sound of their approach, she turned. Her eyes were rimmed with red, her hair was a damp tangled mess, and she wore nothing but a hospital gown.

"Thanks for coming," she said.

Stacy had stopped at the door. Trying to be sensitive to her feelings, Dillon didn't pull Chantel into his arms. He wanted to hold her and rock her and bathe her face with kisses—anything to reassure her that he wasn't going anywhere even if the baby died. But he merely ran his knuckles over her arm.

"You sure like to scare everybody," he said, trying to ease the tension in the room.

She made an effort to smile. "I'm sorry I upset everyone with news of a baby and then—" A tremor passed through her, and she didn't finish.

Dillon felt a lump rising in his throat and tried to swallow it down. "Have you already lost it?"

"Not yet. The doctors gave me a muscle relaxant to stop the cramps, but they're not going away."

Forgetting about Stacy, he cupped her chin in his hand and tilted her face toward him. "You really want this baby, don't you?"

Fresh tears streamed down her face as she nodded.

"So do I," he said.

A noise at the door told him Stacy left. Part of him wanted to go after her and apologize for what she had to be feeling, but he couldn't leave Chantel standing vigil over their baby alone. He'd talk to Stacy later.

"Did you tell her?" he asked.

Chantel closed her eyes. "I never got the chance."

"Then how—"

"Wade."

A curse hovered on Dillon's lips, but for Chantel's sake he didn't utter it. There was no need to upset her any more, especially when the damage was already done. He promised himself he'd have a little talk with Wade, though, when this was all over. "So did you tell her how it happened?"

She shook her head. "It doesn't matter. She won't believe me, anyway. Not after hearing it the way she did, and not after what happened with Wade ten years ago."

He smoothed the hair off her forehead. "But she brought you to the hospital. She could have left you to make it here on your own."

"She's a nurse. She would have done as much for anyone."

Dillon's heart twisted. Chantel had lost her career because of Wade. Now she was going to lose their baby. And she felt like she'd already lost her sister a second time.

"Are you sorry about that night in the Landcruiser?" he asked, knowing she had to be and wishing he'd somehow been able to keep his hands off her.

A smile curved her lips, but her eyes drooped again, and he realized she was growing sleepy. The relaxant the doctor had given her was finally taking effect. "Are you kidding?" she asked softly. "That was the best night of my life."

He stroked her hair and bent down to kiss her temple. "I'm just sorry it's cost you so much, babe."

Her eyes flicked open, and her hand went to her stomach. "It gave me what I wanted most. If only I can hang on to it…"

"You can hang on to me," he whispered after a few minutes, even though he knew she'd fallen asleep. "If this baby doesn't make it, Chantel, we'll do whatever is necessary to make another one. And we've got my girls." He paused. "I think I'm ready to share them with you."

CHAPTER EIGHTEEN

STACY DROVE OUT of the hospital parking lot without a backward glance. She knew her sister would probably lose the baby, but she wasn't going to hang around long enough to find out. She was too numb to care; too much had happened. And Chantel had Dillon, anyway. What more could she want?

The rain started again, but Stacy didn't bother with the windshield wipers. It was only sprinkling and there wasn't much traffic. She stared beyond the water beading on her window at the wet streets and remembered the concern in Dillon's eyes the moment he arrived at the hospital. Then there was the gentle, almost reverent way he'd touched Chantel when he'd rushed into her room, and the conviction in his voice when he'd said how much he wanted their baby.

All of it told Stacy he was in love—head over heels in love—and the jealousy that stemmed from this realization almost overpowered her. It was one thing to think he and Chantel had had a steamy sordid affair. It was another to think they cared for each other.

Stopping at a traffic light, Stacy smacked the steering wheel. Why couldn't he have returned *her* feelings? She'd mooned over him for two years! And he'd just started asking her out when Chantel came on the scene.

Stacy chuckled bitterly. *Well, let them have each other. I've lived without my sister before, I can do it again. Only this time, there'll be no turning back.*

CHANTEL AWOKE to the sound of Dillon's voice, hushed as he spoke on his cell phone. "Can you get them off to school for me, Mom…? I know, but I don't want to leave the hospital… Tell them I love them and that I'll see them after school… Okay, I appreciate it… No, there's a van from Children's World that picks them up… You bet… Thanks."

He punched the "end" button, then glanced over his shoulder and gave her a welcoming smile when he saw she was awake. "How are you feeling?"

"Better." She expected the cramping to set in again, but it was gone, at least for the moment. Had she lost the baby while she slept? She was too afraid to ask. "What time is it?"

"Just after seven."

She carefully surveyed the room, searching for any evidence that something significant had occurred, but everything looked as it had the night before. Except Dillon. Lines bracketed his mouth and eyes, revealing his exhaustion, and a dark shadow of stubble covered his jaw. He'd stayed with her all night?

"You look tired."

"I dozed a little—" he indicated an orange vinyl chair that hadn't been there when Chantel had fallen asleep "—but they had a drunk-driving accident about four in the morning, and this place turned into a zoo. I didn't get much sleep."

"You shouldn't have stayed."

He raised a hand to caress her cheek. "I wanted to."

A warm feeling began in the pit of Chantel's stomach and radiated out to her limbs, as though he'd just wrapped her in a cozy quilt. But then she remembered her sister, and the warmth disappeared. "Where's Stacy?"

Compassion flickered in his eyes. "She left."

"When?"

He paused, obviously wishing he could soften the truth for her, then said, "Last night, shortly after I arrived."

"She thinks we've been seeing each other behind her back. I tried to explain, but she wouldn't listen. She was too hurt."

"She'll come around," he said, and Chantel tried to act as though she believed him. There was no need for him to share her guilt. He'd done nothing. She was the one who'd betrayed Stacy with Wade. She was the one who couldn't stop herself from wanting Dillon. And she was the one who'd told him she couldn't get pregnant, ensuring they used no form of protection.

"Hello." A doctor who looked wide awake and freshly scrubbed stepped into the cubicle. Evidently there'd been a change of shifts, because Chantel didn't recognize him. "I'm Dr. Wiseman. How are you feeling this morning?"

"My cramps are gone."

"Good. Let's take a look at the bleeding."

Dillon left the room, giving her some privacy.

Dr. Wiseman made a cursory check. "There's some spotting," he said, pushing her gown higher so he could place his stethoscope on her abdomen. She knew he was listening for the baby's heartbeat. She prayed he found one. Otherwise, they'd do a D&C and finish up what the cramping had started.

He frowned in concentration as he moved the stethoscope to a new place.

Please, oh, please, oh, please, Chantel chanted to herself.

Dr. Wiseman shifted the cold metal end of his stethoscope again, and frowned harder.

"Dillon!" Chantel called to him despite her state of undress. She felt vulnerable, exposed, but she couldn't take the news alone. Not when he was standing right around the corner and could be holding her hand...

The doctor raised his head as Dillon entered the room. "I can't get a heartbeat," he said, straightening and letting his stethoscope dangle around his neck.

Chantel clenched her fists and silently stared up at Dillon. She expected him to comfort her in some way, but he looked almost as bereft as she felt. "Are you sure?" he asked.

The doctor seemed slightly offended. "I just examined her."

"Check again, please."

With a sigh Dr. Wiseman bent over Chantel's belly. Again she felt his impersonal fingers and the cool metal of the stethoscope sliding from place to place. Then he froze and listened for several seconds.

"I've found it," he said at last, blinking in surprise. "The baby's still alive."

"WHO IS SHE?" Dillon's mom asked, once he had Chantel situated in his bedroom upstairs.

Dillon smiled and leaned against the kitchen counter, still euphoric from their victory at the hospital and from Chantel's willingness to let him bring her home so he could care for her. "She's going to be my wife," he said.

That made his mother choke on her coffee. "*What?*" she sputtered. "But you've never even mentioned her before."

"I haven't known her very long."

Her browns descended. "And you're planning to *marry* her?"

He smiled devilishly. All his mother's suggestions came out as commands. He wanted her to think he'd actually followed one for once. "I'm just doing what you told me to, Mother. Didn't you say it's time for me to find another wife? Don't tell me you've changed your mind."

"I meant you should start dating. I didn't mean you

should pick up a woman at the hospital and move her in with you.''

He laughed. ''Well, it's a little late for clarifications now. You should be more specific when you tell me what to do with my life.''

''Dillon Broderick, you're a contrary one. You always have been. Why couldn't you be easy to raise—''

''Like my sisters?'' He grinned. ''I have news, Mom. I am raised. We all are.''

''But you're not acting like you have a lick of sense, marrying a complete stranger. Didn't Amanda teach you anything?''

The mention of his ex-wife sobered Dillon, and he turned away to stare out the window. ''She called me yesterday.''

''Amanda?''

He nodded.

''What did she want?''

''Money. She plans to leave her new husband.''

His mother shook her head as if to say Amanda was no good and never would be. ''Already? You didn't give it to her, I hope.''

''Not yet.''

''That sounds like you will.''

Dillon didn't have to see her face. He could hear her disapproval. ''Probably,'' he admitted. ''She'll come back and fight for custody of the girls if I don't.''

''What makes you think she wants them? She abandoned them just a couple of months ago—''

He raked a hand through his hair. ''I'm sure that on some level, she wants them. She's just so screwed up right now. Besides, without the girls she gets no child support.''

His mother grimaced. ''Talk about taking advantage of the system.''

''Bottom line is, I care less about the money than I do

about keeping the girls' world stable and positive, especially with my wedding on the horizon.'' He shrugged. ''If Amanda fights me, I'll be spending money on attorneys.''

''Then make her sign over custody before you give her a dime.''

He took a sip of his coffee, which had been sitting on the counter ever since his mother had poured it. ''I hate that everything seems to come down to dollars and cents. It shouldn't be that way when you're talking about children. But I'll admit I'm tempted to use whatever leverage I've got.''

His mother stirred another spoonful of sugar into her coffee. ''Do the girls miss their mother?''

That was something Dillon had wondered many times. Brittney and Sydney had to feel Amanda's loss, but they rarely talked about her, unless he didn't allow them some treat or indulgence they were used to getting. ''I don't know. I think they're hurt, angry, probably confused.''

''Still, they're better off without her. I'm glad she ran off.''

Dillon was glad the girls were living with him; he just wished it hadn't happened the way it did. ''I'm going to take Chantel something to eat. Why don't you come up with me and get to know her a little?''

He rummaged in the refrigerator, retrieving the sliced turkey breast and other sandwich makings.

''She sure is tall,'' his mother commented. ''Even with you carrying her, I could tell that.''

''She's beautiful, isn't she?'' He heard the wistful adoration in his own voice and nearly chuckled at himself. He sounded like a lovesick boy.

But if his mother found Chantel as beautiful as he did, she was reluctant to admit it. Her lips pursed as she sipped her coffee. ''What does she do?''

"She works for a state senator. But that may not last long."

"Why, for heaven's sake?"

Dillon looked up from spreading mayonnaise on two pieces of whole-wheat bread. "I guess I forgot to tell you. She's having my baby."

His mother's cup hit its saucer with so much force Dillon was surprised it didn't shatter. "How did that happen?" she asked.

He showed her his dimples. "In the usual way."

"DILLON TELLS ME you're pregnant."

Caught completely off guard, Chantel put the sandwich Dillon had brought back on her plate and shifted in the bed. Avoiding his mother's stern gaze, she quickly swallowed the food in her mouth and sought Dillon out where he stood leaning against the bedroom wall. But he merely folded his arms across his chest and smiled innocently.

She cleared her throat. "Yes, Mrs. Sutton, that's true."

Sitting on a chair not far from the bed, Karen Sutton clicked her tongue. "You don't think it would've been wiser to wait?"

"It probably would have been, yes. But we didn't, um, well, we didn't exactly plan for this to happen."

Chantel sent Dillon another glance, this one more pointed than the last. After his mother left, she was going to kill him for putting her on the spot like this.

"Dillon says you're nearly thirty."

Old enough to know what causes these things. The words went unspoken but hung in the air all the same. "The doctors told me I couldn't have children," Chantel explained, knowing she couldn't expect anyone, much less his mother, to understand how it had been that night in the snow. She'd nearly died, he'd saved her life, and she'd fallen in love with him—all in the same night. In the real world it hardly seemed plausible.

Mrs. Sutton sat up taller. "My son's more virile than most," she replied. "Lord knows he has enough testosterone for two men."

At that moment Chantel's discomfort fell away, and she could no longer keep a straight face. The harder she bit her cheeks to stop herself from smiling the more tempted she was. "He's quite a man," she murmured.

Dillon waggled his eyebrows at her, making it even more difficult not to laugh.

Judging by the unchanged tone of his mother's voice, however, Karen Sutton missed these undercurrents and thought they accepted her words at face value. "At least he's doing right by you."

Chantel had no idea what Mrs. Sutton meant—probably the fact that Dillon was taking care of her now. But she'd finally caught on to Dillon's tongue-in-cheek manner where his mother was concerned and realized she shouldn't take her too seriously. "Yes."

"So when's the wedding?"

"Wedding?" Chantel echoed weakly.

"When are you getting married, dear?" his mother asked, obviously trying to hide her impatience.

"We haven't decided on that yet," Dillon said smoothly, finally coming to her rescue. "We'll let you know as soon as we set a date."

"Well, you don't want to wait too long. It won't look right."

"No," Dillon agreed. Chantel made no comment.

"I'm exhausted," Mrs. Sutton announced abruptly. "I need to go home to my husband. He's not used to being without me."

"Mom's a newlywed herself," Dillon said.

"That's wonderful," Chantel replied. "You sound very happy, Mrs. Sutton."

"We are, but it took me long enough to find the right man. I hope you and Dillon have better luck." She stood. Only five-three or so, she looked especially small next to her tall strapping son, but the force of her personality gave her an undeniable presence.

"If Chantel's feeling up to it, why don't we have a family get-together this weekend?" she asked Dillon. "I'm sure your sisters will want to meet your fiancée."

Fiancée? Wedding? Chantel wondered if something had been decided at the hospital, something she didn't know about. When had they gotten engaged? When had they even talked about marriage?

Dillon sent her a sheepish look. "I think she has enough to get used to for the time being. Let's not scare her away before the vows are spoken."

Mrs. Sutton didn't blink. "Nonsense. She'll love Janet and Monica. We'll make it a picnic, on Sunday. Brittney and Sydney will enjoy it."

Dillon didn't argue, but neither did he let her commit him. "It depends on how Chantel's feeling."

"We'll see you on Sunday, dear," his mother said, and suddenly Chantel understood where Dillon got his stubborn streak.

Their voices dimmed as Dillon walked his mother out, leaving Chantel to wonder why he'd let Karen Sutton blindside her like that. She could tell he thought it was funny, but she'd hoped to make a much better impression on his family, if and when they actually met. Blurting out their news about the baby was emphatically not how she would've done it.

"Would you mind explaining that to me?" she asked as soon as Dillon returned.

He shook his head. "My mother's not easy to explain. She's tough as a Sherman tank and twice as direct, but for all that, she has a soft heart. I learned long ago that the only way to handle her is to let her go, and just focus on damage control."

"That smug smile you were wearing while she was grilling me didn't suggest much worry about damage control."

"I knew you could handle her." He sat down on the bed and took her hand to kiss the very center of her palm. His lips felt so good on her skin. Her irritation started to seep away, and she knew then just how terribly hard she'd fallen for this man.

"I didn't want to 'handle' her," she said, her voice calmer now that her attention was on his mouth—and on the possibility that he might kiss her elsewhere. "I want to get to know her. I want her to like me."

"Mother likes anyone she can't bulldoze."

Chantel bristled. "See what I mean? That might have been good information to share *before* you brought her up here."

He chuckled but was quickly becoming absorbed in running his hands through her hair and entwining the strands around his fingers.

"Why did you tell her about the baby? Couldn't we have talked about it first?"

"I wanted to let her know up front that she didn't have a choice about whether to accept you. A mom can behave almost like a jealous lover at times. I didn't want to leave that door open even a crack. Besides, I don't like secrets." He bent to kiss her neck, and Chantel closed her eyes, her body warming in response to the gentle insistence of his touch, the subtle smell of his aftershave.

"Stop it," she said halfheartedly.

"Why?" he murmured, trailing kisses up to her earlobe, which he took in his mouth and tickled with his tongue.

Chantel shivered. "Because you're making me forget that I'm mad at you."

He pulled back, looking wounded. "Why would you be mad at me? I'm the father of your child, remember?"

He slid a possessive hand up her shirt onto the bare skin of her stomach, and Chantel couldn't resist the smile that started in her heart and spread through her whole body. She could be mad at him later.

"God, I love it when you smile at me like that," he said. "It lights up your whole face and makes me feel as if I'm the only man on earth." Finally he kissed her mouth. As his lips moved over hers, Chantel decided he kissed the way he lived the rest of his life—with passion, confidence and complete absorption. At that moment she felt more desirable, more beautiful than ever before.

"Take this off," she murmured, yanking on his shirt. Then she threaded her fingers through the shiny black locks of his hair and kissed his neck, enjoying the salty taste of his skin and the sensation of his heart beating beneath her lips.

He immediately removed his shirt and let her touch what she'd longed to feel again, ever since the night of the snowstorm: the hard sinewy muscles of his arms and stomach, the soft hair that swirled on his chest.

Dillon was nothing like Wade, she thought distantly. To others, he was probably less attractive. But the strength of his character, combined with his raw masculinity, was a potent combination Chantel could not resist. He was capable and confident, but not conceited. He was possessive, but not selfish. He was a leader, but not an autocrat. The biggest difference between the two men, she realized, was in her own response—because she not only loved Dillon, she respected him. He was far more admirable than most men, and old-fashioned enough to marry a woman simply because he'd gotten her pregnant. But she didn't want Dillon to feel obligated to do the "right" thing. She wanted him to love her.

"Why did you tell your mother we're getting married?" she asked.

He propped his head on one fist. His eyes, darkened by desire, caused Chantel's stomach to flutter, tempting her to throw her pride to the wind. She loved him, and he was willing to marry her. Did the reason he was doing it really matter?

To Chantel it did. The fact that she'd wound up pregnant was her own fault. She wasn't going to use her baby to force Dillon into something he wouldn't otherwise have done.

"Because we are getting married, aren't we?" he said.

"I don't remember ever talking about it."

He stroked her arm, obviously still distracted by the passion that had flared so quickly between them. "Then let's talk about it." He pressed a kiss to her lips. "There're several reasons. One, you might not be able to work through the pregnancy. You need someone to take care of you, and I want that someone to be me."

Chantel cringed to hear that she'd been right.

"Two, I want my baby to carry my name."

Of course he'd want that. He was too proud and responsible to accept anything less.

"And three?" she asked hopefully.

He nuzzled his face in her hair and breathed in. "Three, my daughters are living here. I can't have you sleeping in my room unless we're married." He flashed her a grin. "And I'd go mad if you slept anywhere else."

Chantel's desire fled, leaving her cold. He'd just given

her three reasons to marry him, and not one of them was the reason she needed to hear. Trying to hide her disappointment, she slid away from him.

"What's wrong?" he asked.

"While that was definitely a most romantic proposal, I'm afraid I must decline." She hoped he couldn't detect the slight wobble in her voice.

His brows knitted together. "I don't understand. We're going to have a baby—"

"There's nothing to understand. I said no. You didn't really ask, but I'm telling you, anyway. I'll share our baby with you, but I won't foist myself on you as your wife."

He sat up, looking angry. "Who said anything about foisting?"

Chantel blinked rapidly, refusing to cry. "You did."

CHAPTER NINETEEN

WITH A HAND on her chin, Dillon forced Chantel to look at him. "What are you talking about?"

"Nothing. I'm just trying to say it's my own fault I'm pregnant."

"Oh, really? Last time I checked, it took two."

"But I'm the one who said we didn't have to worry about birth control, remember?"

He did remember. He also doubted it would have made much difference. Not that night. "We didn't have anything *to* use."

"We might have been more careful—"

He cocked a skeptical eyebrow at her. "If you think that, then you're more optimistic than I am. Or you weren't feeling what I was feeling."

She blushed. "I think we were feeling the same thing. But I'm happy about the baby and willing to take care of him on my own."

"That's what you keep saying, but who's going to take care of you?"

"I'll manage."

He sighed and glanced at his watch. "Unfortunately we're going to have to finish this discussion later. I have an appointment. You rest. I'll go to work, then leave early and pick up the kids. We'll get some take-out dinner—keep things simple. You and I will talk more tonight."

"Let me pick up the girls."

"I don't think you should get out of bed."

"I won't need much energy to drive to the school, and having company will keep me from getting bored. I can do homework with them here on the bed."

Dillon considered this, wondering if he dared let Chantel take the risk. They'd come so close to losing their baby. But it wasn't very realistic to expect her to do absolutely nothing for the next seven months. And a drive over to the school did seem fairly undemanding. "If you're feeling up to it," he said at last, climbing off the bed. "I'll call the school and let them know you'll be getting the girls. But check in with me before you leave here. If you don't feel well enough, I can do it or they can go to Children's World for an hour or two. Do you know my cell-phone number?"

Chantel nodded.

"Good. I'll bring you some catalogs and brochures to look at tonight."

"I have plenty of reading material at my place. We just need to go over and pick it up."

"Do you have *Bride* Magazine?"

Her delicate brows lowered. "No."

"Then the reading material you have isn't the kind we'll need. We have a wedding to plan." He grinned and ducked out of the room before she could argue. She was going to be his wife. He'd eventually convince her. He had to. Regardless of the baby, he couldn't face the thought of losing her.

BRITTNEY AND SYDNEY chattered happily as they sat on Dillon's bed, telling Chantel all about their day at school.

"This boy in my class named Ryan grabbed my ponytail and pulled so hard it almost made me cry," Sydney complained.

"That means he likes you," Chantel replied, glad that

Dillon had let her pick up the girls and that they had this time together.

Sydney's eyes rounded in protest. "Ryan doesn't like anybody. He's just mean. He's always getting into trouble and—"

"I saw him on his way to the principal's office yesterday," Brittney chimed in.

"He has to go there all the time," Sydney added, as if this confirmed how rotten Ryan truly was.

Chantel chuckled. "Well, this boy might not be all bad. I think your dad probably visited the principal a time or two."

"For what?" they asked in unison, sounding shocked.

"Probably for pulling a little girl's ponytail."

Sydney looked skeptical, but it was Brittney who responded. "I don't think so."

The doorbell rang, and both girls scampered off the bed and charged out of the room to answer it. Chantel could hear them talking and giggling all the way down the stairs, but then they fell silent. "Who is it?" she called.

A feminine voice Chantel didn't recognize floated up to. "Where's your father?"

In her haste to get up, Chantel missed the next exchange between the girls and their visitor. But the woman's voice came through loud and clear when she said, "Get your things. You're coming with me."

A shiver of apprehension slithered down Chantel's spine as she hurried to the top of the stairs. Below she could see a woman standing just inside the front door. A woman about her own age with brown shoulder-length hair and dark eyes, wearing slacks, a shirt and sweater vest, and a pair of pumps. She was hugging Sydney, who looked just like her.

Brittney seemed less sure of giving the woman such a

warm welcome, and Chantel didn't need anyone to tell her why. It was Amanda, their mother.

Clearing her throat, she smiled as Brittney and Sydney glanced up at her expectantly, a hint of fear and worry in their eyes. "Do we have company, girls?"

Brittney nodded. "It's our mom."

"Wonderful. I've never had the opportunity to meet her." Trying to remain calm, Chantel descended the stairs and crossed the floor. "I'm Chantel Miller, a friend of Dillon's."

The woman didn't take her outstretched hand. After an awkward moment, Chantel dropped it to her side, but she kept her smile stubbornly in place. "Unfortunately Dillon isn't here right now, but he'll be back shortly. Would you like to leave him a note?"

Amanda chuckled humorlessly. "No. I didn't come to see him or to write him any notes. I came for my girls. I'm back in town now, and I'm ready to have them come home." She gave Sydney a slight push to prompt her into motion. "Hurry up. Grab your stuff, honey. Mommy's got to go."

Chantel swallowed hard. She could not allow Amanda to take the girls. What if Dillon couldn't get them back? "I'm afraid they can't go with you right now."

Amanda's brows rose toward the widow's peak at the center of her forehead. "I'm sorry?"

"I said they can't go."

Her eyes hardened, but Chantel stood her ground. She could see why Dillon would have found this woman attractive, physically. She had a small compact figure, a pretty face and obviously took good care of herself. What her personality offered was yet to be discovered, but Chantel doubted she'd be impressed there. Divorce often turned both people into the worst possible versions of themselves.

"Who are you to say anything?" Amanda demanded.

"I told you. I'm a friend of Dillon's and I'm watching the girls until he gets home from work. I can't let them go anywhere until he's back."

Chantel stood a good six inches taller than this woman, but Amanda didn't seem intimidated. "They're my kids."

"I realize that."

"Then you should also realize you have no right to keep them from me."

Chantel stepped between the girls and their mother. "Go upstairs, Brittney and Sydney, and finish your homework, please. When your daddy comes home, he'll work all this out, okay?"

Craning her head to see around Chantel, Amanda snapped, "Forget your things. Just come on. This lady is nothing to you. You don't have to listen to her."

The girls looked torn. Brittney moved toward the stairs, but Sydney hovered in the middle of the floor and started to cry. Chantel lowered her voice. "See what you're doing to them? Please, just come back when Dillon's here."

"You're the one who won't let them come with me. They want their mother."

Chantel drew a deep breath and lifted her hand to the open door. "I think they wanted their mother a lot more two months ago. Now go, or I'll call the police."

"You think the police will support you over me? I should call the police myself. They'll come and escort the girls out."

A glance behind her told Chantel Brittney and Sydney were standing on the stairs, watching the drama unfold. Concerned that they might hear, she spoke softly. "Not after they learn that you abandoned them," she said.

Amanda's face went red, and she put up a hand to keep Chantel from closing the door. "You think you know the whole story?" She laughed, then dropped her voice. "Did you know Sydney isn't Dillon's? One blood test is all it would take to get her back, regardless of what I've done. And Dillon wouldn't want her separated from her sister, now would he?''

''No, he wouldn't.'' Both women looked up in surprise as Dillon came around the front walkway and entered the house. They'd been so immersed in their power struggle that they hadn't noticed his car pull up. Jaw clenched, eyes grim, he glared down at his ex-wife. ''And I don't ever want to hear you say that again.''

She gave a brittle laugh. ''It's true. Remember that good-looking trainer at the gym? Phil?''

The muscles stood out along Dillon's shoulders and back, and Chantel could only imagine the powerful emotions he was feeling. Her heart twisted—for him and for the little girl in danger of overhearing and understanding the significance of what her mother was saying. ''The girls...'' she warned.

They turned to see Brittney and Sydney inching toward their father, but Amanda didn't seem to care if they heard her ''It would only take a blood test to prove—''

''Shut up,'' Dillon hissed. For a moment Chantel thought Amanda might defy him, but the expression on his face succeeded in quelling her. When she fell silent he beckoned Brittney and Sydney the rest of the way into his arms, hugged them close, then pointed them back toward the stairs. ''Mommy and I have to talk for a little bit, okay? You girls go to your room. I'll come up in a minute.''

Reluctantly they obeyed. Chantel began to follow them, to give Dillon and his ex-wife the privacy they needed, but Dillon took her hand and guided her outside with them.

''I don't care whether Sydney's blood father is some trainer named Phil or the man on the moon,'' he said when the girls were safely out of earshot. "She's mine. I'm the only father she's known."

"If you want to continue as her father, I'd suggest you let the girls come home with me. I'm their mother."

"Then start acting like it."

"I will as soon as you start paying your child support." Amanda angled her chin up at him, obviously thinking she'd played the trump card, but Chantel could see from the anger flashing in Dillon's eyes that his ex-wife had pushed him too far.

"I was going to offer you a deal, Amanda. I was going to pay for the divorce and help you get back on your feet if you signed custody of both girls over to me. But you know what? I've changed my mind. You can sink or swim on your own. And if you think you can win and don't mind every sordid detail about your past being dragged out for the world to see, then take me to court."

With that, he turned on his heel and opened the door for Chantel to precede him.

"That'll get expensive," Amanda taunted. "It would be cheaper just to cooperate with me. I'll let you see the girls whenever you want."

He turned back. "Seems I've heard that story before. Only this time I'm not buying. It's over, Amanda. You're not having the girls because you weren't taking good care of them, and I have no reason to believe you'll do any better in the future."

"How dare you criticize me! You have no idea how difficult it is to be a single mother!"

"You're not single very often."

"But I love them!" Bewilderment emerged beneath her anger, and Chantel felt a moment's pity.

"You sure have a funny way of showing it."

"So I messed up, made a mistake. It's not like *you're* perfect."

"Then pull your life together and we'll set up some visitation. I'm not trying to hurt you, only protect them."

"That's not true! You're trying to punish me for the divorce! But it's not going to work. You'll pay through the nose if you try—"

"Cost doesn't matter anymore, Amanda. Only what's right and fair," he said, walking inside.

"You won't be saying that when the blood tests come back!" she flung after them. "I'll get the girls! You wait and see!"

Chantel felt Dillon flinch and wished she could shield him from the pain. "I can only hope you love Sydney half as much as I do," he said softly, and closed the door behind them.

THAT NIGHT Dillon worked late in his study, trying to finish a set of plans that were already two days late. He struggled to put Amanda and her threats out of his mind, but there was no escaping the terrible fear that clutched at his belly. How vengeful would his ex-wife be? Ever since the divorce, he'd pulled his punches, hoping to protect his girls from the worst of the emotional trauma and confusion. But now he realized there was only one way to achieve the peace and consistency he wanted. Which meant the situation was going to get a lot worse before it got better. Was it fair to drag Chantel through a lengthy court battle?

Dillon thought of her upstairs, sleeping in his bed, and wanted to go to her. She'd been so quiet earlier, all through dinner and putting the kids to bed. He'd wanted to hear that she agreed with how he'd handled Amanda, but he hadn't been ready to reveal his own troubled feelings. So he'd let her go to bed alone.

Now he longed to have her arms around him, her voice whispering in his ear. But she wasn't even sure she wanted to marry him; he could hardly ask her to tackle his fight to keep the girls. Maybe that was what frightened him, kept him from going to her. That and the fact that she had enough to worry about just hanging on to their baby.

Another difficult subject. He gave a frustrated sigh. How did he tell the girls about the baby? He'd told his mother already, so the news had to come out soon. But first he and Chantel had some decisions to make.

DILLON SHOWERED as quietly as possible, hoping not to wake Chantel while he got ready for work. But as he stood in front of his dresser, looking for socks to match his suit, he realized she was watching him.

"You didn't come to bed last night," she said.

"I slept on the couch. I didn't want to disturb you."

She didn't say anything for a minute. "I think you should take me back to the condo. I refuse to put you out of your own room."

"You're not putting me out of my room. I was pretty distracted last night and I couldn't sleep until late. Plus, I had some work to finish."

"I'm feeling better today. I can take care of myself."

He crossed the room to sit on the edge of the bed. Yesterday he'd been so certain they should get married. Now he wasn't as convinced. For the first time he realized, as more than just a passing acknowledgment, that a stepparent situation wasn't hard only on the kids. It could be difficult for parents, too. He wondered if that difficulty was what had caused his mother's many divorces and feared that, by marrying again, he'd be asking for the same kind of trouble. "Are you upset about what happened with Amanda?" he asked.

Chantel shook her head. "I'm not upset, just worried. About you and the girls."

He eyed the sack that held the bridal magazines he'd brought home yesterday. He'd had such high hopes when he'd bought them. But after Amanda's appearance, he hadn't even taken them out of the bag.

"Do you think she'll go through with the blood test?" Chantel asked. "Surely she can see that it's not what's best for Sydney."

"I don't know what she'll do anymore. She's not the same person I married."

"And if she does go through with it?"

"I'll have to comply."

"And then what?"

"And then pray she's wrong."

"But you don't think she is."

Dillon let his doubt finally show on his face. He'd carried it inside him for so long, so deeply hidden. But now that Amanda had confirmed his worst fear, he couldn't hide it anymore, at least not from Chantel. Worse, now that his ex-wife had pointed the finger at Phil, he thought he recognized similarities between Sydney and the muscle-bound trainer. He hated that he saw them, wondered if his mind was playing tricks on him, but there it was. "I don't know what to think," he said at last. "But I know I want you here with me."

He held his breath, waiting for her reponse, and finally she nodded. "Okay."

THE NEXT MORNING the girls came up to say goodbye to Chantel before thudding down the stairs again and slamming the door. She heard the engine of the Landcruiser roar to life, the higher whine of reverse, then nothing. Just silence.

Poor Dillon. She remembered Amanda's vindictive threat

and the pain in Dillon's eyes, and felt the same anger she'd felt yesterday. She was glad Dillon planned to fight for his girls. But she feared for what he might have to endure before it was all over. Sydney didn't look much like him. Given Amanda's past, it was easy to believe the child belonged to someone else, and because of that, Chantel didn't hold out much hope that a blood test would prove Dillon's paternity. But in his heart, where it mattered, Sydney belonged to him, and Chantel ached at the thought of his daughter being torn from him.

If the worst happened, maybe their baby would help ease the loss. She knew one child couldn't really compensate for another, but hoped a new life might do something to fill the absence Sydney would leave behind. Dillon wouldn't be the only one hurt—Brittney would be devastated.

The phone rang, and Chantel scooted over to the nightstand to answer it.

"If this is Brittney, you've grown up awfully fast." The voice was raspy and held a hint of surprise.

"This is Chantel."

"Oh, yeah? Seems to me I've heard that name a time or two." There was a pause during which Chantel didn't know what to say, couldn't imagine whom she was talking to— and then the man finally identified himself. "This is Dave, Dillon's uncle."

Dave. Fleetingly Chantel remembered Dillon's mentioning something about his uncle Dave the night they met. He was like a father to him, wasn't he? But he didn't live close by. "It's nice to talk to you, Dave."

"Did I miss Dillon?"

"Yes, he just left to take the girls to school. Then he's heading to the office."

"Well, I don't need anything, really. Just wanted to call and give him a hard time. His mother phoned here yesterday, saying he was getting married. You wouldn't happen to know anything about that, now would you?''

She could hear the teasing in his gruff voice and liked him instantly. "Actually I wouldn't. I haven't agreed to anything of the sort.''

"You're making him work for it, huh? Well, nothing wrong with that. Reva made me sweat for two weeks before she gave me an answer.''

Chantel heard a woman's voice in the background but couldn't quite hear what she was saying. Dave laughed at it, though.

"I'm not trying to make him sweat,'' she told him. "I just want to be sure he's doing it for the right reasons.''

"He's an honest boy. You ask him. He'll tell you why he's doing it.''

"Are you sure he won't just tell me what he thinks I want to hear?''

"Positive.''

Yes, Chantel liked this man. He looked at things in their simplest form. He trusted Dillon, and his trust was absolute.

"He's been goin' through a lot with that ex-wife of his,'' he added. "You hang on, little lady, and I think you'll be glad.''

"I'll hang on,'' she said, realizing that, at least in one sense, Dave was right. She'd wanted Dillon to woo her with words of love, to hear him speak his undying devotion, but he was dealing with a lot at the moment, and had been almost since they'd met. She'd been so caught up in her own concerns over Stacy, perhaps she hadn't given enough consideration to the obstacles he faced. He wanted to be part of their baby's life. He needed someone to help look after the girls and to take care of him, whether he knew it or not. And Chantel had nothing but time. Why not marry him and let him think he was doing the right thing, taking care of *her?* There were certainly worse things than marrying the man she loved! She stifled a giggle.

"When will I get to meet you?" she asked Dave.

"You tell me when the wedding is, and me and Reva, we'll be there."

Chantel laughed. Everyone was so sure there was going to be a wedding. She was beginning to believe it, too. "Dillon and I will call you tonight."

With a smile Chantel hung up and dialed the senator's office. She had to tell Maureen about the pregnancy and see what her options were at work. She wanted to keep her job, but the next few months presented some uncertainty.

"Senator Johnson's office."

"Getting tired of answering the phones?" Chantel asked, recognizing Maureen's voice.

"We've been busy," she admitted. "How are you feeling?"

"Better. I'd like to come back next week."

Maureen hesitated. "The senator's here, Chantel. He wants to talk to you."

The senator? Chantel's stomach tightened. She hadn't talked to him since before she got sick, but she'd often wondered what he must think of her extended absence. Surely his patience was coming to an end. And now she had to tell him about the pregnancy. Yikes!

Chantel took a deep breath as the senator's voice came on the line. "How are you, Chantel?"

"Better, Senator, thanks."

"Are you ready to come back to work? We really need someone here."

"I understand, sir. And I am ready. But before we make any plans, there's something I should tell you."

"What's that?" He sounded leary, and for good reason.

"I just found out a few days ago what's wrong with me.

I'm pregnant.'' Squeezing her eyes shut, she awaited his response.

"That's good news, isn't it?'' he said.

"It is for me, sir. But I know you need someone you can depend on, and this is a high-risk pregnancy. The doctors don't know how much of the next six or seven months I'll be able to work.''

There was a pause. "Do you want to keep working?''

"Yes, sir.''

"Then I'm sure we can figure something out. Why don't you start again on Monday and we'll go from there. If it turns out you can't handle full-time, we'll cut back your hours and hire someone to help you.''

"Really? You'd do that for me?'' Chantel could hardly believe it.

"I just had a constituent send me a large donation for my campaign because we'd been so responsive to her in her time of need. Turns out you were the one she dealt with here. You're doing a good job. We'd like to keep you.''

Chantel smiled. *You're doing a good job. We'd like to keep you.* Few words of praise had ever sounded better. Chantel just wished her father was around to hear them. *Goodbye New York. Goodbye modeling.* Wade had been wrong all along. She could make it without him. *Goodbye Wade. There's nothing else you can ever do to hurt me.* "Thank you, Senator,'' she said. "I'll be there on Monday.''

She hung up. Then, just because she felt better than she had in a long time, she dialed Stacy's number—and when the answering machine came on, she actually left a message.

She knew her call wouldn't be returned, but at least she'd reached out—again. Maybe someday Stacy would change her mind.

CHANTEL PICKED UP THE GIRLS from school and helped them with their homework. They didn't talk much and said nothing about Amanda, but seemed to be in good spirits.

Thank goodness children are so resilient, Chantel thought.

By the time Dillon returned from work, she'd already fed Brittney and Sydney and had his dinner warming in the oven. And she was glad she did. He looked exhausted.

"How was your day?" she asked.

"Busy, but I managed to stop by your condo to water your plants and get your mail." He piled the stack of letters, bills and junk mail on the counter.

"Thanks. That was really thoughtful."

"It's not hard to be thoughtful when you're all I think about," he said with a grin.

Chantel glanced up the stairs to make sure the girls were still playing in their room, then sauntered closer and put her arms around his neck. "I think that deserves a reward." She kissed him, long and hard and hungry, and when she pulled away, she caught the gleam of surprise in his eyes.

"That's quite a welcome. I could get used to coming home to this."

"Then it's a good thing I've reconsidered."

"What?" He bent his head to look at her.

"Your proposal. I'm going to marry you. We're going to become a family."

DILLON FELT SOMETHING lurch inside him, a combination, he guessed, of fear and excitement. "Do you think we can make it work?" he asked. "Despite everything?"

She reached up to stroke his cheek. "I'm not a quitter. Are you?"

He gazed into her eyes, knowing he'd never needed to

hear anything so badly. "You'll stick it out with me, then, even if it gets rough?"

"Even if it gets rough. We'll just batten down the hatches and weather the storm."

He drew her to him and hugged her tightly, bending to bury his face in her neck and to breathe in her clean sweet scent. Chantel, his Chantel. It sounded good. It felt right. God, how could something so wonderful happen to him right in the middle of his emotional tug-of-war with Amanda? "I'll always take good care of you," he promised.

Chantel murmured some kind of response, but Dillon missed it. Instead, he heard two distinct giggles and looked up to see his girls staring down at them through the banister.

"I told you they were kissing," Sydney announced with another giggle.

Dillon almost pulled away from Chantel, afraid that what the girls had seen would upset at least one of them. But then he realized they weren't upset at all. They were grinning from ear to ear.

"I knew it," Brittney said.

"Knew what?" Dillon challenged.

"That you liked her."

"And how did you know that?"

"Because you always look at her like this." She gave her sister a lovelorn glance, batting her eyes dramatically, and Dillon laughed. He should've known there'd be no fooling them.

"Come on down, you two," he said. It was time to announce the wedding, but he'd save the baby for later. "Chantel and I have something to tell you."

CHAPTER TWENTY

DILLON PARKED in front of Stacy's house and sat in his car for a few minutes, staring at the light burning in her window. She was home. Her car was in the driveway, and he could hear her television from the street. Taking a deep breath of warm spring air, redolent with the scent of gardenias blooming in the neighbor's yard, he prepared himself for the confrontation to come. Stacy wouldn't want to see him, but he had to talk to her, for Chantel's sake. Each day he stopped by her place to pick up her mail and check her answering machine; without fail, the moment he walked through the door at home, she asked if there'd been any messages from her sister. And each day he had to tell her no.

Getting out of his truck and pocketing his keys, he strode to the door, wondering if Stacy would even let him in. He had a high opinion of Chantel's sister, wasn't sure he wanted to see her worst side, but with all the emotional upheavals of late, he figured one disillusionment more or less wouldn't really matter.

The porch light flicked on almost as soon as he rang the bell, but the door didn't open right away. Dillon got the distinct impression that Stacy was watching him from her peephole, wondering whether or not to admit him.

"Come on, Stace."

Evidently she heard him. The lock clicked and the door opened a crack. "What are you doing here, Dillon?"

"I just want to talk to you for a few minutes. May I come in?"

She looked at him warily. "I don't have anything to say to you."

"Aren't you even going to ask if Chantel lost the baby?"

"I don't want to know," she said, but he guessed she'd already asked at the hospital. She wasn't as indifferent as she made herself out to be.

"Well, there're a few other things you should know."

"Like?"

"Like the little-known fact that Chantel and I created the baby before I found out she was your sister and before she had any idea you and I knew each other, let alone had dated."

Stacy's expression was skeptical. "That can't be true—"

"It is true. If you'll let me in, I'll explain."

She finally stepped back so he could come inside, but she didn't offer him a seat. Dillon took one, anyway.

"She rear-ended your Landcruiser," Stacy said. "Don't tell me you were both suddenly so lust-crazed you immediately ran into the woods. Or are you saying you met before the accident?"

Dillon told her about the events of that night, even though there was no good way to explain what had happened between him and Chantel. It was the kind of thing that had to be experienced to be believed, but when he finished his story, Stacy didn't seem as angry as she had when he'd arrived.

"Why did she lie to me?"

"You know why. She was trying to live down what she did with Wade. I wanted to continue seeing her, but she told me she wouldn't risk her relationship with you. She didn't want to hurt you."

Stacy made an incredulous sound. "For someone who didn't want to hurt me, she's done a pretty good job."

"I can't make any excuses for the situation with Wade. But I can tell you that she tried to handle what happened between us in the best way she could. She was afraid you'd never forgive her if she told you what happened during the storm. She tried to diminish what we felt for each other, walk away from it. And I tried to respect her wishes because I care about both of you. But I won't lie, Stacy. I couldn't forget her."

"So you love her?"

Dillon hated the thought that his answer might hurt Stacy all over again, but he knew it was time for honesty. Only the truth could possibly repair the damage to Chantel and Stacy's relationship. "I want to marry her."

A tear slipped out of the corner of Stacy's eye, and she wouldn't look at him. He stood and tried to comfort her, but she swiped at her wet cheeks and pushed him away. "Don't touch me."

He moved back. "I'm sorry, Stacy. Chantel and I didn't plan this. Our meeting was just an odd twist of fate. And if not for the baby, we'd probably still be talking ourselves out of believing that what we felt that night was real."

"Well, I'm happy for you," she said on a sniffle, her voice laced with sarcasm. "Tell Chantel I know she'll make a beautiful bride."

"It would mean a lot to her, to both of us, if you'd come to our wedding."

She chuckled. "Sorry but I'm not a glutton for punishment."

Dillon shoved his hands into his pockets, wishing there was something else he could say or do to soften her heart. But now it was up to Stacy. She understood that neither of them had meant to hurt her. Maybe, with time...

"Chantel may end up having to spend much of her pregnancy in bed," he said. "It won't be easy, but she really wants this baby."

"Yeah. I'd want it, too," Stacy replied. Then there was nothing left to do but see himself out.

MONDAY MORNING Wade sat in the parking lot waiting for Chantel to show up for work. He wasn't sure she was back at the senator's office, but he'd tried her condo a number of times and knew she wasn't staying there. Was she living with Dillon? The thought filled him with anger, but it was an impotent anger. He'd lost her. Ever since the day he'd seen her and Dillon kissing in the white Landcruiser, he'd known he wasn't going to get her back. He didn't even know why he was here, except that he had to see her one more time.

Chantel's car pulled into the lot, and she parked without noticing the Cadillac. She stepped out, wearing a green silk sheath that fell to midcalf, then paused to collect her purse and briefcase before starting toward the office.

Wade had told himself he'd just watch, see how she looked, but he couldn't resist climbing out of the car and waving to attract her attention.

She frowned when she saw him and hesitated, as though tempted to keep right on walking. With the morning sun sparkling all around her like a halo, she made quite a sight.

"What do you want?" she asked before he even reached her.

"Just to see you."

With a fleeting glance at the office door, she paused, and he took the opportunity to study her carefully. "You look good."

"I'm feeling better."

He shoved his hands in his pockets. "You with Dillon now?"

She nodded.

"You pregnant?"

"That's what you told Stacy, isn't it?" Her gaze was cool, level, but not hate-filled. She had class. Wade had to hand it to her.

"I'm sorry about Stacy," he said. "I was angry, jealous. I wanted to hurt you."

"That's always been our problem, Wade. You feel the need to hurt me. But you can't hurt me anymore. I'm in love with someone else."

"Dillon."

"Yes."

He let his breath out in a whistle, surprised at how much that admission stung. "So it's completely over between us?"

"Wade, it's been over since I left New York. I'd already given our relationship all I had by then."

He chuckled without humor. "Well, you tried to tell me. I guess I just couldn't figure out why things had to change, how you could turn away from me. We had it good in New York—"

"You had it good. I was miserable most of the time. You were unfaithful to me. You refused to marry me, to have a family. You blamed anything that went wrong on me and my career—at the same time you spent the money I made."

He stared down at the cement. "Maybe I didn't deserve you, but I thought you loved me."

"I did, once."

"So now what?"

"I'm going to marry Dillon. And I don't think you should come around anymore."

"Don't worry. I'll be heading back to New York, after all. Try to make it on my own."

She nodded. "Then I wish you the best of luck."

He itched to hug her, to pull her to him just once more, but he knew she'd have none of it. Not after what he'd done to her and Stacy. So he started to walk to his car, then turned back.

"Chantel?"

She paused, the door to the office half-open.

"I'm sorry," he said, and for the first time in his life, he meant it.

"SO WHEN'S THE WEDDING?"

Dillon's sister Monica sat at the picnic table across from Chantel. The two of them had been chatting happily almost from the moment they met. Behind them a small lake shimmered like a jewel in a valley created by gently sloping green hills. To their left, Brittney and Sydney squealed on the swing set, playing with their younger cousins and enjoying the warm Sunday afternoon.

Dillon wasn't sure how to answer his sister's question. They'd originally planned to have a small wedding at a church not far from where he lived, but a notice he'd received from Amanda's attorney had changed all that. Now he just wanted to get married, fast so he could deal with the other issues in his life. And Chantel seemed quite willing to revise their plans.

He met her eye before answering Monica. "Because of the situation, I think we've decided to keep it simple. We thought we might get married in Vegas next weekend."

"Hogwash." Dillon's mother held court at the head of the table, where she'd been passing out large pieces of a delicious-smelling oatmeal cake. Her busy capable hands paused in their task. "A small ceremony right here would be lovely. It doesn't have to be extravagant, but Chantel deserves something nice, with a photographer and a real wedding dress. You'll pay for it, and we'll all help.''

''Vegas next weekend is fine,'' Chantel said.

Dillon grinned. ''Good, I'm getting tired of sleeping on the couch.''

''You're getting tired of creeping around your own house, more like,'' his mother put in, ''but you can do it for another couple of weeks if it means giving Chantel a nice wedding.''

Dillon nearly laughed out loud. He and Chantel hadn't been intimate since she'd come to stay with him. The doctor had warned them it might cause a miscarriage, and he wasn't going to do anything that could cost them their baby. Beyond that, he'd been determined to set a good example for his girls. So he'd done his best to put temptation out of reach by working late every night and relegating himself to the living room.

''Amanda's back in town and giving me problems again,'' he said, changing the subject.

''More custody battles?'' His mother grimaced. ''So she's following up on her phone call. Well, let her do what she will. She can't take the girls after abandoning them.''

''Not when you're doing such a good job with them, Dillon,'' Monica added. ''They seem so happy with you.''

Jason, Dillon's nephew by his other sister, Janet, started to cry. They all looked over to the slide area where Janet was picking him up and dusting him off. Evidently he'd taken a little tumble. Mark, Janet's husband, joined her, carrying their baby daughter.

''I know a guy at work whose wife did something similar, and she's never been able to regain custody,'' Monica said, resuming the conversation. ''You're not worried, are you?''

He *was* worried, and with good reason. Chantel reached out to take his hand, and he smiled at her. ''I guess I may as well tell you,'' he said, knowing the truth would come out soon enough anyway.

''What?'' His mother frowned. She must have known she wouldn't like his news, because she abandoned her task of covering the leftover cake and sank onto the bench beside her short wiry husband, who never said a word.

''Amanda's making me take a blood test.''

''Why?'' Monica scowled, her posture defensive.

''She claims Sydney isn't mine.''

Stunned silence met this announcement, and Chantel squeezed his hand. A lump the size of a grapefruit lodged somewhere in his throat. Damn, why had he said it now, in the middle of a family picnic? Because he wished they'd tell him that it couldn't be? That Sydney looked just like him?

He knew better.

His mother was the first to speak. ''Dillon, that child is yours. No matter what the blood test says—''

''I know.'' He cut her off, wishing he could cut his emotions off as easily. He *couldn't* lose Sydney. What would the girls' lives be like, growing up without each other? How many concessions would he be forced to make, being the only one, as usual, who seemed to care about their ultimate welfare? Would he be faced with the decision of letting Brittney go, too?

''When?'' Monica asked.

''The beginning of July.''

''That's more than a month away. Why so long?''

''I wanted to stall as long as possible, just in case…'' He let his words die off and everyone shifted uncomfortably.

''Does Sydney have to go to the doctor's with you?''

He shook his head. ''I'm taking her in separately.''

''What are you going to tell her the appointment is for?'' his mother asked.

"I don't know. Part of me wants to lie and say she's getting a vaccination. The other part is tempted to sit her down and try to explain, so it doesn't come as a worse blow later on. But there just isn't any way to tell her how I feel—" he fought to control his voice "—and how lost I'll be if—"

"I don't think you should tell her anything yet," Chantel interrupted, her voice soft but firm.

"Why?" His mother and sister looked up in surprise.

"I'll admit I've had my doubts. But now…" She shrugged. "Now I don't know. Something's just telling me not to worry. I think she's his."

Skepticism shone in his mother's eyes, but to Dillon, Chantel's words soothed like cool cream on a hot sunburn. If only the blood test proved her right.

"About that wedding," his sister said, obviously trying to move the conversation in a more positive direction. "I think we could pull it together in three weeks. What do you think?"

Chantel's smile remained unchanged, but Dillon caught the sparkle of excitement in her eyes. So, she wanted the wedding, after all. Well, he certainly wouldn't deny her because of his own preoccupations and worries. She deserved a special day, something far nicer than standing in front of an unknown minister in some gaudy Vegas wedding chapel.

"Three weeks from this weekend sounds good," he said, and bent and kissed Chantel on the mouth. He didn't care if they were married in a barn as long as she became his wife. He just wanted her to be happy.

When Dillon drew back, Chantel gazed up at him with those incredible eyes of hers and asked, "Do you think there's any chance my sister will come?"

Dillon remembered his confrontation with Stacy, a meeting he'd never told Chantel about, and knew she wouldn't.

But he didn't have the heart to tell Chantel that. "Maybe," he said hopefully. "We'll certainly send her an invitation."

STACY KNEW it was the invitation to Chantel's wedding before she even opened the envelope. She nearly tossed it in the wastebasket with the rest of her junk mail, but something about the pretty paper made her pause. Was their picture inside?

Bracing herself, Stacy ripped open the envelope to find a black-and-white photograph of Dillon, Chantel and his girls. Separated from it by a thin piece of tissue was a scalloped one-sided invitation.

Holding the picture to the light streaming in through her living-room window, she carefully examined her sister's face, and then Dillon's. Chantel, forever a friend of the camera, looked wholesome and beautiful in a sleeveless dress and straw hat. The girls wore matching chintz dresses, and Dillon was wearing a pair of slacks and a tie. They were standing in the middle of a meadow, the wind rustling through their hair. And they looked happy—like a family.

Stacy sank onto her sofa and read the invitation, which had a pretty piece of ribbon at the top and delicate cutouts along the fancy edges. The wedding was the last Saturday of the month, a little more than a week away. Dillon had told her how much it would mean to Chantel if she came, but the wound was still too raw. She couldn't sit in the audience and watch them promise to love and cherish each other, pledging all their tomorrows.

And yet, despite everything, there was a calmness deep inside her at the realization that Chantel was in good hands at last.

CHANTEL SMILED HAPPILY as she hung up after her conversation with Monica and glanced over the menu they had planned for the wedding. They were going to have a brunch following a midmorning ceremony, instead of a reception at night, and Monica claimed she knew just the caterers to use. Clippings from various magazines lay spread out on the kitchen table, showing different place settings, gourmet foods, flower arrangements and dresses.

She stood and adjusted the blinds to let in more of the midmorning sun, breathing in the scent of the lemon furniture polish she'd just used to dust, then went back to sifting through her clippings. She had to decide on bridesmaid's dresses for Dillon's sisters and Brittney and Sydney. She was running out of time.

Her own dress was draped over the closest chair. With an empire waist, the style was reminiscent of a Regency-era gown; it had a small train and was made of delicate beaded lace over a satin underlining—understated yet elegant. She compared it to an emerald-green dress that could possibly work for the bridesmaids, at least for Dillon's sisters, then hugged herself. She'd been back at work for a whole week, feeling stronger every day, and could hardly believe she was getting married *and* having a baby. How many times had she tried to convince Wade that they should start a family?

Now she was glad he'd never agreed with her. It had been painful at the time, but she knew, deep down, that Wade could never have made her as happy as Dillon. Stacy's stubborn silence was the only thing that spoiled her contentment. That and her worry about Dillon and Sydney.

Chantel heard keys jingling in the lock at the front door and looked up in surprise. It was Saturday, but Dillon had told her he'd be gone all morning, helping his mother trim some of the taller trees in her yard. The girls had been invited over to Mary Beth's for the day. So who was home already?

"Hi." Dillon smiled as he came in, but Chantel detected a certain strain in his face.

"Hi, yourself. Is something wrong?" she asked. "What are you doing home?"

The dimples in his cheeks flashed. "What if I just wanted to be alone with my fiancée?"

"I'd say you weren't having much fun at your mother's."

He chuckled as she met him halfway across the kitchen and pressed her lips to his, but his usual enthusiasm for her kiss wasn't there. He released her almost as soon as he'd hugged her and went to the kitchen sink, where he washed his hands, then gazed out the window.

"What's wrong?" she repeated.

He leaned his hip against the counter and turned toward her. Bits of leaves and twigs still clung to his hair and clothes. "I went to the doctor's and had the blood test yesterday."

"What?" Dread congealed in Chantel's stomach like cold gravy. "But you said you weren't scheduled to go in until the first of July. That's almost two weeks away." *After the wedding,* she added silently.

He sighed. "I couldn't wait any longer. It was driving me crazy worrying about it, wondering whether or not we'd really be the family I want us to become. I didn't want it hanging over us all through our wedding."

Chantel didn't mention that something much worse than not knowing might be hanging over them now. If Sydney didn't belong to Dillon, the truth would be inescapable. How would they deal with all that in the eight days before they got married? "And?" she said quietly.

"The results are right here." He took an envelope out of his back pocket and stared glumly down at it. "I've been carrying it around all morning."

"They didn't tell you?"

"I wanted to talk to you first, make sure you agreed with me that it's best to get this over with and not drag it out any longer." He set the envelope on the counter and they both watched it warily, as though it had suddenly grown fangs.

Chantel knew Dillon had taken Sydney to get her blood test almost a week earlier. They'd told her the doctor wanted to run some routine tests, and she'd complied, if not happily, at least willingly. Evidently Dillon had gone in a few days later, during work hours, so she'd never connect the two appointments.

"Well?" he asked. "What do you think?"

Chantel didn't know how to answer. This was eating him up inside. She wanted it over as much as he did, but she wasn't sure whether it would be better to face the possible bad news now or put it off a little longer. "I think you should do what you need to do, and if that means you open the envelope today, then do it."

He reached out for her, and she went to him, slipping her arms around his waist and tucking her head in the hollow of his shoulder. The smell of perspiration and the outdoors still lingered on his warm skin and clothes. Chantel breathed deeply and the thought that she'd be able to hug him like this every day of their lives made her happy all the way down to her bones.

"How are you feeling?" he asked above her head. "Any cramps?"

"Not since that day in the hospital. I think the baby's going to be fine."

"I hope so." He turned her in his arms so that her back pressed against his chest and his hands were free to cup her belly. He rubbed it gently, his actions telling Chantel that he was affirming the baby's existence. "I like it that you're starting to show."

Chantel enjoyed the feel of his hands and wondered if the baby could somehow understand how badly they wanted him or her. "What should we name the baby if it's a boy?" she asked.

He kissed her neck. "I kind of like Junior."

Chantel chuckled. *Typical male.* "You want to name him after you?"

"Uh-huh. And if it's a girl, we can name her after you."

"No." She covered Dillon's hands with her own and entwined their fingers. "Stacy's middle name is Lauren. I'd like to use that."

He paused for a moment. "I'm sorry about Stacy, babe."

Chantel turned and lifted her chin, giving him her bravest smile. "I haven't given up on her yet."

He frowned. "That's what worries me. I don't want you to be hurt again."

"There are some things you can't protect me from," she told him. "Just like there are some things I can't fix for you." She eyed the envelope again. "Are you going to open it?"

She felt him haul in a deep breath. Then he moved away and tucked the envelope in the cupboard above the refrigerator. "Not today," he said.

CHAPTER TWENTY-ONE

FOR DILLON, the next few days dragged by. The envelope in the cupboard seemed to beckon him every time he passed the kitchen. But then he'd think of Chantel and their upcoming marriage and force himself to move on.

At least the wedding plans were finally set. On Wednesday afternoon, with only two days to go before the big event, he received a call at his office.

"Don't say I've never done anything for you." It was the voice of a heavy smoker—Helen. Dillon recognized his ex-mother-in-law immediately, even though they hadn't talked since Amanda's reappearance.

"I'm afraid I don't understand," he said.

She chuckled, the sound more bitter than sweet. "This is a courtesy call to let you know that Amanda's gone back to her new husband in Salt Lake City."

"What?" Dillon could hardly believe his ears.

"You heard me."

"But what about the girls, the blood test?"

"She wanted to go through with the test, anyway, but I knew it wasn't for the right reasons."

Dillon agreed with this assessment, but he was cautious about jumping to any conclusions. "And that means..."

"It means I won't let her. I told her if she goes through with the test, I'll do everything I can to help you get custody, even if you're not Sydney's real father. And she knows

I'll do it, too." Helen gave a hacking cough. "Anyway, she's agreed to drop the suit."

Dillon couldn't breathe for a minute. The thought of how many times he'd nearly reached for that white envelope waiting at home terrified him. "So, no blood test?"

"No blood test. The girls are yours. May you do a better job of raising them."

A dial tone hummed in Dillon's ear for several seconds before he hung up the receiver. No blood test. No threat to Sydney. They were going to be a complete family, after all.

"Thank you, Helen, thank you." He muttered, and wearing the most carefree smile he'd worn in a long time, he picked up the phone to call Chantel.

CHANTEL LEFT the girls at the kitchen table, where they'd been working on their scrapbooks, to answer the phone.

"Hello, beautiful."

"Hi, Dillon." She smiled, loving the sound of his voice.

"I have some good news."

Chantel waved for Brittney and Sydney to stop fighting over the glue. "What's that?" she asked.

"Amanda went back to Utah."

"To her husband?"

"Yeah."

She glanced toward the cupboard over the fridge, where she knew the envelope with the results of the blood test still lurked. "Does that mean what I think it means?"

"We get to keep the girls. Both of them."

"Dillon, that's wonderful!" The invisible bands that had been squeezing Chantel's heart ever since Amanda had appeared at the door were instantly released, and she felt lighter than air. "You must be so relieved."

"I am."

"Is that Daddy?" Sydney asked.

Chantel nodded.

"Is he calling to tell you he loves you?"

No, he's never told me that, Chantel thought, feeling a flicker of doubt. She wanted to believe he loved her. He *acted* as if he loved her. So she was marrying him on faith. But he'd never said it. "He's calling to say he misses his girls," she filled in.

"Why don't you guys come meet me for lunch?" Dillon asked. "I do miss my girls—all three of them."

All three of them. It wasn't *I love you,* but Chantel was part of the family now. She remembered her own father, and missed him all over again. But the pain of his passing and the regret were gone, because she was finally where she belonged. And somewhere along the line she'd managed to forgive that nineteen-year-old girl who'd screwed up so badly. "We'd love to," she said, and the only empty place left in her heart was the spot she would always reserve for Stacy.

AFTER A LONG NIGHT of tossing and turning, Stacy awoke with her heart pounding. Today was Chantel's wedding. As much as she'd tried to ignore the passing days, her internal clock refused to let her forget.

"I'm not going," she groaned. She hadn't heard from Wade since that day in the hospital parking lot, and she was glad. He had no place in her life. She hadn't seen him around town, either, and guessed he'd gone back to New York, after all. Neither had she heard from Dillon, not since the night he'd come to invite her to his wedding. Her love life was amazingly bleak, but she doubted even a hot new romance would have made any difference to the way she felt today: insignificant, left out, nostalgic, guilt-ridden and confused, all wrapped up together.

She got up and scowled at herself in the mirror. Not a

good hair day. She could tell already. But she wasn't interested in how her lack of sleep had affected her looks. She'd saved a message on her answering machine that she wanted to hear again, just to see if her conscience would let her erase it this time.

"Stacy? This is Chantel. I know you don't want to hear from me, but I'm calling to tell you…I don't know…that I miss you. And that I'm sorry. Not for what I've done. You already know that. I'm just sorry you got stuck with such a lousy sister. You deserve better."

A lump formed in Stacy's throat, but for a moment her finger hovered stubbornly over the erase button. Then she played the message again, and again, until tears streamed down her face. Chantel wasn't such a bad person. She'd been sweet and giving when they were growing up. Until Wade, Stacy had definitely been the more selfish of the two of them. And now, with Dillon, Stacy wasn't sure it was entirely Chantel's fault. When they'd first met, Chantel hadn't known she was dating Dillon. What would *she* have done in a similar situation? With a man like Dillon?

The T-shirt and shorts she'd worn to bed didn't match, but she didn't bother to change before she grabbed her keys off the counter and headed out into the warm July morning. She hadn't been back to Chantel's father's grave since Memorial Day, but she felt compelled to go there now. She missed Grant, needed his advice. If only he was still alive…

The cemetery was large and sprawling, with an older section on the far left and a new section with mostly flat headstones on the right. A small stone structure, built to resemble an ancient Greek temple, sat in the middle; it held, Stacy guessed, the remains of those who'd been cremated.

The scent of carnations and damp soil crowded in close as she walked across the neatly trimmed grass. The sun was beating down, promising temperatures in the upper nineties for the afternoon, but somehow it reminded her of another day, this one in spring.

It was May. She was only fourteen, Chantel not quite eleven. They both stood at Grant's side, gazing at the grave of their mother, who'd died just two months before. It was Stacy's first experience with death and never had she felt so bereft. The one person who had sustained her, loved her, was gone, and now she belonged to a man who had fathered her sibling, but not her.

Would he eventually send her to her real father, a drifter who'd never shown much interest in her? She wasn't sure. She only knew she felt apart from the family, alone, until Chantel had come to stand by her. At that age they rarely hugged, but Chantel put her arm around Stacy and simply stood there until they went home, the contact telling her that she did belong, that she would always be part of the family.

Now Grant, too, was gone. Would she and Chantel maintain their relationship? Was it too late to save what was left of their family?

Stacy sank onto the grass, heedless of the wet ground as Chantel and Dillon's engagement picture flashed in her mind. They'd looked so happy, so right together. Could she really begrudge her sister a man like Dillon? When Chantel was ill with what they'd thought was flu, Stacy had sworn she'd never let anything else come between them. And yet here she was, carrying her old grudge.

Closing her eyes, she said a silent prayer, to God, to Grant, to her mother, to whoever was listening. "Please, help me forgive her," she said. "Neither of us is perfect. But nothing should come between sisters."

STANDING IN THE BEDROOM of her condo, where she'd insisted on getting ready for the wedding, Chantel stared down at her engagement ring. It was a large marquise with a double row of smaller diamonds on each side. She'd never seen a more beautiful piece of jewelry, not even in her New York days, when nothing was out of reach. She and Dillon had gone together to choose their rings, and she'd loved this one from the start. But the price had been exorbitant. She'd immediately shied away and chosen something more reasonable, but Dillon had already noticed the gleam in her eye. After her ring had been sized and they'd gone back to pick it up, she'd stood in the store and opened the plush velvet box to quite a surprise.

She smiled at the memory of Dillon watching her, his eyes warm and soft as the tears rolled down her cheeks. He'd gently wiped them away, put the ring on her finger and pulled her into his arms. "I'm a lucky man," he'd said, but he still hadn't told her he loved her.

He did care about her, she told herself. He showed it in every possible way, down to the flowers he brought home at least once a week.

If only he'd say the words…

Taking a deep breath, Chantel stood and surveyed herself in the mirror. She was wearing her wedding dress. The ceremony was in less than an hour. Then she'd be Mrs. Dillon Broderick. She put a hand to her stomach, which bulged slightly beneath the concealing folds of her dress. Her baby would have its father's name and grow up under his protection. Fortunate child.

"It won't be long now," she whispered as the telephone rang. Even before she answered it, she knew it was Dillon.

"How's my beautiful bride?" he asked.

She smiled to herself. "I'm almost ready."

"Can I come get you?"

"No. I'll drive myself. You can't see me until I walk down the aisle, remember?"

He groaned. "I can't wait. For the wedding—or for to-night."

Chantel thought about sleeping with Dillon again, feeling his bare skin against her own. Unity, love, had no better expression. "No more couch."

"Never. But we'll be very careful of the baby. Don't worry."

"I know you'd never do anything to hurt me or our baby."

"I'm glad you know that, because it's true. I'll see you at the church."

She hung up feeling nervous yet happy. She coiled her hair into a fancy style she'd once worn on the cover of *Elle,* situated her veil and collected her keys. But before she could walk out the door, something called her back into the living room. Stacy. She had to try to convince her sister, one more time, to be part of the wedding, to give them her blessing.

Picking up the phone, Chantel dialed Stacy's number, but got the answering machine. She opened her mouth to leave a message, to plead with her sister to come, but ended up saying simply, "Stacy, I love you."

DILLON'S MOTHER and sisters had done an incredible job decorating the church. Sprays of lilies, accentuated by ivy, lined the steps outside and continued down the aisle. They'd hired a photographer and were serving prime rib and roast turkey at the brunch to follow, along with a variety of side dishes, fresh fruit, breads and gourmet desserts. But the flowers had been the single biggest expense, and now Chantel could understand why. They were everywhere, they were real and they were beautiful.

Her stomach fluttered with nervous excitement as she stood in the small vestibule to the side of the front foyer, watching through the crack in the door as a crowd gathered.

Maureen and her husband went inside, and the senator himself, along with his wife and one of the field representatives, but Chantel didn't recognize anyone else. They were all Dillon's friends and family. He'd lived in the Bay Area his whole life.

According to Dillon's sister Monica, who had met Chantel at the chapel the moment she arrived and whisked her away to her current hiding place, Dillon was already inside. But Chantel hadn't seen him. She imagined him standing at the altar, waiting for her, and felt a tingling rush of anticipation.

"Oh, you look absolutely stunning!" Dillon's mother exclaimed, bursting into the room. She clasped Chantel in a tight hug.

"I'm just glad I'm feeling good enough for this. And I'm grateful you talked us out of going to Vegas."

"Well, if she's lucky, a girl only gets married once."

Chantel smiled, understanding the allusion to Karen's own past. "At least you got it right this time. You seem very happy."

She shrugged. "Dillon doesn't think much of Lyle, but my husband treats me well—and I don't want to be alone."

"I'm sure Dillon will eventually come to like him."

Karen nodded. "He's been through too many stepfathers. But look how well he turned out, in spite of my rocky past. I think he'll forgive me someday."

"I'm sure he already has."

The organ music started, and Brittney and Sydney hurried into the room, wearing their matching emerald-green dresses. "Everyone's here!" they gasped. "Even old Aunt Maude."

"It's going to be a lovely wedding." Dillon's mother kissed Chantel's cheek, then squeezed her hand. "I need to ask you something."

Chantel raised her brows in surprise. What could Dillon's mother want right before the wedding?

"I know we were planning to have Dillon's business partner give you away when Reva got sick and Dave didn't think he could make it. But he flew in this morning and surprised us all. Would you mind if we let him take Simon's place?"

"No. Of course not." Chantel remembered the gruff but warm voice of Dillon's uncle from their telephone conversation. Before her plans to marry Dillon, Chantel had felt so isolated and alone. She'd had only her sister, who wasn't speaking to her. Now Dillon's family would surround her and become her own—an added blessing.

Karen went out and returned with a stocky, ruddy-faced man with salt-and-pepper hair in a buzz cut. "So here's the beautiful bride," he said when his sister introduced them. Instead of taking her hand, he gave her a hug.

"How's Reva?" she asked.

"Her cold turned to bronchitis there for a few days, but she's ornery as ever and on the mend. She sends her love."

Chantel smiled. Somehow, with Dave, it didn't seem strange that a woman she'd never met would send her love.

"I'm glad you're on board for the ride," he admitted. "And I'm glad my favorite nephew has fallen in love again."

"We all love her," Sydney announced, hugging her legs. Brittney stood a few feet away, smiling shyly.

Chantel lifted Sydney's chin so she could see into her eyes. Then she reached out for Brittney. When her small hand slipped inside Chantel's, Chantel squatted down to the girls' level and said, "And I love all of you. We're going to be happy together, aren't we?"

They nodded and hugged her, and Dillon's mother began

to cry. "Everyone's waiting," she said, sounding impatient with her own emotions. "We'd better get started."

Karen disappeared and Dave smiled reassuringly at Chantel as Monica and Janet arrived to take their places. Then the music changed to the wedding march, and Chantel slid her hand through the crook of Dave's arm.

"Here we go," he murmured. "Don't be nervous."

He might as well have told her not to breathe. Chantel braced herself and they set off, with Monica, Janet, Brittney and Sydney following.

Even though Chantel had seen almost all the guests as they came in, she couldn't stop herself from looking for Stacy. She gazed down the rows of pews and searched each face, but mostly strangers gazed back, smiling.

Sadness filled Chantel's heart, but she forced herself to smile, too. She was getting married. She should be thrilled, she told herself, and she was, once she glanced up and saw Dillon waiting at the altar. He looked even better than Chantel had envisioned. His black tux fit perfectly. His hair had been trimmed and combed back from his face but still curled just a bit in back and around the ears. And the dimples Chantel loved so much deepened as he watched her walk toward him. He had to be the handsomest man in the world, she thought. She already knew he was the kindest.

She gave him a tremulous smile, but then the door opened and closed, stealing Dillon's attention away from her.

Something made his eyes sparkle. What was it? Chantel was tempted to see for herself, but everyone was watching her little procession, and she didn't want to trip on her heels and take her bridesmaids down like dominos.

Dave stopped and put Chantel's hand in Dillon's, but Dillon was still looking beyond her.

"What is it?" she whispered.

"A wonderful surprise," he said, turning her around as soon as her bridesmaids had taken their places.

Chantel scanned the pews again, until she saw what Dillon saw. Stacy, sitting in the back row.

Tears burned behind Chantel's eyes and clogged her throat. Even though the minister, Dillon's family and the entire congregation expected her to do something far different, she let go of Dillon's hand and rushed back down the aisle to give her sister a fierce hug.

"Thank you for coming," she whispered.

Stacy pulled back, tears swimming in her own eyes. "You're my sister," she said.

"No. No CLOTHES," Dillon protested when Chantel tried to grab her robe off the chair in his bedroom before they headed down to rummage through the kitchen for something to eat. "I love seeing the curve of my baby in your belly." His hand moved protectively over her abdomen, and he pulled her back against his own nakedness, then breathed in deeply, as though he'd absorb her very essence if he could.

Dillon's mother had taken the girls for a week so that Dillon and Chantel could honeymoon in Hawaii. But they were spending their first night at home. In fact, Chantel wondered if she wouldn't be just as happy staying right where she was and never leaving the bedroom. Dillon had massaged every part of her body with his hands, his lips, his tongue. And while he'd been cautious of the baby, he'd proved himself creative enough to give her a spectacular wedding night, in spite of their restrictions. He'd promised her a nice warm bath next, where he'd said he planned to lather her with soap and...

"What are you thinking about? You're smiling like the cat who swallowed the canary," he said.

Chantel laughed. "I was thinking about what an incredible lover you are."

"Oh, yeah?" He nuzzled her neck. "Tell me more. My male ego is eating this up."

She turned in his arms and pressed her breasts against his chest, then kissed the ridge of his jaw. "Your touch makes me crazy, Dillon Broderick, because you're such a good man, and you're so talented with your hands, and because…"

"And because you love me?"

Chantel drew back to look up at him. "You sound as if you're trying to convince yourself of that."

"Maybe I am."

"Why?" It was well past midnight, but Dillon had insisted they leave the light on. He wanted to watch the expressions on his wife's face when he made love to her, he'd said, and Chantel had enjoyed seeing his expressions just as much. But now she could read doubt flickering in his eyes.

"Maybe I'm afraid you married me for the baby's sake," he murmured. "Or maybe I'm just afraid it's too good to last."

Chantel wrapped her arms around his neck and pulled him into a tight embrace. "You think I might do the same thing to you that Amanda did."

He didn't answer for a moment. "We started out happy," he said at last.

"But you were working and going to school. You were under a lot of stress and you were gone a lot. That can take its toll."

"But she seemed to grow bored so quickly."

"I don't think she really understood what marriage is all about. She still wanted to be young and have no responsibility. And you have to remember that she's a different person than I am, Dillon." At that moment Chantel knew it might take him a while before he could express his feelings for her. It was love that had given Amanda the power to hurt and manipulate him. He was fighting against putting himself in the same vulnerable position again. But he did care for her. She knew that much.

"I love you with all my heart," she whispered, "And I'll never purposely do anything to make you jealous or to hurt you in any way."

She felt his arms tighten around her, crushing her to him as he buried his face in her neck. When he finally lifted his head, Chantel could see he was struggling with some deep emotion. Cupping his cheek in her hand, she smiled up at him. "You'll tell me the same thing someday, when you're ready. Now let's go eat!"

She led him from the room, but he didn't say anything until they reached the kitchen. By then he had his emotions in check and insisted she sit down while he cooked.

They lit a candle, turned off the lights and ate omelets in companionable silence. Afterward Chantel took Dillon's hand and brushed a kiss across the knuckles. "I have a gift for you," she said.

He raised his brows. "I don't think you could give me anything better than what I've already got."

"You'll like it." She went to the cupboard and brought back the envelope that held the results of Dillon and Sydney's blood tests. "The other day, I noticed that this was still here."

He tensed. "I've tried to throw it away several times, but…I can't. I want to put an end to the wondering."

"We're a family, Dillon, a real family. What's in this doesn't matter."

"I know. I think it has more to do with hope, hope that Sydney *is* mine and that Amanda has nothing to come back with."

Chantel smiled and started to open the envelope.

"Don't." Dillon stopped her. "I don't think it's wise. I've debated with myself over and over, and while the wondering's driving me crazy, I think it's better not to look. Let's burn it."

"I said this was a gift, remember?" Chantel touched his cheek.

He didn't answer. He just watched nervously as she pulled out a letter and a report and handed them both to him. Slowly he took the documents from her outstretched hand and, after a final scrutiny of her face, began to read.

"How did you know?" he asked a few minutes later, looking stunned.

"I peeked before you took me home last night. I thought it was worth the chance, and better me than you if things turned out…well, differently from what we hoped. In that case, I planned to carry the secret to my grave."

"She's mine," he said as though he couldn't believe it. "Despite her dark eyes and her small build, despite that weight-trainer guy in Amanda's past, she's mine."

Chantel's grin widened at the incredulity and happiness in his voice. "No one can ever take her away from you again."

"From us," he corrected. "And that's the best gift of all."

CHAPTER TWENTY-TWO

Four Months Later
Lake Tahoe

"HAVEN'T YOU DONE enough?" Dillon asked, coming up behind Chantel at the cabin's kitchen table. "You've been stuffing envelopes for two hours." He grinned. "I'm starting to feel neglected."

Chantel smiled, feeling the same warmth she always felt when Dillon was around. "I'm almost done," she assured him. "I had to finish. I promised Senator Johnson I'd get these in the mail today. The election's close and—"

Dillon slipped his arms around Chantel's bulging middle and kissed her neck. "So is the baby. I don't want you to overdo it. We shouldn't even be up here, so far from the hospital."

"But we had to come and celebrate the first snow." She put her hands over his and threaded their fingers together, enjoying his clean woodsy smell.

"It was nice of Stacy to take the girls," he said.

"Are you kidding? She lives for having the kids come."

"I know, but we should've spent the weekend at home. What if you go into labor?"

"I'm not due for nearly three weeks, and I haven't had any pains. Besides, there's a hospital in Truckee. I'd rather have Dr. Bradley deliver the baby, but if it's an emergency—" she shrugged "—we'll go there." Affixing a stamp to the last envelope, she added it to the gigantic pile of letters encouraging the voters of the seventh district to support Johnson on election day. "Phew! That's the last of them."

She leaned her head back against Dillon. "Did you get the generator started? It's cold in here."

"I started the generator and shoveled the walks—"

"So we can go to the post office?"

"No—so we can make a run for it, if we have to. And I built a fire in the living room. Come sit with me. I've got water heating for some herbal tea."

Chantel stood and tried to stretch her aching back. She loved being pregnant and knowing she supported another life inside her, but it was getting harder and harder to work and to move and to sleep. Gaining enough weight had been difficult, too, but Dillon had made sure she'd eaten properly. And he told her she looked great even when she felt like a moose, which led her to believe he loved her as much as she loved him. Not that he'd ever actually said so.

He seated her on the couch, disappeared into the kitchen and returned with two cups. "I like this place," he said, sitting next to her. "It's certainly a lot nicer than the cabin Stacy rented last March."

Chantel smiled. "It's a lot more expensive, too." Accepting the cup he handed her, she took a cautious sip, admiring the leaping flames beneath the stone mantel, the gleaming hardwood floors, the rough-hewn furniture. "Someday maybe we can afford to buy a cabin up here."

Dillon put his arm around her and pulled her closer, and she curled her legs underneath her and relaxed against him. "We'll build one. I'll design it."

"That would be great. We could bring the kids up whenever we wanted." Her head resting in the hollow of his shoulder, she gazed out the window at the softly falling snow. "Even if I live to be a hundred, whenever I see snow I'll remember the night we met, how you risked your life to save me."

He chuckled. "And I'll remember how you wrecked my new Landcruiser."

She elbowed him in the stomach. "Here I am, being romantic, and you have to bring *that* up. Besides, that accident was your fault. If you hadn't slammed on your brakes all of a sudden—"

"You mean, if you hadn't been tailgating me all the way from Auburn—"

"Then we never would've met."

"And I would have missed the love of my life," he finished.

For a moment what he'd said didn't quite register. When it did, Chantel twisted around to see his face. "Are you trying to tell me something?" she asked, holding her breath and hoping he'd finally grown to trust her enough to talk about his feelings.

"Something that's been true since that very first night," he admitted. "I love you, Chantel. I always have. I always will."

And then he gave her a kiss that told her just how much.

EPILOGUE

Six Months Later

STACY STOOD in the hospital nursery, gazing at the five new-borns who had entered the world during the past twenty-four hours. They were small and shriveled, not much to look at, really, but they smelled sweet and they were so innocent, so dependent. Her heart ached to think she might never have one of her own.

She'd had a birthday since Chantel's wedding and was now thirty-three. She'd hoped to have several children by now. But it was Chantel who was busy raising a family. Grant David Broderick had arrived two weeks premature, weighing only five pounds, ten ounces, but he'd survived and now, at six months, was thriving. Chantel and Dillon doted on him and their girls almost as much as they doted on each other. And Stacy had to admit that she thought the baby was pretty special, too, although it was Brittney and Sydney she'd grown close to over the past few months. They came to stay with her once a week, or as often as Dillon and Chantel could bear to part with them.

"Incredible, aren't they?" A man stood at the entrance to the nursery, wearing blue jeans, a golf shirt and a baseball cap.

Stacy nodded, wondering which baby belonged to this handsome father. She hadn't seen him during the night when she'd helped two mothers go through labor and delivery.

She figured he must be with one of the three women assigned to the other nurse.

"Which one's the Hansen baby?" he asked.

Stacy navigated through the jumble of rolling cradles to a big boy who weighed almost ten pounds. "Here he is," she said, wheeling the sleeping bundle toward the door. She automatically checked the man's wrist for the band that would identify him as the baby's father, but found none, so she kept her hands on the cradle and stopped several feet away. "Are you a member of the family?"

He was staring at the baby, looking awed. A crooked grin appeared on a face badly in need of a razor. He'd probably been at the hospital most of the night and hadn't gone home yet to shave. "His father's in the military and couldn't be here. I'm just standing in. I'm his uncle."

"Well, he's a big healthy boy. I'm sure his father will be proud."

The man nodded. "Any chance I can take him to my sister? She'd like to feed him."

"I can't let you take him without a wristband. But we can go together, if you like."

"That's fine."

As he led the way to room 305, Stacy couldn't help noticing his straight back, broad shoulders and tight behind. It'd been a long time since she'd met someone who'd started her heart pumping so furiously, but this man was *definitely* attractive. And she loved his attitude toward the baby. Was he married? She caught a glimpse of his ring finger, but didn't see a wedding band.

He waited at the door while she pushed the cradle inside. Then he went to his sister's bed and praised the newborn extravagantly as Stacy helped nestle him in his mother's arms.

''It's no wonder we thought you were having twins,'' he told his sister. ''This guy's half-grown.''

Mrs. Hansen was no china doll. Somewhere close to five-ten she had a sturdy frame and looked almost as big as her brother, although he had her beat by a few inches in height. They both had dark hair, hazel eyes and smile lines bracketing their mouths. Stacy imagined they laughed a lot.

''Just hit the call button when you want me to come back for him,'' she said.

''Oh, wait. Would you mind taking a picture of us?'' the woman asked.

''Not at all.'' Stacy listened to the quick instructions Mrs. Hansen rattled off, then admired the woman's brother through the lens of the camera. What a gorgeous man! She pressed the shutter release, heard a soft click and whir, then asked if they wanted another one.

''Get Rand holding Jeremy this time,'' Mrs. Hansen suggested.

Suddenly looking ill at ease, her brother picked up the baby, but held him in an awkward position, away from his body.

Stacy chuckled and moved to show him how to cradle the newborn in the crook of one arm. ''You must not have any children of your own,'' she said.

''Not yet.''

''Do you and your wife live in the area?''

His sister's lips curved into a smile. ''I don't know, Rand, but I think that might be Nurse—'' she leaned forward to read Stacy's badge ''—Miller's way of asking if you're married.''

Stacy felt herself blush at being so easily found out, and stepped away to hide behind the camera again. After she'd taken another picture, Rand said, ''Don't mind my sister. She loves to put people on the spot.''

Stacy set the camera on the table. "I guess I was being a little obvious," she admitted, then tried to bolt before Mrs. Hansen could embarrass her again. But the other woman's voice followed her out. "Rand's *not* married, by the way."

"Ugh, I'm an idiot!" she groaned, and raced for the nurses' station, where she slumped into the seat behind the desk. "Why didn't I just come right out and ask for his number?"

"That probably wouldn't have been a bad idea."

Stacy stopped pounding her forehead against her palm long enough to look up. Rand had followed her. "Oh, God. It gets worse."

He laughed, the sound deep and rich and appealing. "But just for the sake of tradition, why don't you give me yours?"

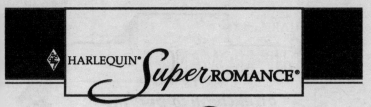